SIN & INK

SIN & INK

NAIMA SIMONE

This book is a work of fiction. Names, characters, places, and incidents are the product of the author's imagination or are used fictitiously. Any resemblance to actual events, locales, or persons, living or dead, is coincidental.

Copyright © 2018 by Naima Simone. All rights reserved, including the right to reproduce, distribute, or transmit in any form or by any means. For information regarding subsidiary rights, please contact the Publisher.

Entangled Publishing, LLC
2614 South Timberline Road
Suite 105, PMB 159
Fort Collins, CO 80525
rights@entangledpublishing.com

Scorched is an imprint of Entangled Publishing, LLC.

Edited by Tracy Montoya
Cover design by KAM Designs
Cover photography by
iulias/Bigstock
magann, fxquadro, and valuavitaly/DepositPhotos
doodko/Shutterstock

Manufactured in the United States of America

First Edition October 2018

To Gary. 143.

"Life is not measured by the number of breaths you take but by the moments that take your breath away."

—Maya Angelou

Chapter One

Knox

Several sins could send a man to hell.

Blasphemy.

Murder.

Idolatry.

Lusting after your dead brother's wife, especially when you were responsible for his death, might not top blasphemy, but it must be on the list.

Which means I have a one-way ticket to hell with my dick riding shotgun.

"It's pretty. You did good," my own living, breathing mortal sin praises over my shoulder. Eden Gordon, my sister-in-law—or former sister-in-law. Shit, I don't know how that works—straightens, and thank God. I can breathe again. With her leaning over me, I drag her scent into my lungs. Like peaches left out under a summer sun—warm, sweet, sultry, and fucking edible.

I bend closer to the young woman in my chair and

finish up the last of the color and shading on her shoulder. Not because I've suddenly developed a Mr. Magoo case of nearsightedness, but to insert even a little more distance between Eden and me. When it comes to her, distance is good.

Sitting up, I shut off the tattoo machine and spray the tat with tincture of green soap and water, washing off the excess ink and blood from her shoulder. Eden's right. The butterfly is beautiful—3D turquoise, purple, and black art that appears to lift from the woman's skin.

And if I have to ink one more goddamn butterfly on another coed, I'm going to junk-punch myself. There are tens of thousands of students enrolled in Chicago's "Loop U," and I swear, it seems as if every female student who enters Hard Knox Ink looking to get her tattoo virginity popped, wants a butterfly.

At least from her squeals and twisting and turning in the mirror, it appears this Loyola student likes it. There's a warm satisfaction in seeing her pleasure—or any client's joy in one of my tattoos—that's incomparable to anything.

"I. Love. It." She whirls around, wearing a huge grin.

"I'll go ring her up," Eden says, laying a hand on my back. *Fuck*. I briefly close my eyes, that simple, small touch like a blowtorch to my insides. There should be branded flesh under her palm because, I swear, the heat burrows past skin and muscle. And I want it. I hunger for the burn.

Nodding, I bend my head on the pretense of removing my gloves and dumping the extra caps of ink. My jaw is clenched so tight, I'm surprised something doesn't snap.

Eden's a toucher; she hugs everyone, sweeps gentle strokes over cheeks, hair, and arms. Affection—and showing it—comes easy to her. Her caring, friendly caresses are every championship win, orgasm, and Christmas morning wrapped into one shiny package. They're also every hell.

And I crave each one, hoarding it like I need an intervention on one of those A&E TV shows.

A greedy, goddamn masochist. That's me.

"Thank you. It's just what I wanted," the brunette continues to gush as she turns back to the mirror for another peek at her new ink.

With her long, shiny hair, jeans with rips that were obviously done at the hands of a manufacturer, and the necklace with its single diamond resting against her collarbone, she looks like one of those girls from the Gold Coast. Or from a North Shore suburb with its mansions, golf courses, and country clubs.

Do her parents even know she's slumming it in a Ukrainian Village neighborhood tattoo shop owned by a former MMA fighter? Highly doubtful. If so, they'd probably be shitting bricks—gold bricks.

"Let me bandage it up for you." I stow the bottles of ink and pull open the second drawer of my work station, removing the roll of gauze and tape.

"A couple of my friends came in a few weeks ago," she says, crossing the room and giving me her back. "They told me you were the best." She glances over her shoulder. Smiles a smile that has my inner *Oh-shit*-o-meter pinging like a ten-alarm fire. From her driver's license, I know she's twenty, but that curve of her mouth and the DTF gleam in her eyes tells me this girl has been around a few suburban blocks. "Now I know they weren't lying. You're great," she damn near purrs.

"Thanks. I'm glad you like it." I cut off a piece of gauze and carefully place it over her skin, taping it down on either side. "Leave that on for at least an hour."

"I will," she promises, turning around to face me. "Is it true you were an MMA fighter?"

I toss the gauze and tape back in the drawer. "Yeah."

Most people would've taken the short, "drop it" tone for

what it was and gotten the hell up out of the room, but not her. She trails her fingers over the tats on my forearm that are exposed by the pushed-up sleeve of my black Henley, tracing the trunk of the family tree inked there. Stroking the faded, brown leaf falling from the branch...

Controlling the urge to flinch, I deliberately move my arm, but she just shifts her hand to my stomach, flattening her palm against the muscle there. That hand slowly slides down, bumping over my belt, and lowering until it's right over my cock. Her fingers curl around me through my jeans. And squeeze.

It's not the first time a customer has come on to me, offered me pussy or head. Hell, it's not even the first time one has grabbed my junk like it was their own personal joystick. And yet, a bolt of surprise still wings through me. A little flirtation, yeah, I'd kind of expected that. But I'd underestimated this girl.

"Another thing my friends weren't lying about. You're hot as hell," she murmurs, lust darkening her blue eyes.

I know what she sees when she looks at me. A big, tatted motherfucker who could be either a fighter or an ex-con. Maybe both. She sees a man who would shut the door, push her up against the wall, and fuck her six ways to Sunday right next to the framed black and white photograph of a woman with my art on her back.

She's not wrong. On either of those. In my twenty-nine years, I've been in the ring and on both sides of the law. And after a match, with the adrenaline still raging through my veins, I had no problem finding a woman at the club, bar, or even around the ring willing to let me pound out the rest of my energy in her body. Even now, I'm far from a saint or a monk. Sex is still an outlet—maybe even more than it used to be since I don't have fighting anymore.

But too bad for her, I don't fuck clients. Or employees. I

never shit where I eat. That's just begging for trouble.

Not that I'd take her up on the invitation in her stroking hand anyway. She's too goddamned young.

She's only a couple years younger than Eden.

Yeah, and Eden is even more off-limits than this coed.

Gripping her wrist in a gentle but firm hold, I pry her hand off my junk.

"Thanks," I reply to her earlier compliment. "You can pay up front."

I half expect her to storm out of here, hissing *asshole* or something, along with a dramatic exit. Instead, her lips curl into a wicked smile that probably has those frat boys at Loyola coming in their khakis.

Damn, I almost feel a flicker of sympathy for her parents. No doubt, they're hosting fancy dinner parties up in their big-ass, gated home, blissfully ignorant, thinking their precious, beautiful daughter is at her school studying and doing sorority girl shit. When, little do they know, she's at a tattoo shop, attempting to give a hand job to an ex-fighter in a neighborhood that would send them into heart palpitations.

This is just one of the reasons I don't plan on having kids.

They never fail to break your fucking hearts.

I should know since I've cracked my parents' hearts into so many fragments, they resemble jigsaw puzzles. With a few missing pieces.

The familiar, corrosive burn of guilt scalds my chest like acid, even more painful because it *is* familiar.

"I'll see you out there," she says, sauntering out the room, the fragrance of her floral perfume trailing behind her. Hell, it smells like it cost a bill. But it still can't compete with the summer and peaches scent that I could identify in a damn perfume factory full of open bottles.

Shaking my head, I grab the bottle of disinfectant. For the next few minutes, I spray and clean the black leather seat and arm cushions on the massage chair I use for shoulder and back tattoos. Collapsing the equipment, I stow it along the wall and head out.

Stepping into the main part of the shop, the loud, grinding mix of metal, electronic, and classical music that is Igorrr's hit song *ieuD* blasts out of the state-of-the-art sound system, one of the first things I had installed after I bought the shop three years ago. The drone of tattoo machines and the hum of voices buzz beneath the pounding heavy metal.

This is home. A home I created for me with the family of my choosing, if not birth.

Pride swells inside me, pressing against my chest wall, as it does whenever I walk in and stop to think how lucky I am to do something I love. The big storefront window still looks out on busy N. Western Avenue and its bars and cafes. Exposed brick still covers one wall, and cubicles dot the wide, open floor plan. Art decorates the walls, along with the hanging portfolios containing stencils, drawings, and pictures of past tattoos.

In front of the long desk stands a couple of glass cabinets stocked with Hard Knox Ink merchandise—shirts, hats, chains, jewelry. That had been Eden's idea. After retiring from the Bellum Fighter Championship, or the BFC, I'd wanted to completely separate myself from that part of my life. Hell, I'd named the shop after my fighting name only at my brothers' insistence. That had been as much as I'd been willing to concede.

But when I hired Eden a year ago as my receptionist and, later, office manager, she'd informed me I would be stupid not to capitalize on my career and reputation. After a lot of nagging, I caved. Honestly, I didn't give a damn what brought people through the door. Every artist here, including me, can hold our own once we have the client in our chairs. Yeah, some people might walk through those doors to rubberneck and find out what happened to Hard Knox Gordon, former two-time BFC heavyweight champion. But most come because our tattoos are the best in Chicago.

"Hey, Knox. What the fuck is this, man?" Hakim Alston yells from his cubicle. The wheels of his stool roll over the tiled floor, and then he appears in the doorway, his long dreads held back from his face by a black bandana. "I mean, some of the shit your brother listens to I can tune out, but this? It's weird even for him."

"I'm sitting right here, asshole," Jude calls from the space that adjoins Hakim's. "And I'm just trying to expose you to different kinds of music, elevate your taste."

"I got one thing that elevates, and I don't need your help with that," Hakim shoots back.

"Yeah." My other artist, Heaven Travers—who refuses to answer to anything but V—chimes in as she walks past us. "He handles that *all* by himself. Emphasis on 'hand.'"

"Now, that's just wrong," Hakim grumbles. Then, as Taylor Swift replaces Igorrr, he shakes his head as V, the resident Swiftie, cackles from her cubicle. "And that's worse. Really, Knox?" he continues. "Isn't it some kind of cruel and unusual punishment to work under these circumstances?"

I snort. "File a complaint." I happen to like Taylor's latest CD and work out to it. Not that I'll admit it to Hakim, or anyone else, for that matter. That kinda shit you take to the grave.

Pausing a moment before continuing to the counter, I peek into his space, checking out the piece he's working on. Daenerys Targaryen and her three dragons cover a wide back from shoulder to waist. Eden is a *Game of Thrones* fanatic, which is the only reason I recognize the characters. Hakim has been working on this guy's back piece for weeks now, between the outline and adding color. And even though it's only the fifth session and about halfway done, it's stunning.

Each of us specializes in a certain style, and Hakim's is realism. The tattoo could've been ripped from the pages of any graphic art book and superimposed on this guy's back. That's how detailed it is, with color that pops off the skin.

"Damn. That's coming along good," I murmur.

"I know." The tattoo machine buzzes to life in Hakim's hand, and he grins at me. "It's what I do."

Shaking my head, I turn toward the counter. And I brace myself.

Back in my private room, I'd forced myself not to turn around and look at Eden. But now, I don't have a choice. And with her profile to me—and those dark, chocolate eyes not fixed on me—I don't hold back.

I drop my gaze, starting at her booted feet, moving up and over the dark denim encasing her toned, slender thighs. She's petite, no more than five-feet-four, but the curves on this woman. I lock down the growl rumbling in my chest and rolling up the back of my throat. She owns a round, firm ass, perfect for filling a man's hands. The dip of her waist only emphasizes the feminine flare of her hips and the fullness of her breasts, which are a shade too large for her small stature and delicate build. In other words, goddamn flawless.

Dragging my starving scrutiny from her tits and up her elegant neck, I linger on the graceful line of her jaw. The sexual invitation that's her mouth. The straight nose and slightly wide nostrils. The spatter of cinnamon-colored freckles across her cheek, nose, the slash of her cheekbone, and her forehead. They were an inheritance from her Polynesian grandmother, along with her golden, hot-sand-on-a-beach skin.

Long, thick, black-brown hair flows over her shoulders and down her back. The color reminds me of the bark on the trees in San Jose's Japanese Friendship Garden. Deep. Rich. When I trained at a mixed martial arts school and gym out there years ago, I would go to that garden to think, to rest.

That's what Eden does to me. Her presence calms me even as she turns my body into a marble statue—hard as fuck.

Even now, I struggle to fight back the lust that's always right under the surface, simmering, just waiting to be let loose like an inferno…or wild beast. Because that's how I feel around her. Like a caged, hungry animal just waiting for one slip, anticipating that one time when the lock on its prison is left open so it can break free and feast.

She brushes her hair over her shoulder, revealing more of her profile. And like the animal I am, I watch her lips curve into her signature sweet smile as she slides the receipt across the counter for the coed to sign. All the while, I'm imagining those lush, sensual lips offering me that same innocent smile just before they part, giving way for my cock. Her mouth has always been my obsession. I want to take it, bruise it, corrupt it with mine, and with my dick. I want to come in it, watch her swallow every fucking drop of me, and then drag her back to her feet and taste us on her tongue.

Yeah, I'm a dirty motherfucker.

And the absolute lowest piece of shit walking to fantasize about my dead brother's wife that way. Especially when partial blame for his death weighs on me like the world on Atlas's shoulders. Connor had been the genius in our family—entering college at seventeen, graduating at twenty. We'd all expected him to be the first of us to get a job using his head instead of his hands or fists. Instead, he'd followed me into MMA. And eventually to his death.

The crushing, smothering guilt wouldn't strangle me so tightly if all I wanted was to fuck Eden. To bury myself balls deep inside her. If that's all I lusted after, then maybe the taint on my soul wouldn't be as black.

But it's not all I hunger for. I want it all. Her body, her affection… I want her to gaze at me the way she used to look at Connor. With that soft, secret gleam in her eyes that said they shared something that was completely mysterious to everyone else but them.

I want her. I have from the first moment I saw her five years ago—even after she met, fell in love with, and then married my brother.

And that makes my sin unforgivable.

I can never have Eden; I can never touch Connor's wife. Because yeah, he's gone, but she will always be his wife. And I am not worthy to breathe the same air, much less touch her. I know it. God knows it… My own mother knows it.

Women who know what's up, who are willing to fuck or blow me in bathroom stalls or in the back room of a bar or club, those chicks are my speed. All I deserve. Quick, emotionless, nameless screws.

Never her.

I made a promise to keep my hands off Eden. And after all the other things I've broken in my life and others'—hopes, dreams, hearts—this is a vow I refuse to break.

"Hey." She glances at me, arching a dark eyebrow. "We're just about done here."

"Thanks." Nodding, I grab the top sheet from a stack under the counter and hand it to my client. "Here's your aftercare directions. Like I told you, remove the bandage in about an hour. Keep the tattoo moist. We have some ointment"—I dip my head in the direction of the merchandise cabinet—"but you can use any petroleum-based ointment or lotion. All the instructions are right there." I tap the sheet. "You have any questions, you can call up here, but everything should be included on the list."

The instructions roll easily off my tongue; I've said them hundreds of times over the years. Still, this is the other woman's first tat. But she's not listening. Instead, she snatches Eden's pen off the counter, rips a corner off the paper, and scribbles on it. I don't need a Magic 8-Ball or an all-seeing-third-eye to figure out what she's writing.

"Thanks, Knox. Hope to see you soon." She grins and pushes the scrap toward me. Both Eden and I watch her stride out of the shop.

"Let me guess," Eden says, turning to me with a smirk. "She offered to give you more than a tip for your fantastic work."

Shaking my head, I pick up the paper with the name and number scrawled on it and toss it in the garbage can. I'm not answering that one.

She snorts, opening the register and placing the credit card slip under the cash drawer. "Hey, can I talk to you?" she asks, dragging a hand over her hair, pulling the strands out of her face.

I narrow my eyes at her. Something's up. Her tells are pathetically easy to catch. How she doesn't quite meet your eyes, or pulls her shoulders back and thrusts her chest out as if daring you to call her on something. Or crosses one foot in front of the other and stands in an awkward ballet position. What is it? Third or fourth? My stepsister used to take ballet lessons, and Dan and Mom used to force all of us to go to her recitals. It was hell.

Right now, though, Eden's giving me all three of those telltale gestures. Whatever she needs to speak with me about must be some serious shit.

"Yeah," I agree. "Hey, Jude, watch the front for a few?"

My brother glances at me, his tattoo machine still buzzing as he hovers above his client. His eyes, the same green as mine—as our father's—shift from me to Eden and back to me. Of my three brothers, Jude and I have always been the closest. Probably because we're only two years apart. So, when I barely jerk my chin up, he gets it. *Ask me later.*

"Got it covered," he says.

"Let's go to the breakroom." I head toward the back of

the shop.

"Can we go to your space instead?" she asks from behind me, her fingers grazing my hip.

My gut clenches at the light touch, the muscles wrenching hard. What would she do if she guessed the extent of her effect on me? How would she react if she knew that every time I look at her, inhale her scent, hear her throaty, 1-800-Fuck-Me voice, I fight the urge to shove her against the nearest wall, bury myself inside her, and pound into her until her screams break around my ears and her nails leave dents in my skin?

Would she run from me? Glare at me with disgust? Make sure she was never alone with me?

Like she is now.

Yeah, if Eden had the faintest hint of how dirty I want to get with her, no way in hell would she be asking to see me behind a closed door, away from prying eyes.

But the truth is there's no one she's safer with than me. And not just because she's Connor's wife or I'm chained by a promise. It's because Eden doesn't want me. From the moment I laid eyes on her five years ago and craved her, she looked past me and only saw Connor.

Shaking my head against the memories and the old, acrid bitterness crawling into my chest, I enter my room and, crossing my arms, wait for her to close the door.

"What's with all the secrecy?" I press, deliberately focusing on her face and each adorable freckle instead of the curves of her breasts beneath her form-fitting black sweater. Especially because she's doing that shoulders-back, chest-out thing again. Sighing, I cock my head to the side. "What are you nervous about, Eden?"

She frowns as if I've offended her. I smother a snort. More like called her on her shit. "I'm not nervous," she objects, moving farther into the room and closer to me. So close, I can easily catch her sunshine-and-fruit fragrance.

Would that scent be heavier, more saturated, like rain-soaked earth when she's aroused? When she's wet?

Fucking *focus*.

"What's going on, then?" I demand, the warring need to get closer and need to escape roughening my voice. "Something has you wired."

"Fine," she grumbles and blows out a breath. "I checked your schedule, and you don't have any appointments booked for the rest of the evening."

"Okay." Not surprising. It's a Tuesday, and the beginning of the week is always slower. "So?"

"I—" She breaks off, drags her fingers through her hair, and looses a soft chuckle that slides over my skin like a silken caress. "I have no idea why this is so hard for me to say. I'm twenty-four, damn it, not four." Her gaze locks with mine. "I want a tattoo."

Surprise whips through me. Yeah, because I expected something more…I don't know…cataclysmic, given her behavior. But also because Eden is a tattoo virgin. Even though she's worked in my shop for the last year and has been surrounded by people who wear more ink than clothes, she hasn't ever expressed a desire to change that status.

"And I want you to do it," she adds. "Will you?"

Have my hands on her body? Skin to skin? *Hell no*. "Yeah."

Relief crosses her face, and she nods. But there's more; she's not finished. I can tell by the ballet position. Unease curls inside me, squirming and coiling. I almost tell her "never mind."

"I'm moving out of your parents' house."

Well, fuck.

I don't know about cataclysmic, but shit's definitely about to hit the fan.

Chapter Two

Eden

Knox stares at me. Blinks. Stares some more.

I think I've sent him into shock.

That blink is a dead giveaway. For Knox The-Sphinx-Ain't-Got-Shit-On-Me Gordon, that one tiny tell is the equivalent of me knocking him on his ass.

"Well?" I press, fighting not to tangle my fingers together and twist them in front of me like some damsel in distress. Or a teenager being called on the carpet by a parent. Growing up in a house with an alcoholic father, I used to be as nervous as the ex of a rapper with a single about to drop. Finger-twisting is just one of my habits. But over the years, I've learned to control them, hating any sign of weakness. Except around Knox. Nothing—or no one—can bring out my nerves like Knox. He can be…intimidating. Yet, there's no one I trust more. "Say something."

Another blink. "Something."

A startled laugh escapes me before I can catch it.

Sometimes I think Knox was born centuries too late. With his huge, powerful, warrior's body, razor-sharp intensity, and laconic manner, he could've been a Spartan. Which is why, when he reveals his dry humor, it always catches me off guard and gives me an inexplicable little thrill of delight. While my feelings tend to explode all over the place, splattering everything and everyone like a paintball gun, Knox is a vault, with every emotion locked up tight behind that broad chest. Even when Connor died, that stoicism didn't crack. I half hated, half envied him that at the time. The only instances I've seen him lose that impassivity is in the ring...and the one memorable time I accidentally saw him having sex.

My belly twists, and the ache that pulses there slides lower at the memory, leaving a warm, bright trail. By the time that sweet pain settles between my legs, I'm surprised my flesh isn't lighting up like a damn glowworm.

So inconvenient and inappropriate, this raging case of lust for my brother-in-law.

"I know this is"—I shrug, searching for a word and coming up with a lame—"surprising."

He arches a dark eyebrow. "Surprising," he repeats. "That isn't the word I would've chosen. *What the fuck* fits, though."

"Those are three words," I mumble, and then I sigh because, yes, I'm stalling. Jesus, sometimes I still feel like that scared kid afraid to speak her mind, terrified of disappointing someone. Of making them mad. Bad things happened when you annoyed or irritated a drunk. But Knox isn't my father. One, I've never seen him down more than two beers in a night. And two, I've never dreamed and touched myself to visions of my sperm donor. Eww. Mimicking Knox, I cross my arms. But while his stance screams badass, mine probably radiates, "I'm trying to keep my shit together." "I can't live in Dan and Katherine's house for the rest of my life," I say, hearing the defensiveness in the tone.

"I agree."

That steals some of the steam building up inside me. Scrubbing my hands down the fronts of my thighs, I cross the small distance to the black, leather tattoo chair and drop down onto it.

"They aren't going to see it that way," I murmur, not needing to clarify who "they" are. His mother, stepfather, and I are close—even more so after Connor's death. I close my eyes and release a slow, deep breath. Used to be a time when I couldn't even think those words—Connor's death. Connor died. Connor. The pain would flay me, stripping emotional skin from my bones. I didn't scream aloud, but the cries would echo in my head like a crazy-ass banshee. Now, two years later, the agony had dulled to a sore ache. Still there but bearable, a reminder of an injury. Even forgotten for small stretches of time.

But for Katherine, the suffering hasn't diminished. Her sorrow is as sharp as the day she found out her son had died in a stadium locker room from a ruptured brain aneurysm. Connor was—is—her son, and I can't imagine losing a child, no matter his age. She's clung to her family to get her through. Well—I glance at Knox and meet his shuttered, dark green gaze—most of her family. She considers me her last living piece of Connor, and my leaving is going to hurt her. Badly.

But I can't let that keep me frozen in this...half-life anymore. Moving is just the first step. When I met Connor, I dropped out of college, choosing to move in with him, to support him and his career. To just be with him. Now, I'm a twenty-four-year-old widow with no college education, living in her in-laws' house. Not what I envisioned for myself. I enjoy working at the shop as the manager—really love it. I'm good at it, and I have so many ideas how Knox can grow, expand his brand, maybe open more tattoo shops. To gather the courage to approach him with my thoughts, I need to learn more about marketing, promotion, and business. And to accomplish that, I have to return to school.

That's step two.

Yeah, I'm trying to become a big girl.

"No, they're not," he agrees once more. There's no softness or gentleness to his voice, but I don't need either at the moment. If he did soften, I might cave and decide to put this move off like I've done for a couple of months now. "Are you ready to face it?"

Again, we're on that same wavelength, and I don't need to ask what he's referring to. "Face their sadness? Hurt? The sense of betrayal?" I shake my head and spread my hands out, palms up. My heart pounds, lodging in the base of my throat as if I'm telling them at this moment. "How the hell do I prepare myself for that?"

Knox snags his chair and lowers his big frame into it, never removing his steady, piercing gaze from my face. Jesus, he's... Handsome isn't the right word. That's too anemic, too...tame. Even though I can tell from the strain around his eyes and the tautness of his skin over his slanting cheekbones that he had a rough night, there's still a wildness, a harsh rawness in his fierce, angular features that isn't softened a bit by the lush fullness of his mouth or the dark brown scruff that's a little thicker than a five o'clock shadow but nowhere near verging into *Duck Dynasty* territory. Thank God. He's beautiful in the way of a black leopard—powerful and dangerous, muscles covered in sleekness. And all that focus and intensity. When he fixes that on a woman while he's fucking her, it must be exhilarating and terrifying at the same time. An image flashes across my mind before I can strike it down.

His hard, relentlessly male features are dark and stamped with a carnality that is both cruel and sexual. Green eyes hooded; skin pulled tight over sharp cheekbones; full, sensual mouth even fuller, more sensual, the corner curled into a small snarl.

Fuck.

I struggle not to fidget but fail. A small, subtle shift of my hips, and heat licks at my sex, flicking my clit. Please God, let him take the betraying movement as nerves rather than arousal. Catastrophic doesn't even begin to cover the mortification that would consume me if he discovered my inappropriate, damn abnormal fascination and... preoccupation with him. Yes, preoccupation sounds so much better than obsession. Still, doesn't matter what you call it. Fascination, preoccupation, obsession—they're all so wrong when I possess them for my dead husband's *brother*.

In some people's books, it would make me a slut, at best. A deviant, at worst. Or a deviant slut.

One of those books would belong to Katherine and Dan. And the thought of hurting them, of piling more despair on top of Katherine's already fragile shoulders... I'd die rather than do that to the woman who's been more of a mother to me than the one who birthed me.

"You can't," he answers my question. "You just do it and brace yourself for the fallout." His eyes narrow on me. "Are you ready for this, Eden? To move out and live on your own?"

If it'd been anyone else asking, I might take offense. Might, hell. I would definitely take offense. Just the suggestion that I'm weak, that I can't fend for myself, support myself, sets my teeth on edge. I've survived what most people have only seen on Lifetime movies—a drunk father and not-all-the-way-there mother, homelessness at eighteen, the death of my husband. I might appear like a good Chicago wind could blow me over, but I'm stronger than anything life has thrown at me.

But that's not what he meant. For five years, I haven't

been on my own. Three months after meeting Connor, I moved into his cramped, one-bedroom apartment. Then when he died, I lived with his parents. Am I ready for the loneliness that might eat me alive? For the silence that might press in on me?

The truth?

I don't know.

But I'm ready to find out.

And moving out is just the first step. But it's the most important one.

"If I don't do it now, I might never do it," I reply, shifting my attention to the muscular forearms resting on his thick thighs and the large hands clasped together between them. "It would be easier to stay with Katherine and Dan. But I need to…" *Get on with my life* trembles on my tongue. God, that sounds so cold, so dismissive. As if I'm really saying, *get over Connor*. And maybe…maybe both are right. I'll never forget Connor—how could I forget my first love, my husband?—but I can't remain in this limbo, either. My fingers tangle together of their own will. Though I despise the gesture and what it reveals, I can't stop the restless, anxious twisting. "The house. It's…" The words stick in my throat, and I swallow to force the explanation out. "I love your parents, but I feel like I'm not progressing there. At first, I needed to be there, for them as well as myself. But sometimes I feel like I'm… like I'm suffocating." Horrified at what I just said about his parents, I jerk my head up and stare into his eyes. "I'm sorry," I whisper. "I didn't mean…"

The guilt gnaws at me, because I *did* mean it. It makes me a selfish, ungrateful bitch, but I did.

"Don't apologize for being honest." His fingers curl, and for a breath-stalling moment, I think he might hold my hands, hug me. Except for the odd, rare embrace and the one time I cried in his arms, Knox doesn't touch me. And he doesn't now, either. He straightens, his back pressed to the chair. "I know they lean on you more than the rest of us. Especially Mom. To her, you're all she has left of Connor, and she clings tight to you. She's"—he pauses, his mouth hardening a little—"fragile right now, and to keep the peace and keep her steady, we've all allowed it. And that's not fair to you. So, no, don't apologize. This just means we have to step up."

I stare, barely managing to keep my jaw hinged shut. That might be the most I've heard him speak at one time.

"So, umm..." I clear my throat. "Can I ask a favor?"

He arches a dark eyebrow.

"I plan to tell them Sunday." Sundays were family dinner nights. It'd been a tradition I'd been folded into when I started dating Connor. Since his death, they hadn't been the boisterous, laughter-filled affairs they'd once been. And Knox has only showed up a handful of times. "Will you come to dinner? I know it's a lot to ask," I rush on, because I did recognize the toll these dinners exacted on him. But this past year, especially, Knox has become my rock. Not that I'd ever told him that. He wouldn't appreciate it. No...correction. He wouldn't *want* the burden of it. "But I could really use your support."

For several moments, he doesn't reply, just stares at me with that unwavering, piercing emerald gaze that could burn a hole through you. Finally, he nods.

"I'll be there."

A sigh of relief erupts from me. I'd been ready for his refusal. And wouldn't have blamed him for it.

"Thanks." I lean forward and rest my hand on his leg. The muscles underneath the denim tighten, and my breath snags. Before I can prevent it, my fingers curl into his huge thigh, squeezing. I swallow back a groan, captivated by the strength and...power that seems to emanate from him, to vibrate under my palm. It's like grasping a lion by the tail and waiting breathlessly for him to let you pet and stroke him. Or for him to pounce and snap his mighty jaws around your neck. Did it make me a little disturbed that I didn't know which I craved more?

Yeah. Disturbed.

And more than a little horny.

It'd been two years since I'd been with a man. Screw that. "Been with a man," is just too damn euphemistic. Two years since I've had sex.

Since I've fucked.

It's like my body shut off, went into a cryogenic state after Connor died. For six months, I remained in that frozen condition, no emotions, no needs, nothing. It'd been Knox who forced my return to the land of the living. One afternoon, in his no-nonsense, I-don't-give-a-fuck way, he'd barged into my room at his parents' home, literally carried me out of the bed and into the bathroom, where he'd dumped me into the shower and turned on the water. After much yelling and cursing on my part, he calmly explained that I would be his new receptionist at the tattoo shop. If I didn't show up the next morning, he'd come back for me. I showed up. And when I broke down at the end of that first day, sobbing as the grief and rage poured out of me, he held me, silently letting me cry and scream until I was hoarse and my head hurt. That had been the true beginning of my healing. I have him to thank for that.

I also have him to thank for the reappearance of my sex drive.

Though I'd started to smile and laugh again, that part of me—the need, the arousal—had remained dormant. Then, a year after starting at the shop, we'd all gone out to one of the local bars to celebrate my promotion to manager. A couple of hours in, I'd gone to the bathroom, and on my way back to the bar, I passed a partially closed door. To this day, I don't know what made me pause and glance inside the room. Maybe a sound that caught my attention underneath the throbbing music and shouts and conversations? Maybe some intuition? Either way, one peek into that dark, cluttered storeroom, and the ice that encased my body for so long melted under a fiery meteorite of lust.

Knox.

His back propped against a tall rack, his huge body taut. His hand burrowed in the dark red strands of the woman kneeling in front of him with his dick buried in her mouth. Even now, the heavy, aching pulse that had throbbed low in my belly, between my legs, as I stood frozen in that doorway, resurges. That memory is so damn entrenched in my brain that it torments me when I sleep, when I'm awake. When I'm eating damn breakfast. The wet suction of him driving into her. The woman's ravenous moans. His almost guttural, low growls.

But in the vision, it's me with my fingernails denting his jean-covered thighs. Me, with my lips stretched wide, taking him down my throat. Me, tearing those sounds of pleasure from him, shredding his unshakeable control. Me, staring up at the razor-sharp edges and planes of his face that appeared even more chiseled from stone with lust branded on his face. And those eyes. They'd always been gorgeous to me. While Connor's eyes had been a lovely, pale green that reminded me of spring, Knox's are a dark, deep emerald. Fathomless. And that night…

I shiver. That night from my vantage point, I'd glimpsed that gaze just before he tilted his head back. It haunts me, chases me into my dreams and darkest, dirtiest fantasies. His normally impassive, shuttered gaze had blazed like emerald fire. Like the stalking, predatory animal he'd unleashed in the MMA ring had reappeared with this woman.

In that moment, I'd wanted to be that woman. Craved it.

I'd longed to switch places with her, be full of him, have his taste and power inside me...bring him back to fierce, almost feral life.

Exhaling, I remove my hand from his leg. Dangerous. Touching him is too dangerous when I dance this close to the edge of begging him to take me, to fuck me until every part of me—my sex, my thighs, my belly, my chest, the goddamn soles of my feet—echoes with the knowledge that he's been inside me.

But I have zero doubt Knox doesn't want me like that. Entwined in his life as his brother's widow? As his adopted sister? As his shop manager? Yes. But as a woman he'd press to her knees so he could defile her mouth? No.

I know because he told me as much, a few days after I'd seen him and the woman in the club storeroom. God, I hadn't been able to look him in the eyes, not with the memory of him so entrenched in my mind. I could still hear his grunts, his growled orders... Maybe he'd picked up on my discomfort, or maybe he'd believed I was having one of my "spells" when the grief over Connor just snuck up on me.

Either way, as I cleared off the front desk and shut down the computer, he'd touched me. Which he almost never did. But that night, he broke his norm. Just my hands. He clasped them, his larger ones practically swallowing mine. Such a simple, innocent touch, one meant to comfort, but when I could no longer look at his fingers without envisioning them twisted in my hair... There was nothing innocent about it for me, or about the tight, aching pull of desire between my sex.

I can only imagine what my gaze contained when I tilted my head back. Need? A plea to put those big hands on me? Questions about whether he wanted me, too?

Maybe all of those. Because something entered that hooded, emerald stare. Something dark, cold...forbidding. He'd never looked at me like that before, and icy, skeletal fingers of…not fear, but almost of despair had scraped down my back, infiltrated my veins.

He didn't want me. And the hardness in his eyes had assured me I'd violated the bounds of our friendship by even hoping he would. He hadn't needed words to shut me down. He'd done it with a stare and by walking away without a backward glance.

Then, and even now, I don't resent him for that unspoken but implicit rejection. He's my dead husband's brother, for God's sake. Still… Buried deep beneath reason is that fragile kernel of my sexual confidence, curled into a protective fetal position, shielding itself from any more rejection from the one man it'd shyly awakened for.

"Anyway," I say, lifting my head, forcing a false cheer into my voice and shoving that pathetic memory far, far away. "About this tattoo…"

My voice trails off as I meet his stare, the rapid, heavy thump of my heart replacing my voice. I try to swallow, but I got nothing. All the moisture in my mouth has evaporated under the force of his hooded, glittering scrutiny. It's as if we've traveled back in time in a souped-up DeLorean, and he's in that dim storeroom once again, a single bulb illuminating us. And *I'm* clutching him, starved for him.

"What do you want?" he growls.

I blink, my voice trapped inside my throat. *So much. Your mouth. Your hands. Your body. Your fire. Your rawness.*

You.

"For your tattoo," he clarifies.

The tattoo. Of course. Shaking my head as if that could dislodge those fruitless thoughts that reek of everything taboo and forbidden, I stand on trembling legs. And when I look down at him, his gaze is as impenetrable as always. God, am I so desperate that I superimposed my own lust on him and misjudged what I saw in his eyes? Disgust rolls through me, and I welcome it. *He's just not into you*, my inner know-it-all whispers smugly. Yeah, I remind myself, crossing the room and picking up one of the black plastic portfolios on the glass table in front of his small couch. To Knox, I'm his younger brother's widow. That's it. That's all I'll ever be. Which meant I'd better find another outlet for this desire. Quick. Five minutes ago.

Flipping through the laminated pages, I find what I want in seconds. "Here." I return to him, holding the opened book out to him. "This one."

We both study the watercolor of three flowers on a vine. I know exactly zip about flowers, but they could be roses or peonies painted in soft, varying shades of pink, lavender, green, and brown. It truly resembles something Van Gogh would've created rather than a tattoo. From the first time I spotted the piece a year ago, I've wanted it. Only now, on the cusp of making changes in my life, have I dragged on my big mama drawers to get it.

"It's yours, right?" I ask. When he nods, I trace the first, tightly furled bud. The second one is shyly halfway open, and the third is in full bloom. Spring. Life again. "It's beautiful."

"You should have Shana do this for you," he states in the deep rumble that reverberates inside me like a low drum of thunder. "Watercolor is what she does."

I know this. The other female artist is a genius when it comes to this particular style. But... "I want you."

The three words echo between us, seeming to gain velocity and volume with each beat of silence in the room. Mortification slams into me. *Jesus.* His shoulders stiffen, and his big fist clenches around the edge of the portfolio, the plastic cracking in his grip. Glancing at his face, I see the harsh, sculpted lines are even more stern, more severe.

"If you've changed your mind—"

"No," he cuts me off, closing the portfolio with a slap of

his palm. "I said I'll do it. I'll do it."

"Look, forget it. When Shana arrives, I'll ask her to fit me in." I head toward the door, a little hurt and a lot ready to escape this room that has suddenly become too tiny, too stifling, too hot. Feeling like a nuisance—an undesired nuisance—sucks shit. This was probably all a bad idea anyway...

Two long fingers hook into the waistband of my jeans, halting my march of humiliation.

I gasp. This is the closest I'll ever come to having Knox's hand in my pants, and I'm relishing the kiss of flesh to flesh, which feels more like a brand than a simple touch. Glancing down, I nearly groan. The purple, lace band of my thong rides above my jeans, and when I slide a peek at Knox, his gaze is lasered to it.

I stop breathing, watching the nostrils of his twice-broken but somehow still-elegant nose flare as he sharply inhales. Bracing myself, I expect him to snatch his hand away, but instead, he slowly slides his fingers free, stroking my skin. As if he's savoring the caress.

Only when he turns around, giving me his broad shoulders and back, do I close my eyes and silently, deliberately exhale. Feeling like a newborn colt on shaking, gangly legs, I cross the short distance to the tattoo chair and sink onto it.

Silence permeates the room. The only sounds are the rip of the new needle package, and the open and closing of drawers as Knox grabs ink, caps, and his tattoo equipment. His hands are steady. More evidence that I'm the only one affected by this troublesome, objectionable lust.

Maybe I just need to go find someone to fuck. I spend most of my time with Knox in this shop. That could explain why this...hunger seems to be fixated on him. Shana and V have been attempting to hook me up with guys for months, but I've always claimed I'm not ready. But maybe I should give it a try. I mean, not only would I satisfy this need clawing at me, but it would also be with someone I've never called "brother."

Win-win.

"You ready?" Knox spins to face me on his stool, his expression cool, professional. Like I'm any other client.

Fine. I can be polite, too.

I nod. "Yeah."

"Where do you want it?"

Instead of answering, I scoot farther back on the chair, which wouldn't be out of place in a dentist's office, recline, and lift up my shirt. "Here." I trace the right side of my torso, several inches below my breast. "What do you think?"

Knox doesn't answer. He hasn't moved. He studies my bared stomach with the same, narrowed, fevered gaze I convinced myself I'd imagined moments earlier. Jesus, it's like he's...like he's *touching* me, licking me, devouring me with that stare. Sweat pops out on my palms. My heart slams against my chest wall, bruising it. Liquid heat pours into my sex, and I'm on fire, even as I'm drowning. My thighs quiver, and I squeeze them together to alleviate the ache.

His scrutiny drops, and damn, he didn't miss that telltale movement. I *know* he didn't. Not when the sensual curves of his mouth harden, and the skin over his cheekbones seems to tauten. Embarrassment races through me. But right next to it, keeping pace, is excitement. A shameful excitement. His hooded contemplation slowly travels up my body and settles on the jeweled ring piercing my belly button.

"When did you get this?" he asks, flicking it.

"Last month," I whisper. "Jude did it for me."

"Is it still tender?" he murmurs, flipping the metal again.

Pain in the palest shade of red tinges the pleasure zinging through me and arrowing straight to the wet flesh between my thighs. My teeth sink into my bottom lip, and I can't prevent the slight squirm of my hips.

"A little," I breathe. Then, because I can't hold it in… "Do it again." It's clearly a plea, and I know how it sounds. Greedy. Desperate. Screw it. I don't care. "Please."

That piercing, emerald gaze—with its dark depths and hard edges—bores into mine. Instinct warns me to avoid it, but I don't. Can't. Even if it means he glimpses the arousal that's lighting me up like the Olympic torch.

As if in slow motion, he grasps the tiny jewel in the middle of the ring.

And tugs.

My breath explodes from my lungs, echoing in the room like a cannon shot. It shouldn't feel this good. But God, it does. Maybe because it's him. No, *definitely* because it's him.

"Again," I rasp, my fingernails digging into the leather cushion.

Something spasms across his face, some emotion I can't decipher. But it's dark, a little forbidding, like that night months earlier. A little scary, a little be-careful-what-you're-asking-for. A lot I'll-fuck-you-into-this-chair. Part of me almost rescinds the request, not ready for what that expression promises. But the starving, hasn't-been-touched-in-two-years part drowns out that other half. Yeah, I might not be ready. Doesn't mean I don't want it more than my next lust-infused breath. Especially from him. Especially when I'd convinced myself I'd never have this.

Without releasing me from the visual snare of his eyes, he rolls closer on the stool, lowers his head, and—

Ohhh fuck.

His tongue sweeps over me, curling around the jewelry, gently sucking, pulling. The springy but soft hair of his scruff brushes my skin, adding another sensation to enjoy and covet more of. Pleasure radiates from where his mouth covers me, and my clit pulses like a beacon. My nipples throb, drawing into tight points, and I cover them with my hands, palms pressing into them. But it doesn't ease the ache, just worsens it—or heightens it. Both.

Unable to remain still, I whimper, arching into his wicked caress, my hips rolling, begging for another, harder, deeper touch. Releasing the belly ring, he traces the rim of my navel, dipping inside. Blowing gently on the damp skin.

He straightens, and I almost cry with the loss of that beautiful mouth on me. Releasing one breast, I trail my hand down my torso and stroke the damp flesh he left behind. As if I can seal the impression of his tongue into my skin.

"Lift your shirt higher," he growls. Shock slaps me, and I freeze, my hands—one on my stomach, the other over my breast—going still. Standing from the stool, he leans over me, his big palms resting on the chair arms. A fine tension damn near vibrates from him, his muscles straining against his shirt. The tendons in his neck stand out in sharp relief. He appears one second—or one disobedient act—away from snapping and losing control. "Show me where it hurts."

Is this the same voice he used on the girl at the bar to convince her to enter that storeroom and get down on her knees for him? Because, like her, I'm ready to please him. And all because he asked in that rough, sex-on-churned-up-earth voice. I'm raising my shirt, baring my chest when there's a shop full of people just on the other side of the door. I don't even think it's locked. But at this moment, I wouldn't care if Jude, his client, and the client's mama stride into the room. I just want to give Knox what he wants.

What I need.

And I need to see the desire deepening his eyes to a green so dark, they appear black. I need him to cool the burn, satisfy the hunger. I need to be wanted. By *him*.

"Here," I whisper. Then, another woman—a less inhibited, more sexually confident, don't-give-a-good-fuck woman—possesses my body because I tug down the lace bra, freeing my breasts. Cool air brushes over my flesh, and the nipples bead tighter. But I don't fool myself. It's his gaze on me that has me in this state, not the kiss of air. "It hurts here."

I cup myself, offering...pleading.

And he takes.

A loud, slightly ominous rumble is my only warning before he swoops down and sucks my nipple into his mouth, drawing hard.

A scream shoots up my chest, crawls up my throat, but I slap a hand over my lips before it escapes. I burrow the other hand into his hair, dislodging the bun he binds the thick strands into when he's tattooing. I can't... I can't think. Can't... My muffled cry is muted in the room, but in my head, it's splintering glass. Perking up the ears of dogs. His tongue torments me, each pull and stroke tugging on a phantom cord connected to my sex. There's no hesitation in him. No gentleness.

No mercy.

And I don't want his mercy or his tenderness. For the first time in years, someone is treating me like I'm not this fragile figurine that needs to be delicately handled so I won't shatter. Treating me like a woman.

Lowering my hand, I am riveted by the sight of his mouth surrounding me. Watching him only sharpens the pleasure shrieking through me like the fiercest Chicago wind. With a soft pop, he releases me, and I trace his reddened, swollen lips. Soft, but firm. Generous but a little bit cruel. I've been obsessed with this mouth. What it could do to me. And now part of that fantasy is coming true.

I shiver.

"Kiss me," I murmur, pressing my fingertip to the middle of his bottom lip, groaning as the edge of his teeth grazes my skin. It's a demand. A plea. A wish. I want to finally taste him. Find out if he's a dark, heady flavor that will go straight to my head and leave me drunk for hours. Discover for myself what that other woman knows. Determine if he's as addictive as I think he will be.

I already know the answer to that.

The two words reverberate in the room, and his impossibly long, dense lashes lower. A harsh, serrated breath shudders from between his parted lips. Even before his big body goes rigid, a sickening tightness in the pit of my stomach alerts me that something is wrong. Has changed. Like a ghost suddenly appeared in the room, the temperature seems to drop. But that cold isn't emanating from an apparition; it's from Knox.

His lashes lift, and this time when I shiver, it's not the reaction to lust, but to the ice coating his gaze, chilling the flames there until they're extinguished. Not even embers remain. This look is all too familiar. And I shrink from it now, just as much as I did then.

"Fuck." Knox shoves away from me as if I'm the pox giftwrapped in the clap. I flinch, even though the vicious lash of anger is clearly self-directed. He stalks across the room, thrusting his hands through his hair, completely dislodging the bun I'd loosened. The dark brown and gold strands tumble down, covering his closely shaven sides and falling just below his jaw.

He tips his head back, and if I didn't know he'd cursed God years ago—two, to be exact—I'd assume he's praying. But no. From the tortured frown that creases his forehead, the rapid rise and fall of his chest, and the clenched fists next to his thighs, he's most likely condemning himself to a place the far opposite of heaven.

His obvious shame sends the grit of guilt scraping my skin, leaving nasty scratches behind.

Swallowing back the acidic burn of humiliation scorching my throat, I quickly fix my bra and jerk down my shirt, covering myself. But I still feel naked, exposed. Vulnerable.

This is my fault. I'm so fucking *stupid*. What was I *thinking*? Mimicking his gesture, I bury my hands in my hair, tugging on the strands and enjoying the bite of pain. It gives me something to focus on other than how I damn near *begged* Knox to touch me. Yeah, he might've been a complete guy and responded in that moment, but just looking at him now…

I duck my head, unable to continue staring at him. It hurts too much. The ache and mortification of rejection. The horror that he would now see me as a pathetic, needy woman who he almost pity-fucked in his tattoo chair. The sadness that our friendship might be scarred by this. Because he couldn't have made his regret at putting his mouth on me plainer if he'd branded it on his forehead.

And worse? Worse is my body still hums with unfulfilled need. My nipples are so tight, one touch would buckle my knees. I'm so wet, my panties are probably beyond saving.

I *ache*.

And I need to get out of here before I do something even crazier. Such as climb him like a jungle gym and plead with him to get me off. To finish what he started the night I watched him come in another woman's mouth.

Oh, hell yeah, I need to escape this room.

My feet are moving before the message hits my brain. Survival instincts at their finest.

"Eden."

That gravel-and-sin voice only adds wings to my feet. *Please, don't try to talk to me. Not when I can still feel your tongue curling around my nipple. Please save your apology and "This was a mistake" speech for later. As in, Junevember 56th later.*

"Don't worry, Knox," I say, forcing a nonchalance that is as false as the wig collection on RuPaul's *Drag Race*. I even manage a glance over my shoulder, though it nearly guts me.

He hasn't moved. But the anger and shame are entrenched in every line in his forehead. In the grim set of his mouth. In the darkness of his eyes.

Whipping around, I concentrate on the closed door. On grabbing the knob. Twisting it.

"Don't worry," I repeat, unable to block the hurt from leaking into my tone. Even though my mind acknowledges he did us both a favor by pulling away—that going any further with him would've been a monumental mistake—my confidence is kicked to hell and back. "This was a mistake, and it'll never happen again," I utter the words before he can, trying to salvage some of my pride.

Wrenching the door open, I slip through and close it behind me.

Too bad I can't shut it on the last half hour.

Fuck.

Where's that DeLorean when you need it?

Chapter Three

Knox

It's goddamn Sunday dinner. Not a heavyweight match on a BFC fight card.

Yeah. Then why the hell is my heart pounding like I'm about to enter the ring against a bastard who outweighs me by sixty pounds, has me out-trained, out-matched, out-witted, and totally mind-fucked?

Maybe because that's a pretty accurate description of any time spent with my mother and Dan, my stepfather.

Heaving a sigh, I push open the door to my black Escalade and step out into the driveway of the Edison Park two-story, single-family home I bought my mom with the check from my first championship fight. Yeah, I was a complete cliché, but getting my mother out of that cramped Bridgeport house that we all grew up in had been my dream when I was a kid. And I'd had the sense Dad would've somehow found a way to leave his celestial card game and whatever passed for Guinness up there to come down and slap me upside the head if I hadn't. I close my eyes at just the thought of the big, boisterous, and tough Irishman who'd raised, disciplined, and loved me until I was fourteen and a fatal heart attack stole John Gordon from us. When Mom met and married Dan Keller three years later, I didn't hate or resent him. He was—is—an okay guy. He just isn't my father. Never could be.

Turning around, I stare at my reflection in the window of the truck, going over a mental checklist. Hair pulled back in a short ponytail, beard neat. Mom hates it, but no way in hell am I cutting it. So making it as trim as possible will have to do. A white dress shirt and black pants. Most of my tattoos hidden, except for the one crawling up my neck and the letters on my fingers. I try to conceal everything that might remind Mom of the fighter I was. Remind her of the sport that took her son.

That black hole in my chest expands the tiniest bit. It's resided there since Connor fell to the mat, lying there so fucking still with a thin line of blood trickling from his nose, and has grown and stretched its tentacles like a virus with each passing day, month, year. At some point, I expect that void of emptiness to consume me.

Part of me is looking forward to that day.

Turning, I slowly head toward the front walk and steps. A breeze ruffles my shirt, cooling my slightly heated skin. Mid-September in Chicago, it's still warm enough outside where we don't need jackets. Give it a few more weeks, though, and that's going to change fast. Better enjoy it now.

As soon as I climb the steps to the postage-stamp-size porch, the door swings open. Simon, my youngest brother, fills the doorway. And I do mean, *fills*. Just twenty-two years-old, he's almost as big as Jude and me. At six-feet-four and two-hundred-and-forty-eight pounds, I still stand taller than him by three inches and outweigh him by about twenty pounds. But my little brother is big. And with the same dark blond hair as Jude, and our mom's blue eyes, he can come across as intimidating. The truth is he's the kindest and most sensitive of us all. He was seven when our dad died, and we've all been protective of him since. Not saying Simon can't hold his own. He has a slow-burn temper, but piss him off, and he'll demonstrate he knows how to use those huge fists for more than drawing. Yeah, Simon's a damn good artist getting his Bachelor of Fine Arts in Studio at SAIC, the School of the Art Institute of Chicago. I couldn't be prouder of him.

"Excuse me, sir," he says, frowning. "Who are you? I mean, you look familiar, but we don't really allow strangers to roll up into our house."

I snort. "Very funny."

"No seriously." He palms either side of the doorway. "Do we know you? You kind of remind me of a guy I know. Big motherfucker—"

"Language," a voice calls from inside the house. I smirk as Simon grimaces. If our mother had a dollar for every time she warned us about our mouths, she could own a small country.

"A big mofo," Simon amended with a grin. "Owns a tattoo shop, used to kick a— uh, tail for a living." He squints, rubbing the stubble on his chin. Unlike Jude and me, he can't grow a beard for shit. Isn't stopping him from trying, though. "Yeah, you could pass for him. I mean, you're a little butt-uglier, but still..."

Sighing, I step forward and slam a palm into his shoulder.

"Ouch, dammit," he growls, ignoring Mom's second cursing alert and rubbing the offended spot as I move by him. "You do realize your abnormally large hands—signs of an equally abnormally small brain, by the way—are dangerous to us regular folk?" Grumbling what sounds suspiciously to me like "freakish asshole," he shuts the front door with an exaggerated scowl.

"I take it this is your way of saying you've missed me?" I ask, arching an eyebrow, pausing in the foyer because, if I'm honest, I'm not eager to walk down the hallway that leads to the living room, dining room, and kitchen. To where Mom is cooking. And Eden is no doubt right beside her.

"No," Simon drawls. "That would be my way of saying where the"—he drops his volume several decibels—"fuck you been?"

"Busy." I shrug. The last couple of weeks have seen an increase in walk-ins, and I've had several sessions scheduled for big pieces. Not to mention the BFC 56 event, hosted by Bellum Fighter Championship, was held in Chicago last week. Several fighters came in the shop for new tattoos. That had been bittersweet. I'd been happy to see them and hang out. But the jagged, raw part of me that refuses to heal throbbed at the reminder that they were still doing what I'd walked away from. "I was going to call you tomorrow anyway. I have a client who wants an original piece. Kyro Men from *Star Wars*. Or something like that."

Sometimes Simon draws up art for me when I have certain requests. I'm good, really good, but him? He's fucking brilliant.

"That's Kylo Ren, you ignorant peon." Simon snickers, his eyes gleaming in what I recognize as excitement. Well, that and his rubbing his palms together like a Scooby-Doo villain. "Hell, yeah. I'm down. When do you need it?"

"Wednesday. He's coming in Thursday to approve it. I'll give you forty percent of the fee, as usual." That might seem high, but any tattoo artist knows the art itself is as important as inking it. And Simon should be paid for his work.

"Cool," he agrees. "I'll bring it by since I want some more ink." He grinned. "I'm thinking maybe I could get that hot-as-hell Heaven to do it."

I roll my eyes. Another thing Simon has in common with

Jude and me. Won't keep his dick in his pants.

"You okay?" He frowns, losing all traces of humor. "You look like shit."

Another sleepless night. What else is new? Walking my apartment, fucking, drawing, or sitting up watching old *Murder, She Wrote* reruns are all better than the nightmares. Any day. In the last two years, Jessica Fletcher, a.k.a. J.B. Fletcher, has become my girl.

I shrug in reply to Simon's question, and his frown deepens.

"Are you two coming in, or do you plan on standing there gossiping like teen girls all night?" Eden, arms crossed and hip cocked, smiles at us from the living room entrance. Well, she does at Simon. Me, she skates over, that smile faltering just the smallest bit when our eyes briefly meet.

It's a repeat of the last week. The past few days, she's been her usual open, affectionate self. But there's been a strain between us. One that didn't exist before she walked out of my tattoo room after I tasted her body for the first time.

No, that's not true. There was that night months ago in the shop after closing. There'd been a strain then, too. Then, I thought it'd been one of those periods when memories of Connor drew her into a funk. So, against my better judgement, I'd risked it and touched her. And for a moment, desire had darkened her gaze. For an instant, a fierce, almost excruciating joy had pierced my chest, but then the inescapable truth had slammed into me. She was grieving for her husband—my brother. That arousal that shined in her eyes hadn't been for me. It'd been for a ghost.

I could've touched her, kissed her. Maybe she would've let me fuck her against that desk. But the regret that surely would've crowded into her eyes afterward would've ripped me apart. So I ignored it. Walked away. And I'd been right. Because everything had returned to status quo fairly quickly.

Meaning me craving her, and her treating me like her brother-in-law, the eunuch.

But a week ago, in my chair...

Yeah, I fucked up and let the beast slip the chain.

Days later, and I'm still gripping that chain so tight, my palms are torn up to hell. How could I have touched her? My dead brother's wife. There's no other woman on this planet more off-limits than her. This insane, selfish need for her was manageable before.

Before she placed that delicate hand on my thigh, only inches from my cock.

Before she lifted her shirt and bared all that silken, dusky skin.

Before she asked me to give her pleasure...and a little pain.

Before I found out for myself the size and shape of her nipple with my tongue.

But now? Now, I've spent every damn second warring to not drag her back into my room, stretch her out on my chair, and finish what she invited me to take. Need, hard and ruthless, squeezes my chest, grips my dick. For the hundredth time tonight, I consider turning around, walking out, and not returning. I've never backed off from anything in my life—not taking up responsibility for my younger brothers after Dad died; not a fight against the biggest, toughest opponent; not purchasing and running my own business.

Eden has me in full retreat.

Because keeping my hands off her had been hell when she hadn't twisted and moaned so sweetly, when she hadn't demanded I kiss her. Now it's a torture that would make interrogation by the Spanish Inquisition look like a game of Twister.

It'd been that breathless request that had snatched me back to cold, brutal reality. A reality where she was Connor's wife, and I was the man who'd introduced him to the sport that had cost him his life. A reality where I had no right, where I wasn't worthy to put my hands—or mouth—on her. A reality where a rage-and-grief-stricken accusation bound me to an oath I can't break. Not if I don't want to destroy a relationship that's already dented and bent, almost beyond repair.

My reality.

"Well, I don't know." Simon holds his hands up, pretending to study them. "Knox did promise to paint my nails, sooo…"

She laughs in the way that's strictly hers—a loud, joyous crack that sounds like thunder breaking across the sky. Connor used to say her laughter was God snorting. I'm not anywhere near that damn poetic. But yeah, my little brother might've had something there.

Simon strides down the hall and swoops Eden up in a bear hug, her feet dangling above the floor. There's nothing sexual about the embrace, yet as her giggles reach me, I still want to tear down there, grab her out of his arms, and pull her into mine.

Instead, I wait until they both disappear into the living room. Only then do I follow. Taking my time. Preparing myself for the evening ahead. Between pretending everything is normal between Eden and me, bearing Mom's silent accusation and disappointment, and bracing for Eden's upcoming announcement, I wish I had something stronger than the wine served at every Sunday dinner.

Sighing, I scrub a hand down my face, my beard scratching my palm. As always, I pause and study the framed photograph of Dad and me in front of Wrigley Field when I was thirteen. And as always, a tight fist squeezes my heart as his big, booming laughter from that day faintly echoes in my head. It's one of my happiest memories. Dad was a diehard

Cubs fan, and we never missed one season opener. I haven't been to a game since he died.

This picture used to hang on the wall at the old house. It says something about Dan that he allows photos of his wife's first husband to be displayed so prominently. He's a good man. I can admit that, even though we've never been close.

"Dinner's ready," Mom calls, stepping out of the kitchen entrance. She catches sight of me, and after a beat of silence, nods. "Knox. I didn't think you were coming today."

Nothing in her voice telegraphs if she's happy I showed up or wished I'd stayed away. There'd been a time when her face would've reflected every emotion tumbling inside her. Even Dad's unexpected death hadn't managed to douse her light, steal her joy. Dimmed it for a while, but hadn't snuffed it out.

Connor's death had accomplished that.

I missed the mother who laughed easily, teased with a soft smile, loved with a big heart instead of a shattered one. I haven't seen that version of her in two years, and I mourn it just as much as I grieve for my brother.

"I hope it's okay," I reply. Once, that statement would've been unnecessary. And I would've received a pop for even uttering it.

"Of course," she says and, turning, disappears into the kitchen.

Slowly, I exhale. This is going to be a long evening.

An hour later, seated at the dining room table, I felt like a clairvoyant. Hell, set up my own 900-number, assume a name and a fake accent, and I'd be in business.

Picking up the bottle of beer I'd found in the bottom drawer of the refrigerator, I lean back in my chair, letting the hum of conversation flow around me. Dan shoots me a chagrined frown, and I shrug. Yeah, it's one of the bottles he always keeps stowed away because he's a beer man through and through. But sorry, that sweet Riesling Mom serves just ain't cutting it. And hey, I didn't touch the remaining three bottles in the vegetable crisper drawer.

"He went on and on about how smart Connor was. About how much they liked and respected him," Mom says, continuing her story about bumping into a former college classmate of Connor's at the bank. "Imagine, the Assistant Vice President praising him like that." She shakes her head, her smile trembling as she blinks quickly. Battling back tears.

My chest tightens, and I look away. Not before Dan covers her hand with his and squeezes.

"Yeah," Jude chimes in from beside me. "And he was never shy about letting you know just how smart, either. 'Jude, dude, Occam's Razor states that all things being equal, the simplest explanation is usually the correct one.'" Jude's imitation of Connor's proper, hint-of-frat-boy speech is dead on. I snort, lifting the beer to my mouth. "'So if your girl's car was parked in front of your friend's building at 2 a.m., more than likely they weren't binge-watching *Gilmore Girls*.'"

Laughter erupts around the table, and even Mom smiles, eyes damp. I can't help but glance across the table at Eden. Maybe it's some kind of masochistic punishment to see her face brighten at the memories of her husband. To glimpse the love and sadness in her dark eyes. I need both to remind myself who she belongs to. To emphasize that man's not me. Could never be me.

As if she can feel my scrutiny on her, she shifts her attention from Jude, and our gazes meet. Or clash. My gut hollows out, as bottomless as the depths of those chocolate eyes. It's like we've suddenly been cast in one of those soap operas that Mom watches religiously, and everyone else at the table fades away into a shadowed, hazy mist. Yeah, corny as hell, but I can't deny that I don't see anything else but the spray of Eden's cinnamon freckles across her forehead, cheekbones, and the bridge of her nose. The sensual, sinfully full curves of her wide mouth. The delicate jaw and slightly pointed chin. The fall of her thick, black-brown hair over her shoulders, hiding her breasts from me. Doesn't do shit for my thoughts, though. Without the slightest effort, I can still picture the rounded, perfect flesh that fit my hand as if created for it. Or the beaded tips the color of henna tattoos.

I curl my fingers into my palm, my skin retaining the imprint of her breast and nipple like a brand. What I wouldn't give right now to have my cock experience that same heaven. To cup her, rub my thumb back and forth over the tight peaks while thrusting between that soft flesh. To have her tongue flick over the head at the end of every stroke...

Lust hammers into me harder than a double-fist punch to the chest. It burrows deep, hardening my body until even breathing threatens to crack me into pieces.

Her eyes widen slightly before falling away, the pulse at the base of her throat throbbing so hard the thin, fragile skin lifts under it. I wanted to suck on that spot, drag that little, hungry whimper out of her like at the shop.

Lifting the beer bottle to my mouth again, I down a big, healthy gulp. Too bad it does fuck-all for the heat raging through me like the fire that almost took out all of Chicago at one time.

"While talking to Connor's friend, I couldn't help but wonder where he would've been today if he'd gone straight into the graduate program or to a real job." The soft wistfulness in Mom's voice, or that she probably didn't intend her words as a jab, doesn't lessen the sting of them.

I've been involved in MMA since I was fifteen. Trained in one of the best gyms in the world in San Diego. Have competed in MMA organizations all over the world—California, Singapore, and Japan. I'm a brown belt in Guerrilla Jiu-Jitsu, a black belt in Brazilian Jiu-Jitsu, and a two-time heavyweight champion. Now, I'm a business owner. But none of that equals a "real job" to my mother. Because none of it included a suit, tie, desk, and annual salary. Security. That's what she'd wanted for Connor, knowing she wouldn't get it from her other sons. Not with Jude apprenticing in a tattoo shop before he even graduated from high school, and Simon's love of art and drawing. So when Connor chose to follow in my footsteps into MMA, she'd been deeply disappointed.

"He wouldn't have been happy," Eden says into the strained silence. "There were several offers from big accounting firms waiting for him when he graduated. But the thought of being locked up in an office all day and chained to a desk made him feel like he was suffocating. He would've been miserable."

"But he would've been here." Mom's voice cracks on "here." "Alive."

She glances at me, and the guilt that always weighs me down until I choke with it increases in size and weight.

"You did this! He's dead because of you! You and that damn fighting. Now my boy, my baby is gone..."

I blink, and the image of my mother crumbling onto the floor, her face ravaged by tears and grief, evaporates. But her screams continue to batter my ears for a few seconds longer. Other than her broken, hoarse outburst the night we arrived here to tell her about Connor—and other equally devastating words she yelled at me—she has never come out and blamed me for his death again. But she doesn't need to vocalize it. The accusation is there in every sideways look, every moment of her suffering, every heavy silence.

Like now.

Shoving back my chair, I stand and stride for the kitchen. Tipping up the bottle I'd carried with me, I drink the last of the alcohol and grab another beer from the fridge. Half of it is gone before I turn and head back into the dining room and reclaim my seat. This time, Dan doesn't bother with a those-are-mine squint. Maybe he believes I need whatever I can get to make it through the rest of this dinner.

Jude arches his eyebrow, silently inquiring if I'm okay. I answer yes with a jerk of my chin.

"...was thinking we could repaint your room." Mom pats Eden's hand. "Or redecorate it. Really make it yours," she continues, not noticing the wince that flashes across Eden's face.

Oh damn. It's showtime.

Eden peeks at me, and I nod my head, encouraging her. Letting her know I'm here for her as promised, in spite of the tension permeating our relationship this week.

"Katherine, Dan," Eden begins. Stops. Starts again. "I have some news. I—" She breaks off and slides her fingers from under Mom's, hiding both of her hands under the table. Probably to conceal the twisting and clenching she's certainly doing.

"What's wrong, Eden?" Dan asks, concern evident in his frown. Though Connor had been his stepson, he'd loved him. Had been the closest to him out of all of Mom's kids. And that love spilled over to Eden. "Is everything okay?"

From beside Eden, Simon frowns, stretching his arm across the back of her chair. "What's up, sis?"

"Nothing's wrong," she hurriedly assures them. Closing her eyes, she mutters, "I'm making a complete mess of this." Inhaling deeply, she meets Mom and Dan's gazes. "You two have no idea how much I love you and appreciate everything you've done for me. You're closer to me than my own parents. Which is why knowing this is going to hurt you kills me. I'm... moving out."

"Oh *shit*," Jude breathes.

For once, Mom doesn't reprimand him about his language. She's frozen, staring blankly at Eden.

I don't breathe. Just wait. And prepare to do what I can to deflect the shitstorm that's about to whirl in here like a demented ballerina on crack.

"Wh-what do you mean?" Mom croaks, shaking her head. "I don't understand. This is your home…"

"Did we do something, Eden? We didn't mean—" Dan whispers.

"No," she denies, voice firm. "Absolutely not. You guys have been nothing but good to me. It's just… It's time for me to stand on my own. To try and make it on my own."

"But why?" Mom's confusion and distress is so obvious, I force myself to remain in my chair and not go over to her, hug her. "This is your home," she repeats.

Eden presses a hand to Mom's arm. "It's not," she softly counters. "This is *your* home. Yours and Dan's. And I thank you for opening it to me and giving me a soft place to land for a while. But that's all it was intended to be—for a while. I'm stronger now than I was two years ago. That's thanks to you and your family. I don't want to hurt you," she murmured, her voice cracking on the last word. "It's the last thing I want to do."

"Then don't go," Mom pleads. A note of sharp-edged panic pitches her quivering voice higher. She grabs Eden's hand, grips it like she's the last piece of driftwood sweeping past her, saving her from being battered and swallowed up by treacherous, dark rapids. "First Simon, now you…"

Simon bends his head, his fingers tightening around the fork in his hand. A small muscle pulses along his clenched jaw. He left the house a year ago, moving in with a friend in an apartment closer to SAIC, where he's a senior. He'd stayed at home longer than he'd intended because of Connor's death, to be close to Mom. For her to throw that low, guilt-inducing blow, even if it'd been unintentional, had to piss him off. And hurt him.

"Katherine," Eden rasps.

Though her head is turned toward Mom and I can't clearly see her eyes, the anguish of causing the woman she considers a mother heartache rolls off her. She's wavering, caving. I can hear it in the tremble in her voice. In the weakening of her tone. With her big heart, Eden would rather sacrifice her own needs and wants than inflict any emotional damage to Mom and Dan.

And Mom must sense it, too. She clutches Eden's hands tighter, drawing her closer. "Don't go," she insists again, more fervently. Desperately. "You're all I have left of Connor..."

"Well, fuck," Jude mutters, the same mixture of sadness, helplessness, and anger broiling inside my chest darkening his harsh words.

Pressure shoves against my rib cage, an exact replica expanding inside my skull. *Keep your ass still and mimic a mute*, the self-preserving side of me orders. That's what I usually do at family get-togethers, and I'm able to come through relatively unscathed, my armor just scratched, not dented.

But the other half of me—the emotionally suicidal half whose purpose and calling is to protect Eden—growls and snaps with the need to defend her. She asked me to attend this dinner to back her up, to stand by her side. I can't sit here and be a mime when she's hurting. Even if the cost is going to mentally bankrupt me.

"Staying here, wrapped in a cocoon, isn't what Connor would've wanted for her," I interject. "He would approve of her being independent, of her taking this step to stand on her own two feet and start her life again."

Mom jerks as if an electrical current zipped through her. Slowly, she releases Eden and turns to me. Thick cotton fills my throat, my mouth, my nose. The pounding of my heart is a sonorous drumbeat in my head. Like the death march of a man on his last trek to the gallows.

I wait for it. Knowing what's coming.

Because I willingly asked for it.

Twin red flags slash across her too-prominent cheekbones, all the brighter for her pale skin. Her mouth flattens until it almost disappears into a thin line, and bitterness gleams in her diamond-blue eyes. She's a stranger at this moment, but familiar. I met this woman the night of Connor's death.

"You're behind this, aren't you?" she snaps. "I should've known. It's not enough that you took my son from me; now you're trying to steal the last part of him I have, too."

The pain. The goddamn pain. It burns, leaving its poison in every organ, so I embody it, breathe it. If I could breathe.

I expected it. Braced myself for the impact. But that preparation was for shit. I can't move, can't... Just can't.

"Are you kidding me?" Jude spits, the shout hitting my ears as if it traveled through a long tunnel first. His fist slams against the table, the plates and silverware rattling in protest.

"The hell, Mom," Simon demands, and his hurt, his disappointment barely penetrates.

I want to calm both him and Jude, assure them I'm fine.

But that would be a bald-faced lie; I'm not.

Horror creases Mom's face, bleaching what little color she had from her skin. She covers her mouth with her hands, her eyes filling with tears. One drops, rolls down her ashen cheek as she stares at me, stricken.

"I can't believe you would say that to him," Eden whispers. "I asked him to come here, to support me because I knew hearing my news would upset you. If you want to attack someone, here I am. But you have no call to do that to him. To say..." The screech of wood meeting wood sounds as she shoves her chair back from the table and jumps to her feet. She glances at me, and the stark agony in her eyes accomplishes what my brothers' rage and my mother's regret and dismay haven't. That anguish reaches me. Pierces the layers of numbness starting to encase me.

Before I can react, she rushes from the dining room.

Mom's first sob is a ragged, terrible thing, and it ricochets in the room, filling it. The harsh cry burrows into the opening Eden left behind, and I can't take it. My lungs seize, constrict, and I'm seconds away from scratching at my throat like an animal fighting for survival.

Pushing away from the table, I launch out the chair and stalk from the room, ignoring my brothers calling me back.

I don't stop until I'm in my truck and cranking the ignition.

Tires squealing, I back out of the driveway and roar down the street.

My guilt chasing me.

Chapter Four

Eden

I raise my hand to knock on the closed door in front of me. But something keeps my fist from connecting with the thick wood.

Something.

Bullshit. I recognize what has me lowering my arm back to my side.

Fear. Anxiety… Excitement.

It's the last one that has me rethinking this impulsive decision to show up at Knox's apartment above the shop unannounced. Only a couple of hours ago, I watched his Escalade speed away from the house as if Hell had sprung a leak and demons chased him. Maybe that isn't such a far-off comparison. Knox has demons—dark, heavy, unrelenting.

Yeah, me, too. Some warped with age and dusty. Others new and hungry.

My old ones, they wear the face of my father. Of my insecurity, shame, and sense of unworthiness that are inheritances from an alcoholic parent to a neglected child.

The new ones... Well, they resemble the man behind this locked door. My lust for him is my dirty little secret. Even guilt over wanting my husband's brother can't stop the filthy dreams, or the need that reminds me that I didn't die with Connor.

That need is what has me hesitant to knock on the door. Last time we were alone, I bared myself to him—literally. And he'd ended up rejecting me.

But it'd been for the best. Though humiliation still stings me like a thousand angry bees, I can accept the truth of it now. Sex with Knox—my employer, my friend, my *brother-in-law*—is about thirty-one different flavors of crazy. "Inappropriate" doesn't even begin to cover it. But "forbidden" and "practically incestuous" does.

And shit, I can just imagine Katherine's reaction to finding out. She would disown both of us. The scene at dinner trips across my mind, the audio twisted up to maximum. My less-than-successful announcement of moving out. Katherine's small, desperate pleas for me not to leave her. Knox's rumbled defense.

Katherine's ugly accusation.

Nausea churns and rolls inside me. Jude had told me about those words she'd hurled at Knox on that terrible night that's both fuzzy and seared into my brain. But she'd been inconsolable and incoherent with grief then. Tonight... Yes, she'd been emotional, her fragile stability shaky, but there'd been no excuse. She'd inflicted a horrible wound to Knox. I glimpsed it in that green gaze that usually hid all manner of secrets. But he couldn't conceal the hurt.

No, with Katherine and Knox's already strained relationship, I can't be responsible for irrevocably tearing them apart.

And then, as selfish as it is, there's my need to have

Katherine and Dan in my life. My own parents were... Yeah, there's no other way to put it. They were fucked-up individuals. Just because people are able to reproduce and have children, doesn't mean they should. And my parents are included in that group. When I met Connor, I didn't just gain a lover, friend, and later a husband. I was gifted with a family— brothers and loving, affectionate parents. They filled a hole in my soul that I'd convinced myself I didn't need or want filled anymore. I can't lose that connection. That acceptance.

With that resolve lodged in my chest like a hard chip of ice, I lift my fist again, and this time, it connects. Several seconds pass, and I rap the door again. I know he's here; his truck is parked downstairs.

"I'm not going away, Knox," I mutter, raising my hand to knock again. Harder. Pound if necessary. I'm not going anywhere.

The door swings open, and Knox stands in the doorway.

Bare-chested.

Sweaty.

Breathing heavy.

Fuck.

Images of what he could've been doing before answering the door flood my mind like a swollen, overflowing river. And they all include a woman under him. In front of him. Over him.

Mortification blasts through me, a sharp-toothed emotion, as green as Knox's eyes, nipping at its heels. What the hell? I have no right to be jealous. He's not mine, and we don't have that kind of relationship, regardless of our little...slip days ago. But logic does nothing to ease the burn in my veins or the tightening of my stomach over a nameless, faceless woman.

A woman who knows what it's like to have Knox straining over her, those lean hips flexing, his cock powering into her, filling her...stretching her...

I suck in a breath, expanding my suddenly constricted lungs. Hoping to cool the furnace that has clicked on under my skin. Even the thought of him with someone else can't douse this inconvenient lust for him and his warrior's body.

"What are you doing here?" he demands, gravel in his voice. Frowning, he grabs the doorjamb, black wraps covering his hands from wrists to knuckles. Relief slaps me like a wet rag across the face at the sight of those wraps because that means he's been working out, not fucking some woman. I blink, a little shocked at the intensity of it.

Fascination with Knox. Crazy. Inappropriate. Forbidden.

I chant the last three words like a mantra over and over in my head. Reminding myself why I can't ever suck on the skin right under his navel like it's a Jolly Rancher.

"I came by to see you, obviously," I reply, focusing on his scowling face. Not waiting for his invitation—because I know there's a good chance there won't be one—I slip under his arm and enter his apartment.

It's been a long while since I've been up here—the night I broke down after my first day at the shop, actually—but now, as then, I'm struck by the simplicity of the place. The same exposed brick from downstairs forms two walls of the living room that opens into a shared dining room, with a galley kitchen to the left. Two large windows that almost stretch to the ceiling permit the pale glow from the streetlights into the room, adding to the light from the vintage brass and smoked glass chandelier that hangs from the ceiling. That chandelier is the fanciest thing in the apartment. Generic, mismatched furniture occupies the rooms like strangers who just happen to be in the same place at the same time. Nothing personal like framed pictures or knickknacks or even his artwork like he has hanging downstairs in the shop decorate the cherry wood coffee table or walls.

If not for the gym equipment that I glimpsed in the second bedroom the last time I was here, and the incredibly large collection of anime DVDs stored in a glass cabinet, this place could've been rented and lived in by anyone. In spite of all the money he earned fighting, nothing but the shop, that expensive workout collection, and the house he bought his mother shows it.

No one could ever accuse Knox of being a hoarder.

The door shuts behind me with a quiet click that seems more ominous than a slam. Apprehension tickles my spine. Not for the first time, I'm questioning my sanity for following him here.

"What do you want, Eden?" He stalks past me, and the scent of his sweat-dampened skin is a sultry, potent caress that goes straight to my head like a shot of one-hundred proof whiskey. Rich, bold, heavy with the balsamic and cedar fragrance that reminds me of the incense he burns in the shop—it's earthy, like a dark forest with a dash of cinnamon and Christmas, of all things.

"I couldn't sleep." I hate the hint of breathlessness my voice contains as he turns and leans against the edge of the small dining room table and starts to loosen the bindings around his hands. But goddamn. I left my very tarnished halo in the back of my closet along with my chastity belt. And he is a work of art. No, a sculpture or painting is too cold, too dull. He's...him.

Power and beauty. Beast and man. Tightly leashed control and wild, violent passion.

Unable to help myself, I study his smooth, golden skin stretched taut over rock hard muscle and roped tendons. Tattoos—heavily black with splashes of red, blue, and green—swirl down both arms, over wide shoulders, and scroll across the vast expanse of chest that simultaneously intimidates and invites someone to trace with her lips. Flat, small, dark brown nipples tempt the same someone to nip, lick, tease. A better woman than me wouldn't long to climb that staircase of ridged abs like a roofer on a ladder. Or trail her fingers along that delicious V above his hips that disappears into the same pants he wore to dinner. They ride low on his waist, a challenge to find out just how much force it would require to drag them down.

He starts tugging at the wrap on his left hand to remove it. I know perfectly well that he can take them off himself, even if the process is a bit awkward, but I unglue my feet and move toward him anyway.

"Here, let me help," I rasp. If my head contained just the slightest bit of intelligence, I would remain in place with the distance of half the apartment between us. But I have little sense when it comes to him.

I gently cup his hand and take over, slowly unwinding the wrap. I repeat the action with his other hand and drop the bandage-like fabric on the table behind him. Instead of releasing him, I turn his hands over and brush the word STILL on the backs of his fingers and thumb, and the I RISE on the other five. Oh, how I'd love to unravel the mystery of how an Irish boxer ended up with the words from a Maya Angelou poem inked on his skin.

"So who sent you over here to check up on me? Jude or Simon?" he questions. "Sending our sister over here? Pussy move."

Our sister. Anger flickers in my chest. That's a pile of flaming shit. I may have only finished one year of college, but I don't need a psychology degree to recognize deflecting when I hear it. *Sister.* Fuck that. Not when I can still feel the imprint of his lips and tongue on my nipple.

"No one sent me over here like you're some errand that needs to be taken care of," I say, not even bothering to keep the bite out of my tone. It occurs to me I'm still holding his hands when my grip on his tightens. "And I'm not your sister."

So what if I'm stating the words to his chest? If I look into his eyes and glimpse that he's thinking of his mouth on me, his breath bathing my bare skin, all bets—and my panties—might be off. Resolve to not get involved be damned. Yeah, chest-to-eye contact is much safer.

Knox stiffens; his fingers curl around mine, his hold firm, forceful. I swallow a gasp, shoving down the whimper crawling up the back of my throat. Not because he's hurting me. He's not. No, I'm being offered a hint of how being possessed by him would be like. He would be strong and demanding, in control but careful. Maybe even tender sometimes. If I wanted that.

Shifting forward, he slides off the table, his abs brushing my knuckles seconds before he releases me. Such a simple, there-and-gone touch, but it slips inside me, feathering a caress under my skin. Heat blooms in its wake, and again, I'm finding it difficult to not stare at him. Long for him. For his big, hard hands on me. Again.

Helplessly, I study him as he moves in that graceful, silent way of his into the kitchen. He pulls open the refrigerator, withdraws a bottle of water, and downs at least half of it. We watch each other, the air quivering with the tension of things said, unsaid, felt, and unexplored. Or that could just be on my end. He could just be really thirsty and waiting for me to leave his apartment so he can continue lifting, beating, or stretching whatever gym machine he'd been busy with.

He lowers the bottle and props a shoulder against the jut of wall that separates the kitchen from the dining and living rooms.

"You can see I'm fine, like I told you at the door. There wasn't any need for you to come all the way over here."

"Liar," I whisper. His eyes harden into emerald chips, and I shiver. But I still press forward. "You're working out on a Sunday. Monday through Saturday, early mornings, yes. But Sunday is your rest day. You shouldn't lie to someone who knows you like I do."

"If you *know me* so well," he counters, his voice a low, smooth, almost menacing weapon of beauty that warns me I'm not going to like what's about to come out of his mouth. "Then you should realize I mean what I say." He shoves off the wall and stalks a couple of steps closer to me, his gaze narrowed. "You shouldn't have come over, and you can go." He doesn't shout it, doesn't snap it. But he doesn't need to; the words have the desired effect. And I almost turn to give him what he wants...

Then I remember that shuttered, cold expression when Katherine blamed him for Connor's death. I remember the small, involuntary flinch he probably didn't have time to control.

I remember the flash of glitter-bright pain in his eyes before they, too, darkened and shut out every emotion.

Before I can talk myself out of it, I rush across the short distance separating us and fling myself at him. Wrap my arms around him. Press my cheek to his hard, naked chest. My heart strikes my sternum like a snare drum, and my breath explodes from my lungs. Nerves and fear catch up with me after my mad dash, but make up for lost time, berating me for being so damn impulsive. For setting myself up for his rejection of the comfort I'm trying to jam down his throat.

"Goddamn it, Eden," he growls, palming my shoulders and pushing against them, trying to detach my spider-monkey grip on him.

I lock my fingers together behind his back. Hold harder. Squeeze tighter.

"You won't ask for this," I whisper. "But please take it, Knox. For me. If you'll only accept it for my sake, then... please." Emotional blackmail. Dirty and not fair. I don't care.

My conscience has no place here.

Seconds, minutes, hours pass. And I still cling to him. Willing him to take the comfort I'm offering...the comfort I need, too. Finally, just when I'm about to admit he's not going to concede, his arms close around me. Some of that awful tension melts from his muscles. A groan of relief escapes me, and I burrow my face in his chest.

He doesn't utter a word—doesn't make a sound. But his arms... God, his arms are unyielding bands surrounding me, clutching me so tight that breathing becomes a luxury, not a necessity.

Yet, I don't move.

I close my eyes. Every sense heightens, is magnified. His heart thuds beneath my ear, a deep, reassuring echo. That rich scent is more concentrated, more enticing... Delicious. It wraps around me as securely as his arms. His skin, taut and hot, warms me like a living electric blanket. With his wide shoulders braced against the wall, his solid, huge thighs press against mine, supporting my weight, and driving home his strength and power. And his cock...

I shiver.

Oh God. His cock, thick and hard, digs into my lower belly. Knox. Is hard. For *me*.

This could very well be an aberration like in the shop. Maybe he hasn't fucked in a while, and any woman would have him sporting wood. Maybe the adrenaline from his workout is still running through his veins, his blood's pumping, and his body is reacting.

Could be. Maybe. I don't give a damn.

None of those reasons matter when an answering arousal is burning so bright and insatiable inside me, I can barely keep still. All I want is to grab his shoulders and hike myself up his body so I can settle his rigid length where I need it most.

It's wrong. So very wrong. All of the arguments why I should maintain that line in the sand with Knox and never cross it are still as valid as they were when I arrived on his doorstep. I should drop my arms, disentangle myself, and walk away and through that front door. Yeah, that's exactly what I should do. Right now...

I brush my lips over his chest.

Knox stiffens.

I drag my mouth over his nipple.

A hiss slides through the air above me. His arms constrict around me in a silent but demanding command to cease and desist. He's so right. I should stop...

I graze the small, flat peak with my teeth, capturing it and tugging, then soothe any sting I might've caused with a long, slow lick.

His arms drop from around me so suddenly I stumble backward. But then one hand cups my ass and the other tunnels through my hair, grasping the back of my head and steadying me. Before the frigid shock of his palm molded to my butt can wear off, he grips my hair, jerks my head back so far my neck arches. The tendons send up a grumbling protest at the slightly uncomfortable position, but my brain shoots them a stern order to shut it. Knox is touching me, his bright green gaze scorching my face as he studies me with a narrowed, dark intent. My thighs clench, my sex pinching in avaricious expectation. Hope.

A dull, steady throb sets up camp deep inside me, and I can't help it. I shift closer to him. Spread my legs just a little so the steel length of his thigh presses against the already wet, aching place I need it most. Just one little rub. That's all I'll take.

Rolling my hips, I stroke my jean-covered flesh over him, and *whoa*. My eyes damn near roll in the back of my head. The delicious, rough friction of denim and muscle massaging my clit shoves me so close to orgasm, it's humiliating. But mortification is overrated. Especially when the searing, swollen pleasure building low in my belly heralds release just on the horizon.

I do it again. And again. My lashes lower, concentrating on the swelling need. And so I can shut out the taunting image of me riding his thigh like some desperate, fumbling teen.

"Open your eyes," Knox growls, and I obey, the primal, carnal part of me kicking in before my head can. I meet his hooded stare, lust gleaming and diamond-bright. So is the anger, though. Whether it's directed at himself or me, I don't know. And if it makes me a shitty person right now, with my nipples beaded and tingling, and my panties soaked, I can't care. "There you go," he rumbles, shifting slightly against the wall so I lean more heavily into him. "Look at me when you use me to get off."

Oh fuck. I groan. I *am* using him. And God, that should have guilt chafing my conscience. Instead, a filthy little thrill spirals through me. Sinking my teeth into my bottom lip, I slip my hands up his chest and over his shoulders, clutching the dense muscles and holding on. Widening my legs, I fully straddle his thigh. The heat in that jeweled gaze flares brighter, hotter. Digging my fingers into his shoulders, I settle in for an unhurried, savor-every-damn-second-of-this ride.

The first buck of my hips, and my whole sex gets what my clit has enjoyed so far. Another moan escapes me as pleasure, thick and drugging, surges and undulates. I start to close my eyes, but then his command echoes in my head, and I fight to keep them open. Even though peering into his piercing stare is so intense, too…intimate. It dredges a vulnerability out of me that I prefer to leave buried.

He releases my hair and strokes that hand down my back and hip, to join the other one on my ass. Before I can guess his intentions, he whips around lightning fast, and our positions are reversed. My spine aligns with the wall, and his big body covers me. Hiking my leg up, he cradles the back of my knee and lifts it, spreading me open. Never breaking our visual fucking, he bends his knees, notches his hips under mine, and slowly straightens. Dragging his dick up my folds. Grinding against my clit.

The breath in my lungs explodes past my lips. I writhe and twist against him, my fingernails denting his skin as I chase the pleasure that's part blessing and curse. Jesus, this is what I needed. I shake like an earthquake just rocked the street. I'm so close...

"This is what you really want, isn't it?" he asks, the faintest bite of a snarl hardening his coarse voice. He torments my sex again with a slow, lush circle of his hips.

I don't answer. The last time I uttered something while he touched me, I ruined whatever lust-tinged craze had fallen over us. Nope. I'm a quick learner. If he stops at this moment before I come, it might crack me right in half. I'm two steps from insane with the need to slide into that sweet oblivion, so no, he won't get any words from me. But I can't do a damn thing about the whimper that scratches its way free.

"No." He shifts away, taking his beautiful, orgasm-blessing dick away, and I choke on a scream of frustration and deprivation. "*This* is what you need."

In seconds, my jeans are unbuttoned, unzipped, and his hand is inside my embarrassingly soaked panties. Cupping me. I stiffen, going so rigid, my muscles vibrate in complaint. Part of me is too shocked to comprehend, to accept that a man—Knox—is cradling my sex, grinding the heel of his palm over my clit. That same, anguished part of me looses a small, mourning cry. Because the last man to touch me had been...

My mind slams down on that thought, shutting the door so quick, I physically flinch. I close my eyes, disobeying Knox as I struggle to stay firmly entrenched in the here and now.

"Eden."

I shake my head, eyes squeezed shut.

"Eden." This time firmer and accompanied by the grasping of my chin. Reluctantly, I give in and meet his gaze. And am struck by the turbulence of emotion swirling there before it becomes inscrutable. But my brain snapped a Polaroid of what it'd seen. Foremost was disgust I have no doubts was self-directed.

And the understanding.

He's not a fool; he gets what's churning inside me. That doesn't stop him from continuing to play my flesh, from teasing the grasping, hungry entrance to my sex with his fingertips. My mind might be waging a war between the past and the present, but my body is all about chasing the ecstasy Knox is stirring within me. And as he slides his fingers up my slit, stroking it, then drawing concise, teeth-clenching circles around the sensitive bundle of nerves at the top, my mind waves the white flag, surrendering to the promise of even more pleasure.

Maybe his all-seeing scrutiny catches the exact second of my mental and emotional capitulation because he rakes one more caress over my clit...and thrusts a big, long finger inside me. The scream I'd been containing rips out of me, and it scrapes my throat. It feels so...so...*good*.

"So goddamn tight. How can you possibly be this—" He breaks off the question as if afraid I'll give him the answer. Dark brows pulled down in a fierce frown, with arousal staining the skin above his beard in slashes of red, he eases his finger out of my clasping, quivering flesh. Then plunges it back inside. Another cry, sounding strangled and so, so needy, peals out of me. "Offer me what you did in the shop," he growls.

He doesn't expound, and I don't ask what he's referring

to. I know.

Releasing his shoulders, I grab the bottom of my shirt and jerk it up my chest. Without needing to be told, I yank the bra cups down, and my breasts spill out. The cool air whispers over my flesh, and my nipples draw tighter. I guess I should be at least a little embarrassed or shy. And maybe I would if his finger wasn't fucking me. If a low, deep, animalistic rumble didn't roll from him at the sight of my bare breasts. If I didn't stand on the crumbled edge of an orgasm.

If he didn't bend over me and suck my breast hard and deep into his mouth.

Oh. God. I swallow the wailed words before they can bust past my lips. But they echo in the arch of my back, the unrelenting grip on his bound hair, the buck of my hips. It's as if the nerves in my nipples are connected directly to my sex, and each tug, stroke, or lap sets off sparks deep inside me. And the finger I'm riding is stoking the flashes of fire higher, pushing me closer to the release that I need so damn bad, it's become my sole source for existing.

"Please," I beg on a cracked, hushed plea, breaking my own rule about not speaking and ruining this moment. My fingers flex in his hair, and he glances up at me, his harsh angles even harsher, his mouth damp, swollen. "Don't stop," I whisper, uncaring how desperate or panicked I sound. "Please, Knox, don't stop."

With his gaze refusing to let me go, he parts his lips and delivers a slow, long lick with the flat of his tongue. And below... Oh God, below, he curls his finger and rubs a spot high inside me. A spot that makes a keening wail erupt from me seconds before I explode. Detonate. Shatter.

"*Fuck*," he swears, the guttural curse a hot puff of breath across my skin as he drives into my spasming flesh over and over, not gentle or merciful, but dragging the orgasm out until all I can do is whimper and wilt against the wall. My knees are a useless waste of joints, and only his solid, big body holds me up. Ripples of pleasure ebb through me as I return to myself. The short, heavy rasps escaping me eventually ease to soft pants.

But with the return of sanity comes…more sanity. I shiver, the sweat dotting my chest, throat, and face turning slightly clammy on my skin. The last of the lust-thick haze evaporates, and like mist parting on the dawn of a cold, stark morning, reality greets me. Reality and an overwhelming sense of grief and guilt that almost crushes me to the floor.

No longer can I say that the last man I was intimate with was my husband. I was a virgin when I met Connor. And before that, growing up in a house with an alcoholic who loved to party? When the drinks flowed, so did the unsound decisions. My introduction to sex had been at ten, walking in on my father fucking my mother's "best friend" on the living room couch, empty bottles of alcohol littering the floor. In contrast, Connor taught me sex could be beautiful between two people who loved each other. He'd been the only man I'd trusted with my body…until now.

Dark, twisted sorrow wraps around my chest like barbed wire, tightening, drawing emotional blood. It feels like I'm snipping another string, another tie that binds Connor to me. And a small part of me screams and rages for picking up the scissors and willingly slicing it.

I hadn't experienced this sadness when Knox had touched me in the shop the first time. Maybe because it hadn't gone as far. Maybe because he hadn't been *inside* me. Turning me into this sexual, moaning creature I didn't recognize.

Giving me a cataclysmic, mind-bending orgasm when release had only occurred a handful of times with Connor.

That's the betrayal.

How dare my body, my mind explode for him—a man I care for, but don't love—the very first time he'd penetrated my body, when it'd taken over a year of being together before I reached it with the man I adored. And even then, not very often. But there'd been intimacy, affection, commitment, and love between us. Here, with Knox, it'd been purely physical except for a familial love that had just now been conspicuously absent.

A part of me reverts to the devastated, raging widow I'd been right after Connor's death. And that part resents my body—resents the need that even now stirs as Knox slides his finger free, and my sex clenches around it, already feeling empty and aching to be filled again.

Tears scald my eyes, my head a noisy, confused blender of grief, anger, guilt...and desire.

Gentle hands zip and button my jeans, then rearrange my bra and shirt. I stand there, motionless like a doll, unable to meet his gaze. How can I explain to him what I can't grasp myself? I wanted, *hungered* for the pleasure he gave me, never expecting this barrage of emotion to flood me. Never even suspecting it was there. How can he even look at me now?

How can I look at myself?

"Knox," I say through a dry, constricted throat.

"You should be leaving for home before they start wondering where you are," he interrupts me, his tone flat, detached, as if we'd never touched. As if he'd never made me come so hard, I shook and screamed for him. His hand, though... It's tender as he strokes my hair down my back. Brushes rough, calloused fingers across my jaw. "Let me pull a shirt and my shoes on, and I'll walk you downstairs to your car."

He stalks away, and only then do I lift my head, stare at him when he can't return the favor. The sleek muscles in his wide back flex, tapering down to a lean waist and firm, tight ass I didn't have the chance to grab or dent with my fingernails. Some midnight, silken instinct whispers Knox would like that. To be marked.

I whirl around, squeezing my eyes shut.

Resignation creeps into the maelstrom of emotion. Because even though guilt has a stranglehold on me, a flicker of heat still kindles low in my belly. Just one look at Knox stirred and poked the embers.

Knox's heavy footfalls echo on the hardwood floors, but I don't turn to face him. He pulls the door open, and I follow him out to the landing, down the stairs, and out into the dark Sunday night. The muffled chords of a guitar and the thump of drums pour from the live music venue across the street. The laughter of patrons echoes in the cool air as they enter and leave the building as well as the café next to it. But on our side of the street, it's quiet, nothing or no one occupying the shadows but us.

It's the safest—and most dangerous—place for me to be at this moment.

Bending my head, I approach my twelve-year-old Nissan, the same car I drove from my childhood home in Tampa, Florida, to Chicago all those years ago. The key fob has long been lost, so I slip the key into the door and open it. An urgency is riding me hard. An urgency to drive away and return home so I can lock myself in the room that became my sanctuary after Connor died, and sob until my throat and eyes feel like sandpaper.

"Knox," I say, gathering my courage and lifting my head. His hair, still tousled from my fingers tangling and clutching the dark strands, falls around his face, mingling with the coarser hair of his beard. Those green eyes seem to absorb the shadows surrounding us, and they suck the moisture from my mouth. A pit yawns wide in the bottom of my stomach because I know I contributed to that darkness. My lips part, but all that comes out is, "I'm sorry."

"You have nothing to be sorry for." He steps back, farther into the shadows. "Drive safe."

He's wrong. I initiated what happened upstairs between us; I wanted it. And staring at him, the very recent memories of how he'd stroked me, sucked me, finger-fucked me, gave me such unbelievable pleasure...I still want it. In spite of the emotional storm battering me, I can still feel the heavy, heated brand of his length between my legs. And I crave more of it.

I'm conflicted, one of those old-fashioned spinning tops that wobbles back and forth, teetering between sorrow and guilt and lust. Even as I drop into the car and pull away, a sibilant, murky thought slides through my mind.

I'll come back here.

I don't know if I can stay away.

Chapter Five

Knox

Don't stop.
 I'm sorry.
 Don't stop.
 I'm sorry.

Eden's plea and apology from the night before loop through my brain like a scratched vinyl record. This album has been playing all night, and even now, as I bully this workout into submission, it's still going. And going. And going.

Clenching my jaw, I cross the floor of Jake's, the Bridgeport gym where I first started boxing and later trained from when I was fifteen years old. There are many gyms between this old building on Halstead Street and my place in Ukrainian Village. More stylish, modern ones that don't smell of stale sweat and bleach, have updated the decor since 1990, and sit in better neighborhoods. But the forty-minute drive doesn't matter. Other than the shop, this is home. It was once my refuge, my salvation. Hell, who am I shittin'? It still is.

At six a.m., only a couple of other guys occupy the place. Jake's isn't your sleek, watch-the-news-and-listen-to-yourself-help-audiobooks-while-you-exercise kind of place. No desk jockeys or nine-to-fivers here. Yeah, there are treadmills and stationary bikes, but also punching bags patched up with gray electrical tape, assorted exercise equipment, including free weights, huge, scuffed-to-hell-and-back tires, a ring set up in the middle of the cavernous area… It's a place for fighters. Which is probably what drew me to it as a raging teen on the verge of spinning out of control in the first place.

Stopping in front of a punching bag, I settle into a stance that's as familiar and natural as breathing. Fists up and aligned, I inhale. Exhale. And begin assaulting the bag with varying punch and kick combos. Usually, all my focus is centered on the burning in my muscles, the control of my body. But there's nothing usual about today.

I made Eden come. Made her scream. I deliver a vicious blow to the bag, sending it swinging, as if punishing my fingers for still feeling the tight, hot grip of her pussy. Fuck. Dropping my arms to my side, I bend my head, staring at the scratched floor, chest heaving.

I'd seen it, the moment Connor first invaded her thoughts. But instead of backing off, I'd pushed her, soaking my hand in the cream damn near coating her sex. Stroking that perfect little clit that quivered and pulsed against my fingertips. Circling the small, fluttering entrance to her body. Yeah, selfish bastard that I am, I'd made her focus on the pleasure I was giving her. Made her focus on *me*. And she did. I watched those gorgeous eyes darken, glaze as the orgasm took her hard. Obsessively studied every taut line of her face, every tremble of her soft lips, memorizing what lust looked like stamped on her delicate, beautiful features.

And then the past intruded again.

No, not the past. Her husband.

As I slid my finger from her, reality kneed me in the balls, wearing a Joker's smile and baring razor-sharp teeth. Reminding me, it's not me she wants…loves.

That man will always be my brother.

I've had a rib busted, my nose broken, my body bruised and battered, and countless jammed fingers over the years. Climbing your way up the BFC ranks to become a mixed martial arts heavyweight champion wasn't for wimps.

Yet, those injuries felt like love taps compared to how I felt standing there as she went rigid, the color leaching from her skin. Her anguish—her regret—reached out like ghostly, bony hands, dragging their ragged nails down my chest.

I'd done that to her. If I'd called a stop earlier instead of pushing, she wouldn't have been there, drowning in remorse. I'd walked away, but not before touching her one more time… the last time. Because even then, I couldn't help myself.

Mom was right. I had no business with her.

I would break her as surely as I'm breaking my promise.

Sucking in a breath, I throw a hook punch, the impact of the bag singing up my arm into my shoulder. I welcome it. Shoving down everything but the sweet relief of working my body, I move onto plank jacks and fat-bar pullups, losing myself in the routine.

"Knox." The hoarse, rode-hard-and-put-up-wet voice that was the result of a jab to the larynx years ago comes from behind me. I rise from my bench dip, turning to face Jake Reece, gym owner and my first and former trainer. My best friend and father figure. "You're here early. Can't sleep again?"

That's Jake. No fucking around. Other people who were close to me either tried to subtly prod about my insomnia and the nightmares and ask if I was okay, or they said nothing at all. But not him. Blunt. To the point. His favorite saying? "Do I look like a fucking gardener? I don't cover shit with flowers."

I shrug, but unlike Simon, who asked me about it last night but let it go, Jake doesn't. "How many nights is it now?"

"Two," I grunt. I might as well answer; like a stubborn, mean pit bull with lockjaw, he's not going to relent.

"Shit, Knox," he growls, glaring at me. With his crossed arms, dark eyebrows and eyes, and gleaming shaved head, he resembles Mr. Clean. But not the mop-wielding, smiling domestic god of the porcelain. No, he looks like the Mr. Clean who will toss your ass out in a back alley and skull-drag you for missing a spot on the toilet. "What the fuck do you think you're doing? You know better than to be here if you've gone so long without sleep. That's a dumb-shit foolish move."

"I'm fine." I strip my shirt off over my head and toss it to the floor, then grab the bottle of water next to the weight bench. Tipping it, I down almost the entire contents.

Yeah, I'm tired as hell, but I've gone longer than forty-eight hours without sleep before and functioned. Since Jake would probably turn this gym blue with curses if I admitted as much, I keep that info to myself. Sooner or later, my body and brain will crash, and I'll grab a few hours. The best thing about that coma-like sleep is there are no nightmares of my younger brother lying unconscious on a mat inside an eight-sided metal structure.

"Peddle that bullshit somewhere else, I'm not buying it. And you're no good to me if you're exhausted and sick."

"Good to you?" I ask, bending and swiping up my discarded T-shirt. "What're you talking about? You want me to help with the Grayson kid again?" Every now and again, Jake taps me to help with a couple of the younger fighters. But Jake, one of the first professional fighters when MMA was young and just being recognized as a sport, is more than capable. After all, he gave me my start.

"No," he says, then stares at me, his gunmetal gray eyes narrowed. He silently studies me for several quiet moments, and I meet his piercing gaze. Jake is the only person who I don't have to hide parts of myself from. He's seen me as an angry, hurting teen, raw and unfiltered. He knew me as the fiercely focused, win-or-die-trying champion. He sat with me, a silent, strong presence, when I sobbed out my grief and rage over Connor's death.

The only thing I've kept from him—from everyone—is my dark, fucked-up obsession with my brother's wife. Some secrets are too deep, too sinful to share.

"I just got a call from Mitchell Reyes," he continues, a glint entering his stare. Mitchell Reyes, the CEO of Bellum Fighter Championship. I go still. "He knows we're close. Wanted me to talk to you about the next BFC event in Reno. They want you in an exhibition rematch against Clarkson."

Shock rolls through me, encasing me in ice. *Bellum Fighter Championship... They want you... Rematch against Clarkson...* In Reno. The city where I won my last fight and Connor lost his against death. Still, Jake's words ricochet off my skull in a rapid-fire report. Israel Clarkson was the last person I fought. My last win. I briefly close my eyes. Beneath the ice... No, I can't touch what's stirring beneath it. It's too sore. Too...starved.

"No," I state, shaking my head for added emphasis because Jake is already scowling. "I have my shop. The people who work for me." I shake my head again. "I'm not trying to give that up for a few more years, at most, of fighting. That's in my past."

And it's true. If fighting was a dark, deep ocean, letting me drown in my fifteen- and sixteen-year-old anger and sadness without destroying myself, then my art was the lifeboat, dragging me back to the surface for air.

Yet...

"Do I look like they just popped me off my mama's titty this morning?" He snorts. "If that was true, you wouldn't still come in here training like you were preparing for an upcoming fight. Tell yourself what you want, but you haven't dug that fire out of you. Look me in the eye and tell me a part of you still doesn't crave it."

I don't say anything. I haven't been training for the grueling five-minute rounds in a metal octagon.

At least, not consciously.

Suddenly, all the weariness and exhaustion that I've been fighting death-drops on my chest like a three-hundred-pound free weight. Because I can't deny what Jake said. The way I retired—walking away—has always left me feeling... unfinished. Incomplete. But there's no going back. Can't change that.

"Jake," I murmur. "I..."

"You think I don't know why you quit?" he demands. It's on the tip of my tongue to correct him. Retired. I'd retired. But I don't say a word. We both know the truth. I did quit. "Martyring yourself didn't bring Connor back, and he wouldn't have wanted you to abandon the sport for him like some sort of sacrifice to the forgiveness gods." He swipes a hand over his head, anger and sympathy an odd, warring combination on his tough face. "Just...don't say no, okay? Think about it. Give it a few days—hell, a week. You don't have to give Reyes an immediate answer. Think on it and let me know."

Before I can reply, he pivots and strides across the gym toward the locker room and his office.

I stare after him, my heart a less-than-steady hammer in my chest, his words ringing in my head. *Martyring yourself didn't bring Connor back... He wouldn't have wanted you to abandon the sport for him... Think about it...*

That flame deep inside me that I snuffed out two years ago flickers to life, demanding to be fed. But I extinguish it before it can burn too bright.

No, I can't. Fighting took one of Mom's sons. I don't know if I could face the hurt or accusation in her eyes if I returned to the sport she blames for his death.

But, *fuck*.

I want to.

Chapter Six

Eden

Okay, yeah, so I'm standing in the middle of my new apartment on a Sunday afternoon, hands on my hips, and grinning like an idiot.

But I can be excused, because, y'know, *my apartment*. Just thinking the words has me smiling harder, wider.

The small, ground-level, one-bedroom, one-bath unit in Roscoe Village might not be much by other people's standards. Truth, it's not a palatial condo on the Gold Coast. But damn, it's *mine*. Spinning in a slow circle, I survey the place as if I haven't walked every inch, peeked into every corner and pine cabinet, mentally filled every spot with real and imagined furniture. A living room takes up most of the space and opens up to a tiny kitchen to the right. A short hallway leads to a surprisingly large bedroom, walk-in closet, and cubbyhole of a bathroom. The true selling points of the place—besides all the utilities being included in the incredibly affordable rent and being just a twenty-minute drive to work—are the fenced-in backyard and small, screened-in porch off the kitchen.

I adore it.

Inhaling, I capture the smell of fresh paint and cleaning products in my lungs. Yesterday, I came over and scrubbed the apartment from top-to-bottom. Not that the previous tenants had left it a pig-sty. I just...I don't know, wanted to put my stamp on it.

These last three weeks since signing the lease have passed by like an ice age. And every day has been a leaden weight. I still feel like a Judas for leaving Katherine, for hurting her. An image of her this morning as I packed the last of my belongings in my car wavers in front of my eyes. Her blue eyes glistening with tears she didn't bother to hide. Her slumped shoulders. The thick sadness in her voice as she wished me good luck.

Sighing, I thread my fingers through my hair, shoving aside the heaviness for the moment. Logically, I realize I can't put my life on hold for my mother-in-law. But it doesn't ease the guilt of hurting someone I love. Someone who's been a mother to me.

"Damn, I'm glad you're on the first floor," Jude grumbled, carrying a large cardboard box through my front door. He set it down on the hardwood against the living room wall with a grunt then straightened. "I didn't realize you had so much shit when I agreed to help you move."

I snort. "Well, my shit and I appreciate your assistance." Walking over to the kitchen, I grab one of the cool beers I had ready for him and his brothers and bring it back over to him. He twists off the cap and tips it back, swallowing a huge gulp. "You know I love you, right?"

"Yeah, yeah. Being sweet will only get you everything." He winks at me and sets the bottle down on one of the new cherry end tables. Since Katherine and Dan would only accept a small amount of money from me for rent while I lived with them, I had a nice nest egg saved. Enough to pay for first and last month's rent, security, and some new furniture to go along with some of the things I kept in storage from my old place with Connor.

"Coaster, man. Get a coaster," I yell, snatching up the small canister holding my equally new, square mats. Slapping one down, I pick up his beer and place it on top.

"What did you do now?" Simon asks, entering the apartment hauling another box marked "kitchen." Probably dishes and silverware.

"You don't want to know," Jude drawls, sliding an amused glance my way. "But a word to the wise. Mark up her furniture with a sweaty beer and die."

"Shut up, you," I mutter, following Simon and handing him his bottle. "Thanks, Simon," I say as he sets the box on the kitchen counter. "You don't complain like your brother." I lower my voice to a whisper. "He's a whiner, that one."

"You know I'm standing right here," Jude objects with a mock scowl. "I can hear you."

"Oops. My bad." I snicker. "The acoustics in this place must be wonderful."

Simon laughs, tossing his bottle cap in the garbage can next to him.

"Hey, where's this box going? It's not labeled." The deep, rumbled question echoes off the cream-colored walls, and as Knox moves into the apartment, the already small place seems to shrink even more.

I'd like to claim that my gaze doesn't roam over his big, muscled, heavily-inked arms and the wide, strong shoulders straining the material of his plain, white T-shirt. I'd also like to positively state that my fingers don't itch at the remembered silken slide of his dark brown and gold hair over my palms and between my fingers. That I don't recall the faint scratch of his scruff against the sensitized skin of my breasts and torso.

Yeah, I'd like to be able to say all of that.

But then I would be a bald-faced liar.

Clearing my throat, I cross the room on the pretense of shifting another box out of the way so he can set the one in his arms down. This way I can pretend I wasn't ogling his brutally masculine face, only marginally softened by his thick tumble of hair and the way it falls past his jaw.

"Here." I wave toward an empty spot. "You can put it there for now."

He nods, and I drag my gaze away from his broad back with the delicious play of muscle under the cotton material. And the firm slope of his ass.

My belly clenches, a dark, sinuous heat pooling low, warming my sex, pinching my clit. It's been three weeks since the night in Knox's apartment. The night when he treated me to an orgasm that could be termed an out-of-body experience. The night I careened into a spiral of grief that required days to emerge from.

Things between us have been...polite. I've longed to talk to him, broach the subject of what happened, why I reacted in the way I did. But fear has paralyzed my tongue. How can I admit that the pleasure he plunged me into felt like a betrayal of my dead husband, his brother? I'm afraid of—shit, I'm afraid of everything when it comes to Knox. Of his rejection. Of his silence. Of hurting him. Of him hurting me. Not physically. Never that. But emotionally? Knox could rip my fledgling, newborn confidence to shreds.

And through it all? I can't. Stop. Wanting. Him.

If one of the lamps that I bought at the consignment shop miraculously housed a genie, my first wish would be that this...this clawing, aching, relentless need for him would disappear. Then, Knox and I wouldn't be circling each other like wary wolves. I wouldn't bear this not-so-secret shame. I wouldn't suffer the constant anxiety that Katherine would somehow figure out that I lusted after her other son.

If only he'd never put his mouth on me. If only I'd never pushed him to touch me. If only I'd never discovered the delicious, sinful pleasure of his fingers inside me. If only, if only...

"Was that the last of it?" I ask Knox, forcing my attention away from the sexual minefield my life has become.

"Yeah," he affirms. "What do you need us to do?"

My brain stops operating at *what do you need*. My nipples bead under my T-shirt, as if offering up their vote. It doesn't take much for me to still feel his mouth working on my breasts, his tongue curling around the tips and tugging, sucking...

For a moment, I freeze and helplessly meet his gaze. Am I imagining the flash of heat in his eyes? The slight firming of his sensual mouth? Swallowing a groan, I jerk my head to the side and blindly scan the organized chaos surrounding us.

Over the pounding of my pulse, I wave toward the fifty-six-inch, flat-screen TV against the opposite wall. "Could you get my TV set up?" Turning to Jude and Simon, I ask, "Would you two mind putting together the entertainment center? I'll order pizza and go pick up some more beer."

The next three hours pass in a blur of work, food, alcohol, and male voices busting each other's balls. By the time the three of them head for the front door, my living room is complete with sofa, coffee and end tables, a chair, and television inside the entertainment center. Satisfaction is a warm glow inside my chest. It's beginning to look more and more lived-in. Like a home.

But as Knox, Jude, and Simon prepare to leave, a sliver of icy panic slides inside my chest. The truth strikes me like a bat across the shoulders. In seconds, I'm going to be alone for the first time since I was nineteen years old. Being on my own is what I wanted, why I moved out of Katherine's home. Yet, now that I'm here, I'm...scared. Which is ridiculous, I know it. Even so, I can't deny that I'm five seconds from begging them to stay for another round of pizza. The new season of *Stranger Things* on Netflix. Counting the knobs on the cabinets.

Yeah, I'm desperate.

Still, I must have some remnants of pride left, because I force a smile and accept Jude and Simon's goodbye hugs and smacks to my cheek. Tension invades me as I turn to Knox, bracing myself for his hands on me. The seed of dread sprouts into twisting vines that wind around my chest, squeezing. What is my problem? I can't count how many nights I spent alone in my house as a child, with my father out raising hell and my mother looking for him. I left home right after high school and drove hundreds of miles to Chicago, slept in my car for months, and attended college—alone. Why am I suddenly tripping at the thought of being by myself in my apartment?

Knox studies my face, his gaze roaming it as if analyzing every feature, trying to probe beneath my keep-it-moving-nothing-to-see-here facade. "What's wrong?" he finally asks.

Embarrassed, I glance behind him, but his brothers have already left, leaving the door open for Knox. "Nothing," I lie. "I'm good. Thanks for all your help today."

His piercing gaze drops, narrowing on my twisting fingers. *Damn.* I smother a growl of disgust and halt the nervous tic. Hiking my chin up and tugging my shoulders back, I silently dare him to call me on it.

Without a word, he kicks the door shut behind him, never releasing me from his emerald stare.

"I'm staying."

Chapter Seven

Knox

What the fuck am I doing?

"What the hell are you doing?" Eden's demand coincides with the growled question ringing in my head.

And the answer to both? *I have no damn clue.*

This is what I get for acting on impulse. But lately, that seems to be my default with Eden. And it's done nothing but get my tongue around her nipple, my finger in her pussy, and a fuckload of guilt crushing my chest. Control is a thing of the past with her. And that's not good. At all. More than any other person, she's the one I need to be most disciplined around. Hell, she *needs* me to be.

Frustration gathers inside me, shoving at my rib cage, and I clench my jaw, locking down the curses swarming up my throat. Dragging a hand down my face, I palm my keys. I should've just followed Jude and Simon out of the apartment.

Maybe that hadn't been panic or fear I glimpsed in her eyes as my brothers and I headed out the door. And maybe those telltale signs of nerves were due to being alone with me. Not that I can blame her.

But still, something nags at me. Insists that those nerves aren't because of me, but from being alone in a new place after the constant company of family for years.

And even suspecting she's going to be sitting here in this apartment, lonely and nervous, has me making decisions that both of us will probably come to regret.

"Look, I'll..." But as I consider starting toward the door, something flickers over her face. Lights up the depths of those dark chocolate eyes. Relief. The vise grip around my chest loosens, and I drop my keys on the small table she set next to the door. "I'll take the couch."

She scowls, crossing her arms over her chest. "I don't recall—what? That couch is way too short for you," she mutters, almost to herself.

The corner of my mouth twitches, but I stride past her before she can catch it. She might fight my staying, but she's already agreed.

"I've slept on worse," I reply with a shrug of a shoulder.

"I bet," comes her low grumble behind me. Hold up. What the fuck does that mean? "Speaking of sleeping in other places," she continues. "Shouldn't you be headed to one of them? I'm sure your plans for the night didn't include planting your Tormund Giantsbane body on my brand-new couch."

I turn, scanning and taking in her irritated frown, the defensive cross of her arms...and her feet in third position. Returning my gaze to hers, I blink. "*Lord of the Rings?*"

Heaving a loud, world-weary sigh, she throws her arms up. "Seriously? *Game of Thrones*, you plebian."

"Same thing." I watch her. And wait.

Her eyes narrow, and fists finding her hips, she leans forward, the corner of her fuck-me mouth curling up in a sneer. *There it is.*

"No, it's *not* the same thing," she snaps. "Seven Kingdoms, Middle Earth. White Walkers, Orcs. Dragons—"

"Dragons," I finish, arching an eyebrow.

"That was *The Hobbit*, not *Lord of the Rings*," she mumbles. Then her chin jerks up, and she studies me for several long seconds before her lips twist into a small, wry smile. "Nicely done."

I don't reply; using the show to distract her was child's play. Besides family, there's one thing Eden is obsessively passionate about—*Game of Thrones*. In the past, I've tried to watch a few episodes of the first season with her. Couldn't do it. Tapped out after Aquaman died.

I drop to the couch—and am now vividly aware of how much of it I take up. Where the hell did she get this thing? Little People 'R' Us?

"Why?" she quietly asks. "Why did you stay?"

The note of vulnerability in her voice has my fingers curling into my palms. I can't touch her. Can't smooth my thumb over the sprinkle of freckles across the bridge of her nose. Can't trace the tempting dent above her top lip.

"Because you wouldn't ask me to." I give her back almost the same words she said in my apartment weeks ago. It's stupid, mentioning that night, because I can't think of that selfless, sweet, completely *Eden* embrace without remembering what came after it. And as I stare into her eyes, and they darken from brown to nearly black, I see the memories there. Whether she wants to recall them or not, she's thinking about grinding on my thigh and then my cock.

When she turns away, rubbing her palms up and down her arms, I wonder if maybe her mind switched to when she froze after coming on my finger. And why.

"Do you want another beer?" she offers, heading toward the kitchen.

I doubt it's a sudden thirst that propels her out of the room and away from me. But I don't call her on it, because I need that space, too. Space and a couple of minutes to remind myself of why I'm here instead of at the bar with Jude and Simon, finding someone who can help me try to fuck Eden out of my system. It hasn't happened yet. But who knows? Tonight could be the night.

Keep hope alive 'n' all that shit.

"Yeah, thanks," I agree, picking up the remote off the coffee table in front of me. Out of habit, I search for the Cartoon Network. Many a night when insomnia has me in its grip, I've watched Japanese anime on this channel and my DVDs until dawn breaks. And now, as Sasuke Uchiha fills the screen, I lean forward, propping my arms on my thighs, and am immediately drawn into one of my favorites. The rogue ninja is in the middle of a fierce battle with his brother Itachi. I've seen the episode before, and this fight is one of the most epic in the entire *Naruto* series.

"I should've known better than to leave you alone with the television," Eden drawls, reappearing next to the couch. I glance away from the screen long enough to accept the beer she extends toward me. "You're lucky you helped me move. Or else I'd confiscate that remote."

"It's cute that you think you could," I murmur as the battle and the episode comes to its conclusion on the screen. I click the guide button to see if another one is scheduled. Damn. No, but *Hunter X Hunter* is. Hunter Gon Freeces searching for his missing father is my next favorite show. Settling in, I stretch my arms along the arm and the back of the couch.

"Holy shit. Did you just"—she releases a loud, exaggerated gasp—"tease me?" She sets her own beer on the table—on top of a coaster—and runs to the window that looks out on West Newport Ave. *What the fuck?*

She jerks back the curtains and peers outside, her head

swinging from left to right.

"What's wrong? What're you looking for?" I push up from the couch, halfway to my feet when she spins around to face me.

"I was looking for the rainbow-pooping unicorn and the pig with wings riding on its back. Because if you're making jokes, they can't be far behind."

I stare at her, my brain taking a moment to catch up with her words. Laughter rolls up my chest, warm and a little unfamiliar. A chuckle escapes me, and shaking my head, I return to the sofa. A smile curves her lips, brightening her eyes until they're soft like melted chocolate. God, that smile. It was the first thing about her that seized my attention five years ago.

Like some cliché romance movie shit, I'd glanced across the VIP section of the club where we'd gone after my fight and seen her. Standing uncertainly by the door with a friend, shoulders drawn back and tense, delicate chin lifted, body poised as if caught halfway between staying and bolting. All the people packed into that room, and it'd been her who had captured my attention.

Nah, that didn't accurately describe what'd happened that night. She'd grabbed every sense, every heartbeat, every organ, every brain cell that made existing possible by the throat and forced them to function just for her. And all because of that smile of shy innocence tinged with the hint, the promise of untapped sensuality. And fuck, had I wanted to be the one to explore it, introduce her to it. Before I could reason with myself that this wasn't some John Hughes '80s movie, my feet had unglued themselves from the floor, and I'd headed across the room. *Mine*. The word—the claim—had echoed in my head like a hammer striking an anvil. Loud. Strident. And over and over.

Then Connor had stepped to her. Blocking my view.

Blocking me.

I blink, the memory shattering like glass but leaving behind just enough shards to remind me that like that night, I can't have her now. Contrary to what my primitive mind had roared back then, she isn't mine. Never has been.

Never will be.

"I need to sit down," Eden says, retracing her steps and dropping onto the chair next to the end of the couch where I'm seated. She smirks, curling her legs under her. "I think you just smiled, and that could herald anything from a patch of the sky plummeting to a zombie apocalypse."

Shaking my head, I take another sip of my beer. "I'm not that bad, Eden."

Actually, I probably am. And from the arch of her eyebrow, she agrees with my inner-me.

"Umm, okay." She snickers, reaching out and snagging the bottle she'd set on the coffee table. If God Himself beamed down on a highway paved in gold bricks and punched the shit out of me, I still couldn't have stopped myself from staring at the gape in her V-neck T-shirt as she leans forward. Blood thunders in my veins. Yeah, the glimpse of sun-warmed sandy skin cupped by black lace would be worth that celestial haymaker.

"I can remember each and every time I've seen you smile," she continues, tilting her head to the side. Peering at me with a scalpel-like perception that has me fighting not to gather up my shit and break the door down trying to get out.

I'm used to MMA fans recognizing me, ogling me, mentally weighing me. In the gym, in the ring, during an interview, and now, from a tattoo chair—they don't bother me. I've become accustomed to it.

But sitting here, one-on-one in a small apartment with only feet of space between us, I feel exposed in a way standing in an Octagon with just a pair of shorts on and cameras and thousands of eyes focused on me never has.

And yet, I keep my ass on the cushion, pinned there by her admission. Why the fuck would she bother counting my smiles? Why would she care? My hungry curiosity trumps my sense of self-preservation.

"Three times." She holds up two fingers. "When Connor graduated college and when Simon graduated high school." Another finger pops up. "And when you won your last championship match."

Shock snaps inside me like a plucked rubber band. Three times in the five years I've known her? I've never been gregarious like Simon, a flirt like Connor, or a charmer like Jude; I've always been intense, even before Dad died. And I know I can be a bit...stoic, but damn, that can't be right.

"I'm not talking about casual grins or laughter like in the shop," she explains, her gaze steady and unwavering on my face. "I've seen you do both more often, but even those aren't a daily thing. I'm referring to the genuine, joy-filled, light-up-your-eyes smiles that remind me of the boy in that picture of you and your father hanging in your mother's hallway."

"Why remember at all?" I ask, resenting the gravel-rough quality to my voice. Resenting that inside my head I'm perched on this couch, arms propped on my thighs, leaning toward her and craving her answer.

She chuckles, the sound wry with the faintest trace of humor. "It's hard to forget when you feel like you've been whacked on the back of your head with a two-by-four." She gives another of those puffs of laughter. "I can usually recall why I was initially intimidated by you, but then there are moments like those and..." She shrugs. "Well, I clearly see that charisma is a Gordon family trait."

I don't know which revelation hits me hardest—that I intimidated her or that she finds me charismatic. And I do mean *hit me*. If I wasn't already sitting, she would've knocked me on my ass.

"I've scared you?" So I guess I'm tackling the first. Maybe because the thought of her being frightened by me disgusts me. "When?" *And why? What did I do?* Swallowing down the need to pepper her with questions like an automatic weapon, I wait, tension damn near vibrating over my skin.

"The first time I saw you. You probably don't remember," she says, propping an elbow on the arm of the chair and cupping her chin. Like fuck. Every second of that night is etched into my memory. "My college roommate invited me along with her to the BFC event. Her boyfriend at the time was one of the fighters. We went to the afterparty at some club and were allowed in the VIP section. As soon as we entered, I noticed you. I mean, it would've been next to impossible not to. Everyone surrounded you or was trying to get closer. And you were…"

She shakes her head, the corner of her mouth quirking. "You. Huge, towering over almost everyone there. Hard. Impassive. But so damn intense. I remember thinking, please, God, don't let him notice me. Because if you did, I would've hated to humiliate myself in front of all those people by fainting." This time her chuckle possesses amusement. "You can be"—she pauses, slightly squints—"a lot to take in. To handle. It's like you shrink the size of any room you enter, suck the air right out of it. That kind of intensity can be, uh, daunting."

Hearing her initial impression of me stuns me into absolute stillness. It couldn't be more different from mine of her if we'd planned it in advance. Shock filtered with veins of anger sits inside me like a block of ice. Is that really how she saw me? Sees me still?

Well, fuck, no wonder she fell for Connor. I'm the icy planet Neptune to his burning Venus. The moon to his sun.

"I'd have never hurt you," I reply, forcing a calm into my

voice that in no way reflects the tightness squeezing the hell out of my chest. "Then or now."

"Of course not." She frowns. "I knew that about five seconds after meeting you. Maybe I've been saying this wrong. You're intense, and that's not a bad thing. I've always felt safe with you. Protected," she murmurs. "I just doubted my ability to not lose my mind if you actually turned that intensity on me."

A serrated crack of laughter scrapes my throat, but at the last minute, I lock it down. Truth, I'd annihilate any motherfucker who dared to hurt her. But the joke's on her, because I'm the biggest threat to her; I'm the wolf wrapped in a slightly less dangerous wolf's pelt. I'd never physically harm her. Hell no. But I could tear her safe, familiar world apart. I could cost her the ones she loves, who love her. I could rip her from that existence of light and extinguish it with the darkness that coats me like thick, dirty oil. That's what my lust would do if anyone ever found out how much I want her. Or, God forbid, believed she ever returned it.

"I've never been frightened of you," she stresses in that same soft voice. It carries a hint of reluctance, of hesitancy as she adds, "At least, not in that way."

The air in my lungs evaporates in the blast of heat that surges through me on a soundless, powerful roar. Every muscle tightens, except for my dick, which swells, thickens, blood pounding in it like the bass in a big-ass speaker. I don't need her to explain that last cryptic remark. I decipher it clearly; if I harbored any doubts, the flush suddenly staining her cheekbones, and how she glances away from me, unable to meet my eyes when she hasn't had any trouble until this moment, verifies my guess.

Yet, I still ask. Because masochistic, dirty bastard that I am, I need to hear it from her own mouth.

"How, then?" That's all I get out, but it's enough.

Her gaze flicks back to mine even as her elegant, long fingers toy with the label on the beer bottle. With how she's tearing up the damp paper, I almost take pity on her and rescind the question. Almost. Add selfish to masochistic and dirty.

"The other night..." She falters, swallows. Begins again. "The other night at your apartment, was—"

"Forget it," I grind out, interrupting her. "You don't have to explain it to me." I was wrong. I don't want to hear her explain how my pushing her into that orgasm, manipulating her body so she didn't think about my brother, scared her. I've beat myself bloody for it.

"Yes, I do." Straightening, she bows her head, and her hair falls forward, partially concealing her face from me. My fingers tighten around my beer bottle, holding on. Either that or I'll push them through those brown-almost-black strands, fist them, and drag her head back so she can't hide from me. Which is completely hypocritical since all I've done from the moment we met is hide. "I should've said something that night, or at least the next day, but..."

She inhales, tilts her chin up, and meets my gaze. It's steady, but I can read regret in the small crease between her eyebrows, the gathering shadows in her eyes.

"I'm sorry," she breathes.

Deliberately, I set the beer on the coffee table and settle my arms on my thighs. No way I heard her right. "What are you apologizing for?" I demand, my voice sharper than I intend.

"That I left, let you walk away from me believing that you were responsible for my reaction. That you'd done something wrong to cause it. When that's the furthest thing from the truth."

I'm shaking my head before she finishes talking. "Eden, you don't have to say anything else. I didn't—"

"Do anything I didn't ask—no, beg for." She cuts me short this time. Her teeth sink into her bottom lip, and the need to stroke my thumb over the tender flesh, trace and smooth it with my tongue, has me scrubbing my hands down my thighs. "I started that, Knox, not you. And I wanted it. You didn't force me into anything, didn't take advantage, and I'm so sorry that I made you carry that burden. It's just... It's been two years since I've had sex. You might not know this, but Connor was my first—and my last. I wasn't prepared for that to change. I had started to think I was. Especially since, in the past few months, I've stopped feeling so dead inside. Physically, I might've been ready, but mentally, emotionally? It caught me by surprise, and I had no defense. The grief, the anger of losing him, the guilt over another man touching me just crashed down, and I..." She trails off, lifting her hands, palms up. "I'm sorry."

"For what? Loving Connor? Missing him?" Her apology is absurd and unwarranted. Still... Jealousy stirs in my chest, a green-tinged spark I hate to admit is there, even while I love and miss my brother, too. "Eden, it's not strange you would regret being with someone else." If I hadn't been so blinded my own lust and satisfaction at having my hands on her, in her, I might've predicted her reaction and avoided it by sending her home the moment she showed up on my doorstep. Vulnerable is not a word in my vocabulary—except when it comes to her.

Christ. The woman is my Bathsheba, my Delilah, my Mary all rolled into one. My weakness, my damnation...my strength.

"No," she immediately objects. "I don't regret it. As much as I might've wanted to close my eyes and not wake up when Connor died, I'm not dead." Her low, hoarse words are daggers slicing through flesh and bone. The thought of losing her forever... I inhale. Deliberately push the breath out through my nose. Focus on her, because she's the only thing chaining me to this couch.

"I need to know that I'm healing, that *all* parts of me are coming alive again," she continues. "And you did that for me. It was just…a little overwhelming. A little scary." She emits a breathless chuckle that smacks of self-deprecation, shrugging a shoulder. "I should've been prepared. I've seen how you…"

I slowly straighten, stiffening. And not just my erection. Tension invades my shoulders, my spine, my stomach. Every sense is tuned into her. I notice the slash of scarlet over her ripened-wheat skin. Hear the slight catch in her breath before she glances away from me. I even imagine I can detect the sharp scent of her embarrassment, as well as the arousal that has the pulse at the base of her neck working double time.

"Eden," I rumble, her name a tumble of ragged edges in my chest. "You've seen what?" When she gives her head one hard shake, I call her again, not bothering—or able—to keep the razor edge from it. "Eden. You've. Seen. What?"

Slowly, she swings her gaze back to me, and there are nerves in those umber depths, nerves and mortification. And lust. Dark and bright at the same time. Shy and bold. The perfect dichotomy that is her.

"Tell me," I order, lowering my voice but not eliminating the steel threading through it.

Fingers twist together in her lap. Shoulders draw back. "The night we went out to the bar to celebrate my new promotion, I saw you. In the storeroom. With a girl." She swallows, and a very fine shiver runs over her. If every bit of my attention wasn't focused on her, I might've missed it. But I don't. And coupled with the flare of heat in her eyes, I can guess the origin of that shudder. It's the same thing that has me so damn hard, my dick could be a newly discovered type of metal. "She was blowing you. Or you were holding her steady while you fucked her mouth. I'm still not sure which one."

God. *Damn.* I remember the woman and the blow job she's talking about. It's all kinds of screwed up, but that wasn't the first time I got head from a woman at a bar, club, or hell, even the gym. The women—we give each other pleasure. But we have a clear understanding that it's only for those moments, that night and nothing beyond. The ugly, asshole-ish truth? None of them are memorable. Because none of them were Eden.

Yet, the thought of her watching me fuck a woman's mouth, take her throat. The knowledge that she stood there and stared at me come…

A violent electrical storm barrels into the room and plows into me, lighting me up, setting me on fire, transforming me into a living, charged lightning rod.

Now is when I need to get to my feet, mutter a goodbye, and haul ass out of the apartment. Away from her. From the temptation of sin and guilt-ridden-but-dick-breaking sex. If I had any sense, any self-respect, any morals, any concern for other people rather than just myself, I would.

But I'm a stupid, contemptuous, depraved, self-serving fuck because I narrow my gaze on her and murmur, "But you want to find out, don't you?"

Her eyes widen slightly, her nude, plump lips parting. I've caught her off guard, but, in seconds, arousal eclipses surprise in that deep, liquid stare. Still, it's several long moments before she dips her head in a nod and breathes, "Yes."

The force of the surging need and lust is a blinking, neon, billboard-sized clue that, again, I should leave. But right now, with her pulse dancing wildly in that dip above her collarbone, and when I can already feel those soft, explosive pants of hers against my lips, I'm willing to shove the consequences into the cross-that-bridge-when-I-come-to-it vault and lock the door.

"Tell me what you saw," I demand, grit scouring my throat and voice.

"I-I already did..." she stammers.

"In detail. Tell me."

Her lids briefly lower, and maybe I've pushed her too far. Shit, I'm probably—what was the word she used?—overwhelming her again.

I should pull back, grant her space and mercy.

Instead, I wait.

"She was on her knees in front of you," she begins in a whisper-soft, halting voice. The tip of her tongue peeks out and sweeps the sensual curve of her bottom lip. I pull a submission hold on the growl churning in my chest and heading for my throat. But goddamn, I can practically *feel* that delicate caress, that puff of warm breath. "Your hand was wrapped around her hair, tugging her head back, and she..."

Eden shifts on the chair. Trying to get pressure on that pretty, fluttering clit? Attempting to ease the empty ache deep inside her? The questions—the answers—send another blast of heat streaming through my veins at warp speed.

"She, what?" I push, unable *not* to. Hearing her narrate this tale in that husky, low voice full of innocence and heavy with lust is ripping a hole in my gut.

"She was sucking you off. Hard. Deep. And you—" She pauses, and her gaze briefly dips before lifting to mine again. "And you were at her mercy. I saw your eyes, your face. She was kneeling, but your pleasure was hers. But at the same time, you were in control, your hold on her deciding how fast or slow. How much of you she took." In a gesture that had to be unconscious, that was both seductive as hell and sweet, she brushes three of her fingers over her mouth. As if she's feeling the stretch of her lips around my cock. "Even when she choked a little, she remained on her knees. Taking it."

"Did she like it?" I press, the question barely audible to my own ears through the filter of dark, thick lust pounding in my head, my body.

"No," she whispers without the slightest hesitation. "She loved it." Her hand drops from her face and settles on her thigh, curling into a tight fist. "And I hated her," she admits, her gaze entrapping me now. Fuck if I'm not a willing prisoner. It's too late to look away, to leave. Much too late for that. "I hated her because I wanted to *be* her."

I wanted to be her.

Her confession, though hushed, echoes in the room like a roar in a baseball stadium filled to maximum capacity.

I wanted to be her.

The irony of it all is, in my head, it probably *was* her.

That's my MO. Close my eyes and imagine it's Eden's mouth sucking me dry. Her pussy I'm pounding into. Her ass I'm sliding in. Her screams assaulting my ears.

A shudder ripples through me, and maybe she sees it. Maybe she can peer beneath the quickly crumbling shields of my control and see the ever-present, always-hungry need to get my hands on her. Because seconds later, she's off the chair and sinking to her knees in front of the couch. Between my legs.

"Let me be her," she whispers.

The last charred vestiges of my conscience are screaming about my impending road trip to hell, but I still slide back on the couch until my spine hits the cushion and lower my hands to my belt. Unbuckle it. Unfasten the button at the waist of my jeans and tug down the zipper. The movements are perfunctory, deliberate. But Eden—her cheeks flushed, her lips parted, her chest rising and falling as if struggling to drag in air—contemplates me as if it's some Magic Mike striptease.

Dipping inside my boxer briefs, I fist my erection. The rush of relief at squeezing my throbbing, hard-as-hell, *hurting* flesh has a groan scrabbling its way up my throat and rumbling out of me. And having her as my captive audience, having her pretty brown eyes fixated on my pumping hand only jacks the pleasure-with-a-bit-of-pain higher.

"Show me," she says. And it's not a plea. It's a softly uttered order. And goddamn if that doesn't stroke over me like an eager, warm tongue. Hers.

I shove the cotton and denim down, needing her to see all of me just as she's demanded. Needing her to crave me with the same gnawing, unyielding greed that has been my normal for years.

Staring into those eyes that have both teased and tortured me, I stroke my fist over my length, slower, harder, letting her discover for herself how I like it. How I fuck my hand in the dead of night when only darkness and the image of her crowd into my head. How I squeeze my cock as if it's her slick, tight flesh I'm barreling through.

Her short, harsh pants punctuate the air like small blasts. Her gaze flicks from my face to my dick, back to my face, then down again. Like she can't decide which to stare at—can't decide which she enjoys watching more. If I had her spread wide on my couch, jeans and underwear gone, I might have the same dilemma.

No, I wouldn't. Her soft mouth, bold cheekbones, sprinkling of freckles, and expressive eyes would ensnare my rapt attention any day. But her naked, wet, swollen folds… Yeah, those would ride a damn close second.

Damn. I briefly close my eyes at the image of what she would look like vulnerable and exposed, offering that perfect sex to be claimed, corrupted, branded. Another groan rolls out of me as I enclose the tip, twisting.

"C'mere, Eden," I beckon, curling the fingers of the hand not wrapped around my dick. "Touch me."

Her long, elegant fingers with their bare, short nails splay on my jean-covered thighs, and the muscles involuntarily contract under her palms. Goddamn, I could come just from that light touch.

Clenching my jaw, I stare down at her, part of me reeling. After five years of secretly lusting after and longing for my brother's wife, she's kneeling before me, hunger darkening her gaze, her hands and mouth only inches from my dick. It's as if I'm trapped in an alternate universe. Or caught in that murky place between deep sleep and awareness, where dreams and reality blend. And I'll kill the motherfucker who dares to shake me awake.

"What do you want?" I ask her, surrendering to the pull of one of my guilty pleasures and burrowing my hand in her hair. The thick, heavy strands slide over my palm, in between my fingers, and my imagination starts to run amok. Picturing them gliding over my bare skin. Wrapping around my dick. My grip tightens at the vivid, dirty visuals, and her breath catches. Her lashes flutter, and a small whimper echoes between us. I harden even more at the obvious signs of pleasure. Because I can, I twist her hair around my hand, tugging again at her scalp. With another of those sweet, utterly sexy sounds, she leans into my hold. God, she's perfect. "Tell me, Eden." When her lashes lift but she hesitates, I urge, "Be brave."

Yeah, I'm a hypocrite, since I've been a coward around this woman from day one. Moment one.

"I want—" She pauses. Drags in a breath and continues. "I want what you gave that other woman. You, in my mouth, your hand in my hair, guiding me, showing me what you need from me. No," she says, her fingers curling into my thighs. "*Taking* what you need from me. Don't be gentle. Don't go easy because of who I am. Use me."

Her words ran into one another the longer she spoke, as if she had to hurry and get them out. Didn't matter; I heard each and every one of them. Damn. *Inhale. Exhale. Inhale. Exhale.* My control is slipping, like delicate tissue paper that is steadily tearing right down the middle. Only she could do this to me with just a whispered plea.

I rub my thumb across her bottom lip, tracing the curve, dipping the tip inside. The edge of her teeth grazes my flesh, and the sensation ripples over my erection. Anticipation rides me, drumming deep inside me, sizzling under my skin. A part of me wants to hold out a little longer, but damn that. I can't. Not when I've been holding out for years.

Taking what you need... Don't go easy... Use me.

The litany plays in my head, a filthy little jingle that's quickly becoming my favorite tune.

I, again, wrap my fingers around the bottom half of my length, and draw her head down, down, down, until... *Oh fuck.*

Her lips kiss the head for a chest-squeezing moment before parting, opening, and I'm sinking into the wet heat of her mouth. My body goes as rigid as a statue. *Christ.* Our moans saturate the air, and as hers vibrates over my flesh, I can believe that she's been waiting for this—wanting this—as much as I have. At least, with my dick encased in the sweetest suction, I don't have to imagine it any longer.

She doesn't wait for me to instruct her; her tongue slides over the swollen tip, smoothing, exploring. I don't stop her. That would require moving. And paralyzed by such sharp pain-edged pleasure, I'm a willing prisoner of her mouth. She dips her head, taking more of me, that agile tongue torturing me with its long, greedy strokes. Only when she withdraws and the cool air whispers over my damp skin does my stupor shatter. With a growl that sounds too damn animalistic, I press her head lower, not easing until her lips bump my fist.

Shit. The sight of her stretched wide around my dick... No fantasy, no porno, none of my reality can compare to it.

The dense fringe of her lashes fan against her skin, hiding her eyes from me, but the eager working of her tongue, the flush across her cheekbones, the bite of her nails through denim telegraph her pleasure. And then there are the moans adding another caress up and down my flesh. It's *so good*.

I can't tear my gaze away from her. Watching her slip and slide over me is hotter than the dirtiest sex I've ever had. I've never been closer to heaven than I am now. She's further shredding my control, and it's only been moments since she slid that beautiful, mind-bending mouth on me. Back and forth, she bobs over me, sucking, licking, goddamn worshipping. And fuck if she doesn't make me feel like a god.

Electrical currents race and pop down my spine, culminating in a crackling pool at the base, in my balls. I grit my teeth, fighting the signal that orgasm is much closer than I want. Releasing my flesh, I thrust the other hand in her hair, both cradling her head and firmly holding her steady. Her eyes flicker to mine, and the lust raging through me rockets from consuming to combustible. Pleasure darkens her gaze so it appears black. A spark of impatience flashes in the depths, and in spite of the need digging its claws low in my gut, a corner of my mouth quirks into a tight smile as feral satisfaction curls in my chest.

"Open," I order, not waiting for her obedience but rolling my hips up and nudging her lips. I press inside, pushing deeper, sinking more than half of my length inside her. She flattens her tongue, offering me a runway straight to the back of her throat. A groan tears from me, a reflection of my control ripping at the seams. "That's it, baby. Let me in." It's a demand, a guttural plea.

Raising higher on her knees, she bends lower over me, and grateful, I lean down, press a kiss to her damp forehead. Then, straightening, I slowly guide her down my cock.

"Fuck," I snap as the head bumps the entrance to her

throat. She freezes, and I immediately pause. This can't be the first time she's deep-throated a man...can it? A visceral, primitive approval roars through me, reverberating in my head. I'm seconds from pounding on my chest like the caveman she's transformed me into. "Easy," I murmur, running a knuckle up and down the front of her neck. "Relax, baby. Breathe through your nose and relax. You can take me."

Precious seconds pass as she visibly loosens under my hands, and only when she dips her head, do I stroke inside her again. And slip a little into that tight-as-fuck channel. I grunt, the only sound I'm capable of uttering. My lungs seize as I withdraw then press forward once more, taking another increment of her throat. Feeling it spasm and flutter around my tip.

"*Goddamn*," I snarl. The last remnants of my control disintegrate, and my dick pistons in and out of her, fucking her. *Use me. Use me.* The words spur me on, and I take her at her word. Her nails pinch my thighs, but she doesn't protest. No, she's sucking at me like she can't get enough, like her entire world has narrowed down to my flesh in her mouth.

Lightning snaps through me, and I hurtle toward an orgasm that might fucking kill me. My balls tighten and draw up, and if unclenching my teeth were a possibility, I would warn Eden about coming. About pouring down her throat. Ask if she's okay with it. But I can't, and I don't.

It nails me, and I explode, growling through it like the beast I've called myself. From my brain to the hot, burning soles of my feet inside my boots, I'm land-locked by pleasure so keen, so sharp, it borders on pain. And I come so violently, a part of me recoils at what I've become. Some feral animal gripping his female tight as he pours into her over and over.

When I'm finally, *finally* spent, I release her head and fall against the back of the couch, harsh bellows bolting from my chest, residual pulses tripping over my skin, down my spine.

Eden places an absurdly gentle kiss on the tip, then lifts her head. With her flushed skin, swollen mouth, gleaming eyes, and tangled hair, she looks like a thoroughly defiled angel. Shame should be crawling in any second now, but I still reach down, ball her T-shirt in my fist, and drag her up my body. She willingly clambers onto my lap, straddling it. Even though I've just come hard enough to forget my own name, my dick thumps. And I can't blame it. Her jeans may separate us, but I swear the heat of her penetrates the denim.

Tipping my head back, I tunnel my fingers through her hair once more. I can't help myself. It's fast becoming my new obsession. I want to see it tumbling down, draped over her shoulders and chest, playing hide-and-seek with her beautiful breasts, stuck to her sweat-dampened skin. I'm hungry to wrap the heavy weight of it around my fist and wrist, drag her head back, exposing that slender throat as I fuck her from behind. Yeah, obsession might not be strong enough of a word.

"Kiss me," I rasp, fully aware the last time the words were spoken between us, it was me who turned tail and ran. Now could be the time when she decides to issue a little payback, and she would be in the right. But since only seconds ago she was tonguing my dick, I'm hoping she won't. "Give me what my dick just had."

She studies me, her gaze dropping to my mouth, then lower to my chest and my semi-hard flesh. When she returns her scrutiny to my face, I'm ready to take the kiss. Suddenly, I'm so starved for it, my gut clenches, going concave. Fuck it, I'm ready to beg.

Lowering her head, she puts her lips on me. But not on my mouth. On my chin. My jaw. My temple. She brushes a caress over the faded, decades-old scar right above my right eyebrow. My heart pounds at the tenderness, the affection in the light touches. *Stop this shit*, part of me barks. Hot, frenzied, filthy. That's what I need, because I can't afford to trick myself into believing she could care for me as more than her brother-in-law and a substitute for her vibrator. But the other part—that part that's like a barren, parched, cracked wasteland—craves each soft sweep. Craves it like a man crawling through that wasteland, palms and feet bleeding, dying of thirst.

My eyelids receive the same gentle, but sensual, treatment. So does the small bump along the bridge of my nose. I hold my breath—literally hold my goddamn breath like some smitten teenager—when those lips hover above mine. And when that first sweet rub of her mouth to mine comes, a shudder ripples through my body, like a fucking earthquake, and as unmanning, as revealing as it is, I remain still, aching for another.

I've never had a kiss like this; I don't think I've ever been innocent enough for one. This is the kind that curious, nervous strangers on a first date would share. The kind that says, *I like you. I want to discover more about you.* One, I've rarely been on a date, unless you count buying a woman a drink at a bar or club. And most of the women I've fucked could care less about finding out my likes, dislikes, favorite foods or movies. They liked my fame and loved my dick. And I didn't care. Didn't need anything more from them.

But Eden...

With a growl that generates from the swirling and ever-tightening knot in my chest, I jerk her head down. Desperate to banish that need for something more than this moment of lust-fueled insanity, I open my mouth under hers and drive my tongue between her lips. Hard. The growl rumbles into a groan at my first hit of her sweet, sultry taste. It's instantly addictive, and though I'm licking the roof of her mouth and curling my tongue around hers, I'm already hurting for the next time, the next high.

There's enough awareness, enough reason remaining in my head that if she had pulled back or resisted, I would've freed her. But no, *God no*, she's all in. She meets me, thrusts, sucks, laps, nips—giving as good as I'm dishing out. And all with a sexy little whimper that I swallow and take as my due. Fingers tangled in my hair, her lips part wider, and she tilts her head to the side, deepening this mouth-fucking innocuously labeled a kiss. 'Cause we're definitely fucking. Screwing. Getting wet, nasty, wild. Tongues glide, coil, and dance. Teeth clack. Lips slide and mate.

And below… Below, she's rubbing that hot, no-doubt soaked sex over my thickening cock.

Dropping both hands to her ass, I cup the firm, rounded flesh and urge her on, helping her find a rhythm that has me gritting my teeth and rolling my hips to meet every downward stroke. I don't give a damn that the denim is chafing my dick. The ball-tightening pleasure renders that small detail incidental.

"Touch me," she whispers against my mouth on the tail end of a moan. "Please."

I can't resist her request or the ache throbbing in it.

Quickly unfastening her jeans and tugging them down a little, I slip one hand inside the denim and glide it over silken flesh. No way in hell can I resist not squeezing her pretty ass before sliding down until my fingertips tease the entrance to her sex. I circle the hole, eliciting a gasp from the woman twisting and bucking on my thighs.

That soft, hungry sound quivers between us, and it goads me on. I dip my other hand between the front of her jeans and lower belly, not stopping until I brush her sweet little clit. She jerks as if electrocuted, her back arching so hard she resembles a tightly drawn bow. Her fingernails dent my shoulders through my T-shirt, and I grunt at the slight sting. Savoring it. Hoping when I look in the mirror tomorrow, there are marks decorating my skin.

Not enough. Not enough. The words chant through my head, gaining volume and speed until it's an erotic drumbeat against my skull. And I surrender to that call without putting up any fight.

I remove my hands from her, and her disappointed, frustrated whimper ends on a shocked note as I wrench her from my lap and swiftly switch positions with her. Settling her in the corner of the couch, I kneel on the floor and yank her jeans and panties down and off. She looses a strangled cry and tries to close her legs, tries to hide her bare sex from me. *Tries.* Because I don't allow it.

Palming the insides of her thighs, I push them apart, widen them so I have an unhindered, front-seat view to the prettiest, lushest, most perfect pussy I've ever seen. Maybe because the dark curls and petal soft, swollen folds are drenched with evidence of the desire I've stirred in her. Maybe because her clit is engorged and pulsing, peeking out from between her lips.

Maybe because it's Eden.

Bending my head, I trail my lips up her leg, nuzzling the crease where the limb and torso connect. Inhaling, I drag her heady, delicious scent into my lungs. Yeah, like I suspected. That peaches and summer heat is the same, just more condensed, muskier. Addictive. I haven't even tasted her yet, but I know it will be. And I'm willing to die from the habit.

Growling, I dive in.

And lose myself.

Long licks up her slit. Thirsty pulls at the pink nub. Hard, insistent sucks at the folds several shades darker than her tan skin. Plunging thrusts of my tongue in her sex. Tilting her hips up and back, I angle my head and bury myself inside her. So good. So fucking good. I can't get enough. God, I'm an animal. A ravenous, insatiable animal who can't help but eat, feed, devour.

Her nails scrape over my scalp, score my shoulders. She undulates and writhes beneath my mouth—trying to get closer or escape me, shit, I don't know. But since her choking screams pepper my ears, and she's grinding her flesh against my mouth, I'm going with getting closer.

"Knox, oh God, please. Please. Harder. More," she begs in a hoarse, almost broken voice.

Definitely getting closer.

I give her what she's pleading for.

Without hesitation, I drive two fingers deep. And damn near howl at the immediate vise-grip of her slick, smooth, muscular walls. My cock, fully recovered and stiff against my lower stomach, pounds in jealousy. It wants in this snug, hot embrace. Yeah, can't blame it.

Lowering my head, I trail the tip of my tongue along the path at the back of her pussy, following the smooth patch to the puckered hole hidden between her ass. She stiffens, displaying the first signs of uncertainty since I put my mouth on her. Doesn't stop me from tracing the back entrance, from dipping just inside.

"Knox," she objects, pushing at my head, and I lift my mouth but replace it with my finger. Not entering but tapping it, delicately circling it. Teasing her with the knowledge that I want in that forbidden tight channel I suspect no one has breached. The realization roars through me with a primal surge that should be a warning I'm headed too far, too deep into this…whatever it is between us.

Rearing up, I latch onto her clit, flick and stab the flesh with the stiffened point of my tongue. Abandoning her ass— for now—I shift my touch back to her sex and drive inside. Finger-fuck her. *Goddamn*. I could do this all night. Screw that. Forever. Just set up camp and establish a frontier town right here between her slender, toned thighs. But her steady stream of cries, her desperate clutching of my head and frantic thrusts of her hips telegraph she's close and isn't going to last. And no matter what I crave, she comes first. Besides, I long to feel that bruising, orgasmic grip again. Want to hear that keening wail. Am hungry to witness the flush and swell of her folds while in the middle of a release.

I capture her clit between my lips, graze it with my teeth. Lightly bite it. Just hard enough to inflict the edge of pain while my fingertips press against and massage that place high up in her core that will set her off like a bomb.

It does. She detonates. And it's beautiful.

She's beautiful.

I don't let up on her, ensuring she receives every last shudder and shake. Only then do I reluctantly straighten, knowing surrender to the urge to continue licking and sucking might be too much for her sensitive flesh. The thought of her discomfort is the one thing that can curb this lust ripping at me.

Standing, I stare down at her. Half-naked, legs still sprawled wide, chest rising and falling on deep, loud breaths... Hair tousled and tangled around her shoulders, neck, and face... Eyes closed as she drifts off to sleep, lashes a dark fringe... For years, I've imagined how she'd looked after having my face between her legs, her taste in my mouth, on my tongue. Nothing my mind conjured can compare with reality. Those past images are blurred, black and white photos, while she is cast in such vivid color and HD clarity, it hurts my eyes.

Unease and a fuck load of *What the hell am I doing?* floods me in a roaring deluge.

Promise me. You promise me, Knox.

The words, the demand sneaks inside my head and refuses to be evicted. Tipping my head back, I wipe my palm across my lips and chin, smelling her on my skin, and it's both a gift and an indictment. The roots of my disquiet and guilt burrow deeper, the gnarled vines twining around my rib cage, my heart, every organ. Because as pleasure and satisfaction ebb, I can't block out the voice that whispers I had no business, no right touching her, enjoying her. That if she had any idea of the truth, there's no way in hell she would've put her mouth on me. Let me put mine on her.

Eden, Jude, Simon, Jake—they've all assured me I shouldn't carry the burden of Connor's death. But none of them know I could've stopped that last fight, but I didn't. Connor had been a good fighter; though he'd chosen to attend college, he'd always trained alongside me. And when he'd entered the BFC, he'd been more skilled than most rookies. But he hadn't been ready for that match. Two years of fighting professionally hadn't been long enough to face light heavyweight champion Jordan McNamara. But the powers that be had wanted to promote an event that included both Gordon brothers. Initially, I'd tried to talk Connor out of it, but he'd been stubborn, a trait all of us had inherited from Dad. The truth is, I'd had enough pull at the time that I could've had them cancel his match. Especially if I'd refused to fight.

But I hadn't.

Several reasons had halted me from pulling that trigger: Connor would've been pissed, and that's putting it lightly; I'd liked the idea of us fighting together in the same event for the first time; and preventing his fight from happening would've meant canceling mine. I hadn't wanted to forfeit the match against Israel Clarkson, three-time former BFC heavyweight champion. Beating him would've helped solidify my reputation and career as one of the best in the sport.

Well, I had defeated Clarkson, and my brother had died.

Because of my ambition, I saved my title but lost one of the people I loved most.

And now, here I stand over his wife—the woman I've secretly coveted for five years—being selfish again.

I grind my teeth together so hard a twinge of discomfort echoes along my jaw.

If Eden had the full truth available to her—how I failed Connor, failed her, failed my family—would she have knelt so eagerly between my legs? Let me fill her mouth, take her throat? Allowed me to spread her open and fuck her with my tongue?

Or would she have leveled me with the grief, betrayal, and hate in her eyes that jerked me awake, sweating and heart hammering, in the middle of the night?

I don't know.

But it doesn't matter because there's one certain thing that can't be denied. I *do* know the truth. And I should've kept my distance from her. Maintained a brother-and-sister-in-law relationship. I don't deserve to try and grab for more, even if it's just realizing the fantasy of touching her.

Even if it means forcing distance, physical and emotional, between us, I have to—because indulging in *this* again isn't an option.

Ignoring the aching clench in my chest, I bend down and slide my arms under her thighs and shoulders. She doesn't lift her lashes but cuddles closer to me as I pick her up. The pinch tightens, but I head toward the short hallway off the living room. Seconds later, I enter her bedroom door and lay her on the bed Jude and I put together only an hour earlier.

She doesn't wake as I slip the sheet over her and close the door behind me.

When she awakens, she's probably going to feel abandoned and hurt that I left. And it's a dick move considering what went down between us. But the alternative, dropping onto the mattress and wrapping my body around hers so my face is the first thing she sees in the morning, isn't possible.

Not with a ghost and my guilt an indestructible wall between us.

Chapter Eight

Eden

"Just sign here." The UPS employee extends her scratched-up electronic pad toward me, and I accept it, smiling as I scrawl my name across the screen with the stylus.

"Here you go." I hand her tools of the trade back to her and force myself not to rub my hands together in glee at the two large and one medium-size boxes in front of my desk at the tattoo shop. "Thanks."

"My pleasure," she says. But instead of leaving and returning to her illegally parked, brown and yellow truck, she tucks the pad away and tilts her head to the side, her gaze flicking down my T-shirt covered chest and ripped skinny-leg jeans.

Hold up. Did she just check me out?

I blink.

"I'm just going to say it," she says, returning her eyes to mine. "You're gorgeous."

I blink again. Okay, this is a first. And I have to admit, I'm a little flattered. Even that dung-brown, curve-obliterating uniform can't hide her lean, toned figure. With her light brown hair pulled into a high ponytail, her hazel eyes, and chestnut skin, she's a stunner. And the appreciation glowing in that pretty stare boosts my Knox-battered-and-bruised pride. For the second time since seeing *Wonder Woman*, I'm kind of bemoaning being strictly dickly.

"Thanks," I reply. "That's sweet." I can't prevent the blush that rushes up my neck and into my face. Compliments aren't my thing. Growing up, I'd very rarely been on the receiving end of them. And even though there hadn't been a shortage of them from Connor, I'd never become comfortable hearing them directed at me.

"If someone isn't telling you that often enough, then shame on them." She reaches into her shirt pocket, removes a white card, and holds it out. I accept, glancing down to catch her name and numbers. Katrina James. "Call me. I'd love to take you to dinner."

I almost give her my usual answer: I'm widowed and not really looking to become involved with anyone, but thanks anyway.

But at the last moment, I stop myself. Not because I want to accept her invitation; no matter how attractive Katrina is, I just don't swing that way. No, I swallow the words down because I'm no longer defining myself by my marital status and life circumstances and using both as excuses to not live.

Maybe that decision happened the morning I woke up naked from the waist down, whisker burns abrading the inside of my thighs, and alone except for the memories of Knox with his head buried between my legs. Maybe it happened weeks before that when I made the decision to move out of Katherine and Dan's home.

I can't say for certain, but I'm determined to move on.

Even if I have to kick my own ass to do it.

"Thanks," I repeat, tucking the business card in my back pocket.

Nodding, she smiles one last time and, turning, leaves the shop. Still a little bemused, I watch until she climbs into the truck and pulls off, disappearing into the busy, Saturday traffic.

"Damn." Hakim whistles from behind me. I lean back against the desk, resting my elbows on the top. The Taye Diggs with dreads lookalike props an arm on the frame of his cubicle wall and grins. "That was hot as fuck. You should bring her to my party tonight."

Bent over a client, Shana shakes her head and snorts. "You're such a man."

"Hey," Jude yelled from his workspace. "I take offense to that. I wasn't picturing Eden and the UPS chick naked and sweaty."

"Shit, I'm a woman, and *I* was picturing Eden and the UPS chick naked and sweaty," V drawled, rolling backward in her chair, her grin wicked and teasing. She wiggles her eyebrows at me, the silver ring piercing the right one dipping up and down.

Snickering, I push off the desk and round it. "Hakim, help me with these? Can you take them to my office?" "Office" is being a bit generous, since it's barely bigger than a closet. But it's mine, and I love it.

"For you? Anything." He strolls over, plants a smacking kiss on my cheek, and hefts one of the two larger boxes in his arms.

I follow him with the medium package, and moments later, I'm taking a pair of scissors to the cardboard containers. I can't suppress the pleased sigh that escapes me as I pull back the flaps and stare down at the array of black hoodies. Pride swells within me. The artwork—two fists with HARD KNOX tattooed across the knuckles, and INK underneath—was my idea. The fists pay homage to and capitalize on Knox's MMA background, while the lettering clearly states what we are.

We. It's true. Even though I'm not an artist and don't know how to wield a tattoo gun, I belong here. I have a second family here, and I'm needed. In this shop, I'm not the drunk's daughter or just Connor Gordon's wife or widow, or even Knox and Jude's sister-in-law. I've found my calling as shop manager, and after years of wondering what I would do with my life, I've discovered I'm damn good at business management. And as boring as it might sound to some people, I find all of it—the organization, paying invoices, ordering supplies, marketing, and promotion—exciting. I can never thank Knox enough for giving me free rein with his shop. He trusted me, and I can never repay that.

Even if our relationship is forever changed because of what's been happening between us, I'll always appreciate him for offering me a chance most businesses would never extend a college dropout with zero experience.

"Yooo, these are dope," V praises, kneeling next to the box of hoodies. I'd been so lost in my own head, I hadn't even heard her stop by or walk into my office.

The tattoo artist removes one of the hoodies and holds it to her chest. "I. Love. This." Her halo of dark curls bobs as she lays the thin jacket out and strokes a hand over the logo. "What else do you have?"

Together, we open the remaining boxes and moan and exclaim over the contents as if they're piles and piles of chocolate and coffee instead of merchandise. Long-sleeve Henley-style shirts, T-shirts for men and women, beanies, baseball caps, custom-made leather wrist cuffs and necklaces… Even jewelry with the shop's initials engraved on the silver. Pleasure swirls inside me, and every time V oohs-and-aahs over another article, my delight increases, mixing with a swelling pride.

"I want one of everything," V announces, stripping off her fashionably shredded shirt and drawing on one of the woman's black T-shirts with the purposefully ragged V-neck. It looks amazing against her chicory skin and her full-sleeve tattoos. "God, this even makes me look like I have tits. Now I can stop calling you a bitch out of breast-envy."

I snicker, replacing all the merchandise in the boxes. "Uh, you know you just bought that shirt, right?"

She shoots me a side glance. "Employee discount?"

"Sure." I nod. "I'm pricing it at $19.99. You can have it at 19.97."

"Gee," she drawls. "That's really magnanimous of you." She tosses one of the pieces of ripped-off shipping tape at me, grinning. "Like that word? The U of C professor I'm dating taught me that one. He helps me in expanding my vocab, and in return, I tutor him in…other things." She releases a frankly lascivious cackle, and I shake my head at her. "Has Knox seen the logo yet?"

And like a needle to a balloon, just the mention of his name takes care of the joy bubbling in my chest.

Covering the elation that whistles out of me like a slow leak, I duck my head and concentrate on closing the packages. "Yeah. After Hakim drew the logo for me, I emailed it to him. He approved it, so I'm guessing he liked it."

Not that I could show him the finished product now. Knox has been noticeably scarce around the shop since the Sunday before last. The Sunday I went down on him on my brand-new living room couch, and he reciprocated with a tongue-fuck that literally knocked me out for the count.

I swallow hard, shoving down the knot of anger and embarrassment that has lodged itself in my throat more times than I can number in the last two weeks. As if waking up alone after being so…vulnerable and exposed with him wasn't enough, I arrived at work Monday to discover he'd left for a tattoo expo in Florida. Convenient.

And from Instagram, I discovered he was traveling with Jenika Travers, a local artist and shop owner who's always nurtured a serious hard-on for Knox and is a doppelganger for Ryan Ashley, the gorgeous *Ink Master* champion. I wonder if he had any trouble sleeping while he was gone. Sex has the habit of tiring people out.

Great. My subconscious has deteriorated into a straight bitch. I hate the licks of green fire that even now scald a hole in my belly as they did when I scrolled through the Instagram posts from the three-day expo. I, more than anyone, accept that I have zero claim on Knox, nor do I have the right to be jealous or resentful. *He's not mine.* Still... None of that prevented the hurt from slicing into me and leaving me breathless.

Knox returned home on Thursday, only to leave back out on Monday for another expo in Detroit. And during that time in the shop, he shut himself up in his room with client after client. Hell, I wouldn't be surprised if he snatched people up off the street and offered to ink them for free if they would just keep him occupied. And too busy to speak to or deal with me.

Not that he's the one doing all the avoiding.

I'm guilty. And there's the key word: guilt.

Unlike the time he touched me in his apartment, when I woke up the morning after we'd christened my living room couch I hadn't been crushed by the weight of unresolved grief and shame. Mainly because my head—and body—had still been reeling from the apocalyptic event that had taken place the night before. God. I curl my fingers into a tight fist to keep from pressing a palm to my lower belly...or lower. Sometimes, especially in the dead of night, I can still feel Knox's mouth. Moving over me. Tugging at me. Licking at me. Fucking me.

The man licked my asshole, for fuck's sakes. And—and I

think I liked it.

I smother a mortified groan. What has he done to me? Transformed me into this sexual creature I don't recognize. Didn't know existed.

Sex with Connor had been gentle, tender, patient, loving.

Knox had been wild, raw, dirty, carnal, and the pleasure had been unmerciful.

He'd swept me up in this maelstrom of passion and ecstasy and left me battered and bruised by it. Confused by it. Because I've known love, affection. So how can I crave something so…animalistic? My mind knows the difference. My body doesn't give a damn.

But this…*thing* between us is wrong. Lusting after, kissing, caressing, and sucking off my dead husband's brother is just *wrong*. Katherine would never understand or forgive it. Neither would the rest of his family—*my* family. They would view it as immoral…practically incest. Maybe see me as a brother-jumping whore with no loyalty. I would risk losing the only family I've had since I was nineteen years old.

And then there's another thought that has been nagging at me for the last two weeks. With the chaotic mess that was my childhood, growing up with an alcoholic father and neglectful mother, I grew to be independent. In my eyes, I had no choice. It was either fend for myself or be broken. And breaking wasn't an option. But after meeting Connor, I lost that independence somewhere along the line. I can't pinpoint where, and I don't know why. Maybe it was the novelty of being loved, cared for, and protected? Maybe, in spite of surviving the hell of my upbringing, some residue of it burrowed deep into my subconscious, and when a man finally showed me love, offered me security, I was willing to do anything to keep him? Including surrender my ambition and goals to his? Not that Connor asked me to do any of that. He never even expected me to put my life on hold to support his dreams. That wasn't him. Yet, I did just that.

I mentally shrink from that thought; it veered too close to who my mother had been. But I can't escape my whirling brain; I can't shut it down. And as my third-grade teacher was fond of saying, "The proof is in the pudding." I'm twenty-four, no degree, about to enroll in college for the second time, and am finding my footing in a new position. Just finding myself.

Yes, my fear is losing my family. But... What if my bigger one is losing myself in Knox like I did with Connor?

"There's a party in here, and nobody invited me?" Shana snaps from the office door, breaking into my troubled thoughts. Thank God for the interruption. I need a break from myself. The petite woman props a hip against the jamb, her arms crossed. But the bark of her voice is offset by the smile lighting her lovely features. This week, her black hair is streaked a vibrant pink and purple. I swear, if I didn't love these women at the shop like sisters, their beauty would wreak hell on my confidence. "Hey, don't worry about my client. I checked him out because I figured you were back here getting ready for your date." She arches an eyebrow that states, *I know you're not.*

I sigh. Right. The date. "No, I'm not getting ready yet. I have another hour—"

"Fuck that," Shana interrupts, flicking my excuse off with a wave of her hand. "Knox isn't here, so that officially makes you the boss. So as the boss, I think you can give yourself permission to clock out an hour early and start getting ready."

"And don't even think about saying you're going home, Ms. Thang," V adds, tossing the hoodie she's holding back in the box. "If you think me and Shana are going to let you out of our sights until you leave for that restaurant, you've obviously been hittin' some of Hakim's weed." She stands and twirls a finger over the packages. "We don't trust you not to hole up in that apartment and chicken out. So, tie all this up so we can get you ready."

"But what about Hakim's party? Maybe I should reschedule the date, since he's my friend and invited me..." Yeah, I trail off, hearing how lame I sound. I'm embarrassed for myself.

"Really, bitch?" V drawls, smirking. "You couldn't come up with a better excuse than that?"

"Seriously." Shana shakes her head. "Go on the date, then swing by Hakim's afterward and give us the dirty details. And *please*, God," she prays, slapping her hands together and lifting her gaze toward the ceiling, "let there be the dirtiest of details."

"Why did I agree to this again?" I groan, but their replies of "Because it's about damn time," and "So your coochie won't shrivel up and fall out," aren't really necessary.

V and Shana have been bugging me for the past six months about starting to date again. I've always said, no, not ready. But then, last week, they approached me again about a friend of V's. I would be lying if I didn't admit that the reason I finally caved might've had something to do with a picture Jenika had just posted on her Instagram account of her and Knox working side-by-side. Damn near shoulder-to-shoulder. Again, that hot, emerald flame had scorched my insides, and I'd impulsively given V the go-ahead to arrange the blind date.

Stupid, stupid, stupid.

Now, as I try to evade V and Shana's stony, I'm-not-taking-none-of-your-shitty-excuses stares, I have no one to blame but myself...and the pointless, ridiculous jealousy over a man that I can't have.

"Fine." I sigh. "Let's do this."

• • •

"Are you sure your friend will be cool with me just showing up with you?" Roman Bethea asks as he extends a hand toward me and helps me from his car.

"Oh, it's no problem at all. Hakim's motto might as well be 'The more the merrier,'" I say, smiling up at my date for the evening.

I have to confess—V has wonderful taste. Roman, with his black curls, dark blue eyes, honeyed skin that reminds me of a hot sun and desert sands, and his tall, wiry but strong frame, is beautiful. I bet the man stops traffic on Michigan Avenue with his looks. Then add his perfect manners, dry humor, ability to hold his end of a lively and interesting conversation, and that sexy way of completely focusing on me even when a gorgeous woman walks past. If I didn't know that V goes for the bad boy, ruff 'n' scruff types, I'd wonder why she was pawning him off on me instead of snatching him up for herself. Because yes, Roman is that wonderful.

And we have zero chemistry.

Damn it.

Even now as we head for the cement steps leading to the front door of Hakim's Andersonville home, I'm kicking my own ass. Or my stubborn, blind hormones' asses. V isn't the only one who apparently has a thing for the bad boy, ruff 'n' scruff type.

Silently sighing, I smile up at Roman and tug on his shirt sleeve. Man, he'd even dressed up for dinner at Gibson's, only the best steakhouse in Chicago, and a movie.

And he'd paid.

Fuck. There must be something seriously damaged about me. Especially since I'm bringing him to Hakim's party to maybe find someone to make up for what isn't happening between us.

Yes, I've friend-zoned him and am now playing matchmaker. Or madam. Not quite sure which one.

"C'mon." I nod toward the house. "Knowing my friend, there's not much food, but the booze is plentiful." I laugh. "Though, since it's almost eleven, even that's debatable."

"Lead the way," he says.

He places a hand on my lower back as we climb the steps. I knock on the door, and seconds later, it swings open and reveals Hakim, beer in hand. Loud hip-hop and a deep, thumping bass pour out of the house behind him. I'd caution him about his neighbors, but having met them, I know they're probably in the house, too.

"Heeeyy," he greets me loudly, drawing out the one word into three syllables. "You know I was gonna show my ass Monday if you didn't show up tonight." He pulls me in for a one-arm hug, then turns to Roman. "This your boy? Not as cute as the UPS chick but, okay. What's up?" Grinning, he hikes his chin at Roman and steps back so we can enter. "Food's in the kitchen, drinks in the living room. Help yourself."

I slip past him, wrapping my fingers around Roman's hand to guide him through the surprisingly spacious three-bedroom, two-bath house. This isn't my first visit to Hakim's home, so I navigate through the thick tangle of people drinking, laughing, grinding together to the music, and smoking in the living and dining rooms. From past experiences, I'm sure some of it has spilled over into the bedrooms, bathrooms, and even the hall closet, which actually happened on one memorable occasion.

We maneuver our way to the table burdened with bottles containing all brands and shades of alcohol and plastic cups.

"Roman!" V's shout comes a couple of seconds before she appears and throws her arms around her friend and smacks a kiss to his cheek. "I didn't know Eden was bringing you by." With her arm slung around his waist, she winks at me. "Did I do good by you, or what? Isn't he great?"

"Uh, he needs to go to the bathroom," Roman interrupts, voice wry. He disentangles himself from V and glances at me.

"Down the hall and second door on the left," I direct him. "And, uh, word to the wise? Knock, then knock again before going in. Otherwise, you might be scarred for life."

He snorts. "Got it."

As soon as he's swallowed up by the crowd, V cups my shoulders and gives me a little shake. "Dish, woman."

I wince, lifting a shoulder in a half shrug. "I hate to break this to you, but…"

"Noooo," she howls, drawing several stares our way and cluing me in that my friend might be a bit tipsy. "You two are so perfect for each other," she whines, throwing her hands up in the air. "Are you sure?"

"Yep." I nod, biting the inside of my cheek to keep from grinning at her antics. "Sorry. He's a nice guy, though."

She huffs, dropping her fists on her hips. "Fine. Well, I guess it's my mission to find him some solace tonight."

"And by 'solace' you mean…"

"Ass." Bending, she flips open the top of a red and white cooler under the table and plucks free two beers. "Here." She shoves one into my hand and heads off in the direction Roman disappeared.

Chuckling under my breath, I twist off the top of my bottle and tip it to my lips. The ice-cold alcohol slides over my tongue, and though the red wine at dinner was nice, this is *good*.

I lean back against the wall, content to be on the periphery of all the revelry rather than in the thick of it. Connor was always the one who'd been the center of attention even before he'd joined the BFC. At first, he'd tried to draw me in with him but soon realized I preferred standing just on the outside, observing, letting him bask in the limelight. Back then, I'd just been happy knowing his light cast on me, warmed me.

On the Bose speakers, BlocBoy JB and Drake switched to Camila Cabello's gritty, sultry voice. Taking another sip of beer, I let my lashes drift down, allowing the beer and the two martinis I had at dinner to do their thing. Swaying to the slow, sexy beat, I lose myself in the music and the sweet call of the alcohol in my veins.

Until I can't.

Because something...someone...won't let me.

It's almost physical, the touch of the gaze on my exposed skin. When I'd entered the house, I'd shed my sweater because of the heat from all the people in one space. But now, I'm glad I removed the clothing for another reason. For the phantom stroke of that electric stare. The charge it leaves behind that dances and sizzles across my flesh, lighting me up. Tightening my nipples into beaded tips. Sliding over my quivering belly. Slipping between my legs, leaving me aching and empty.

Only one man has the power to drag this reaction out of me.

For a second, I squeeze my eyes shut tighter, but I can't *not* look. Can't not see.

Surrendering to the feverish need that's igniting my blood, I lift my lashes.

And my gaze clashes with a deep, shadowed, emerald one.

I'm unable to move. Unable to glance away. Unable to do anything but be owned by Knox's stare.

The lyrics of the song narrate this...this clawing, ravenous thing inside me whenever I breathe the same air as Knox. He is a chemical in my veins, giving me highs and, God yes, lows. I'm the worst kind of addict when it comes to him, a fiend, and I need his brand of dizzying, raze-me-to-the-ground, mind-numbing pleasure. And yes, even that sweet bite of pain.

It's been a week since I last saw him, and my scrutiny of him is probably hungry, and even though my mind is screaming to hide it, to deny it, I don't have the strength to. Because that would require not burning in the flames of that gaze. Not visually tasting the almost-too-full curves of his carnal mouth or tracing the sharp edges of his cheekbones. Not imagining the tangled length of his gold-streaked brown hair and coarse-but-soft beard whispering across my skin.

Not feeling the imprint of that big, hard body against mine. Holding me down. Filling me up.

I suck in a breath, curling my fingers tighter around the bottle, anchoring myself to this spot across the room. Either that or barrel across the room and demand he finish what he started—what we started—two weeks ago on my couch.

Then I see her. The woman with her back to his chest, dancing on him. Grinding on him. Touching him like I shouldn't want to. Like I will never be able to do in a roomful of people, including our family and friends.

She, this random woman, has something of him I can never, and will never, have.

As she spins around and loops her arms around his neck, I turn, too, unable to continue standing there as she uses him like a stripper pole.

Blindly pushing through the thick throng, I move toward the hallway, my only intention to put as much distance as possible between Knox and myself. Grabbing the knob of the first closed door I come to, I twist it and enter the dimly lit bedroom, not even looking to make sure it's empty. But the pale light pouring into the window from the streetlamp reveals I'm alone. Relief shoots through me. The last thing I need is—

The door swings open, and Knox fills the doorway.

I freeze, breath trapped in my lungs, a trembling animal caught in the sights of a prowling predator. And that's what he is. Massive, silent, menacing. The soft but faintly threatening click of the door closing snaps me out of my shock, but it's him slowly, deliberately turning the lock on the door that has me inching backward a couple of steps. Until I realize what I'm doing—retreating. Revealing he is my vulnerability.

Because I can no longer deny it. At least not to myself. Knox is the sexual chink in my armor. My erotic Achilles Heel. Every cliché that describes how he destroys my resolve, my will, my strength. From the moment he first put his mouth on me in that tattoo chair, I've been his to mold, shape... break.

"Who's the guy?" His rough growl vibrates in the room like a souped-up engine, and as he stalks forward, I again have to check the urge to shift backward. But as he invades my personal space, I'm damning my pride. Ceding ground is preferable to inhaling his intoxicating cedar and cinnamon scent. To counting how many centimeters separate his rock-hard, T-shirt-covered chest from my breasts. To remembering how far those wide shoulders stretched my thighs. "Eden."

"A friend of V's," I say, cursing my hurried explanation. As if he deserved one. And why did he sound so pissy? When not seconds ago some chick had been air-reverse-cowgirling him.

"You two came here together," he pointed out in that low voice that contained a hint of thunder.

"Yeah, we had a date earlier." And if there's a bit of satisfaction coating my words, well, so be it. So what if I have zero sexual attraction for Roman? My business, not Knox's.

"You're dating now?" A shadow crosses his expression, a glint of...something flashing in his eyes. On another person, I might call it irritation. Maybe even jealousy. But this is Knox. He doesn't do jealousy. Barely does emotion. And of the number of women he's fucked in the years I've known him, none have been around long enough for him to become possessive over. "So this"—his eyes flick down my body—"is for him?"

This? Okay, the flared skirt of the black dress I'd chosen for the evening hit mid-thigh, exposing a ton more leg than I usually do, but the boat-neck collar of the sleeveless top is damn near demure when compared to the clothes a lot of the women are wearing tonight. Case in point, the woman he'd been entertaining out there in the living room. Her tight, strapless top had barely and valiantly clung to her breasts.

"No," I snap. "It's for me. What're you mad about? That I didn't get permission before going out with a man? Maybe I would've considered telling you my plans if you hadn't been avoiding me like the fucking clap the last two weeks." *Like by going out of state with another woman.* "But this is the thing. Last time I checked, I'm a grown-ass woman, and I don't need your okay."

His eyes narrow, and his mouth firms into a flat, grim line.

"What? No denial about avoiding me?" All the hurt, confusion, and anger seething inside me bubbles up my chest and into the brittle, cracked sound that some optimistic soul could label a laugh. One of two things are about to happen right now: I curse him the hell out, or allow the tears stinging my eyes to fall. Neither outcome is acceptable. "Screw this."

I push past him, but a large hand wraps around my bicep in a gentle but implacable grip that stops me short. In the next second, the solid wall of his chest presses against my back, his thighs columns of marble behind mine. And his erection... My heart flails and whips my rib cage like a cornered creature desperately trying to free itself.

His erection brands my lower back, causing my sex to dampen and my mouth to water. It's on a first-name basis with his cock, and damn if I'm not panting to get them up-close-and-personal again.

"No, I'm not going to deny it," he rumbles in my ear, his breath hot and harsh over the sensitive skin under my lobe. "I left the fucking state twice to get away from you." Before the hurt at his admission can burrow deeper inside me, he grinds his hips against me, his hard length digging into my ass. His palm flattens over my lower belly, holding me in place. Not that I'm trying to escape. No, I'm already rolling back into him, lifting into that stroke. Heat blasts through me, and I'm half surprised I'm not exhaling plumes of smoke. "It was either put as much distance between us as possible or slam you up against the nearest wall, table, chair, or goddamn floor and fuck you until your voice gave out from the screaming."

His hand other hand releases my arm and slides over my shoulder and cups my breast through my dress. He squeezes the flesh, thumbing then pinching the nipple until it's a sharp point through the material. I whimper, arrows of sharp pleasure darting from the tip to my clenching core.

"But I might as well as have saved the money and the gas. It was just geography. Didn't stop me from lying there in that bed, my hand jacking my dick and imagining it was your mouth pulling at me, sucking on me. Didn't prevent me from believing I could still taste you on my lips. Still feel your pussy squeeze my fingers and shiver on my tongue." He shifts forward, moving across the room, and I have no choice but to go with him, his huge body moving me like a marionette, and his frame, his filthy, hot words, the strings guiding me. "Didn't keep me from wanting you and despising myself for it."

I try to smother the caustic sting the last bit of his serrated confession sends blistering through me. He loathes himself for desiring me. Probably resents me, too, although he didn't admit that.

Well, welcome to this tiny club of two.

Before I can reply, my spine aligns with the wall, and he plants his fist on either side of my head, his body looming over me. I'm surrounded by his heady scent, his warrior frame.

"I'm tired, Eden." The hushed words are so at odds with the gritty, carnal language that preceded them that I'm taken aback. Can only stare up at him, struck speechless by the weariness that throbs in his voice and etches his taut expression. Eyes closed, he leans forward and presses his forehead to mine. His breath, a cocktail of beer and a unique flavor that tastes of his kiss, puffs over my lips. And I have to fight the urge not to brush my fingertips over the sensual curves...over the light purple smudges under his eyes that telegraph his battle with sleep. "I'm so fucking tired of fighting." His lashes lift, and I swallow a moan at the shadows darkening them. But not so dark I miss the sadness in their depths. Or the lust. The burning, glittering lust. "Give me the strength, baby," he whispers. "Be my strength to walk away."

That would be the right thing to do—the virtuous, moral thing. But the need blazing through me like an out-of-control wildfire razes morals and virtue to the ground, leaving the ashes scattered in the wind.

Instead, I choose to be his weakness.

Our downfall.

Raising onto my toes, I crush my mouth to his. Plunge my way inside, tangle my tongue with his, demanding he drown with me. Tunneling my fingers through his tumble of hair, I grasp the thick, cool strands, and tilt my head, dive deeper into the kiss, savoring the scratch of his beard over my skin. I'm the driver of this embrace, the taker, the giver, the conqueror. And the knowledge that it's only because he's allowing it licks the flames of desire higher, hotter.

God, he tastes so *good*. I can't get enough. Want more. Fisting his hair, I drag him down lower, raise higher in my shoes. This kiss… It's messy, raw, untamed. Perfect.

His hands drop from the wall and grab my hips in a hold that's so tight, I moan at the possessiveness in it. But as one of those hands falls to my thigh and slides up under my dress, not hesitating in its trip between my thighs, the moan swells into a desperate, ravenous cry. And crests into a scream as he slips under my soaked thong and thrusts two thick fingers inside me. Hard. Deep. Just like I need it. Like only he can give it to me.

I tear my mouth from his, my head falling back and smacking the wall. Blindly, I stare at the ceiling, everything in me drawn tight like a newly strung bow. God, will I ever get used to him inside my body? Just those two digits stretch me, have me dancing on the tips, caught between wanting to escape the invasion and sinking down, demanding more.

"Knox," I breathe, as if he possesses the answer. And maybe he does, because he buries himself deeper, reaching higher. His mouth opens over my throat, and he licks my skin before sucking it. The last remnants of my rationale warn me that he's most likely bruising me, marking me, and I should stop him. But the side of my brain that harkens back to the animal-skin-wrapped woman who judged a man by his power and strength, eggs him on with a hand to the back of his skull.

He glides his fingers free of me, and before I can beg for their return, he pushes back inside again, twisting his wrist, and damn if it feels like he's touching every part of my sex. Again and again, he thrusts inside me, the heel of his palm grinding against my clit, propelling me toward an orgasm that I'm reaching for with desperate hands. That's me. Selfish. So goddamn needy. For him. For the pleasure and sweet oblivion that has become a narcotic, both my salvation and my damnation.

"Not yet," he rumbles a second before pulling out of me when I'm *so close* it almost seems like he's punishing me. I must make a sound—honest to God, I'm not sure of anything I do or say anymore—because he shakes his head. "You've come around my fingers and on my mouth. This time, you're coming around my cock."

He releases me and, reaching behind him, balls a fistful of T-shirt and yanks it over his head, baring that chiseled, muscular chest that eclipses everything else in the room. My fingers itch to caress, stroke, worship. He's a work of art. A sculpture with blood and fire running underneath the perfection of marble.

He's beautiful.

Dropping the shirt to the floor, he pulls a wallet from his back pocket and removes a small foil packet. Letting his wallet fall on top of his clothing, he brings the square to his mouth and rips it open, the other hand tugging open his jeans.

"I could hate you for having that condom," I whisper.

His eyes narrow on mine, hands stilling.

"You came here tonight prepared for sex," I continue. "Not with me, though."

If I could've snatched those last words back, I would've. They revealed too much. My jealousy. Insecurity. Longing. Even though he's in this room with me right now, and I still feel the mark of his fingers inside me, he's not mine. I can't forget that. And I won't try to delude myself that sex with him means I can change that fact.

Slowly, he removes the protection from the wrapper and sheaths himself, his gaze never wavering from mine. Even when my attention momentarily flicks down to take in the wide, flared head and thick, rigid stalk, his scrutiny heats my face.

"I always carry condoms on me. It's just smart," he growls, shifting forward, pressing close. Closer. He palms the backs of my thighs and, in a display of strength that has me breathlessly remembering how he ruled the MMA ring, lifts me, his body and the wall holding me up. On instinct, I wrap my arms around his neck. "And these days, Eden," he lowers his head, so I have no choice but to meet his hooded gaze. But below… Below his finger slides under my panties, jerking the drenched panel covering my sex to the side. I bite at the shocking pleasure of his touch on my bare, exposed flesh. Sink my teeth into my bottom lip as he notches the head at my entrance. Jesus. He hasn't even penetrated me yet, and I already feel bruised, branded. "These days, my dick only gets hard for you. And I could hate you for that."

He flexes his hips, pushing, and the tip opens me, stretches me. Just that bit of him, and nerve endings that have laid dormant for years scream to life.

"Hating you would be easier," he murmurs against my lips.

Then shoves all the way inside me.

Oh. God.

Fire blasts through me, incinerating me. Pleasure, pain. Heat, ice. I'm burning alive and shaking with cold. Filled and empty. Sane and crazy.

I'm fucked.

Burying my face in his neck, I cry out into that sweat-dampened, wood-and-sex scented crook. The stretch, the burn. I swear I can feel every ridge, every vein of his cock. Every throb and pulse. There's no part of my sex that isn't stamped, marked, claimed by him. I suck in a breath. Jesus, he's so goddamn deep in me…

"Easy, baby. Easy," he soothes, even as he lifts me just a bit higher, lodges just a bit deeper. I shudder. I'm caught in that nebulous but vivid place between ecstasy and pain. Where one heightens and sharpens the other, but I'm not sure which one is doing the honing. "Breathe for me. Relax and breathe for me."

It isn't until his hand strokes down my hair over and over like I'm a skittish colt that I realize my arms are damn near strangling him and a litany of shattered, soft cries are spilling from my mouth onto his skin. Deliberately, I follow his instructions and inhale, exhale. Inhale, exhale. I force my body to loosen, to wait and accept.

In moments, that line between pleasure and pain becomes even more blurred, and when he grinds his hips in a circular motion, the base of his cock rubbing against my aching clit, a wave of rapture swells from the point where we're connected.

"Oh fuck, yeah," he mutters against my ear, rolling his pelvis again, giving my clit a tight, dirty massage. "I could come just from this. Just from this filthy little kiss on my dick."

Cupping my thighs, he spreads me wider, then slowly pulls free, the drag of his thick stalk over my overly sensitive flesh rips a groan from my throat. Without warning, he thrusts back in, treating me to that grind at the end of it. Sparks shoot from my sex, up my spine, and manifests in tiny gold and black sparkles in my brain. He continues with those ruthless, just short-of-brutal plunges with the shy retreats and all-business strokes. All I can do is hold on for the ride. And God, is he riding me. Taking me. Molding it, reshaping it to fit only him.

A tiny kernel of trepidation and doubt burrows into the blind lust that has enshrouded my world. Because that's what I'm afraid of—that after Knox, no one will ever be enough. What have I done?

The terrified question slips away into the ever-increasing darkness of the abyss that yawns toward me. Anxiety and thought slip over the crumbling edge, and I'm not far behind. With every drive into me, he shoves me closer and closer. Part of me fights it; I don't want this to end. Don't want that beautiful dick to stop granting me this razor-edged pleasure that has me twisting and dancing in time with his thrusts.

But Knox is the master of this show, and I'm just the puppet. Spreading me wider, he pistons faster, harder, fucking me until I'm no longer standing on the edge of orgasm but plummeting into it.

Everything in me contracts and narrows to the place

between my thighs, then explodes like an atom bomb, the ecstasy mushrooming. I scream into his neck, my teeth clamping down on the tendon running alongside his throat. I'm out of my mind, all reason has left the building, and all that's left is this quaking, shrieking creature that is consumed with the rapture seizing her body like contractions. It's almost too much, yet not nearly enough. Even as the seismic ripples ebb, I'm already craving more.

I'm not aware I'm moving until my back hits the sheet-covered mattress. The material is cool against my overheated skin, and I turn my head, whimpering as I rest my cheek against it.

Impatient, demanding hands stride up my thighs, hook into my panties, and yank them down and off. That same commanding touch palms my knees and pushes my legs up and back until the front of them nearly graze my chest.

Knox leans over me, covers me, and crashes his mouth down on mine as he drives into me once more. Burrowing my fingers in his hair, I cling to him, taking the hungry thrust of his tongue as he slams into me.

This Knox I've unleashed is wild, undisciplined, primal. An animal cut loose from his leash. And I'm its mate, bucking my hips to greet every thrust. He wraps his arms under me, pressing me so close, I can feel his heart beat against my chest. Ripping his lips from mine, he mimics me from seconds earlier and buries his face in the crook where my neck and shoulder meet. His breath is hot and harsh on my damp skin, his hard, desperate grunts punctuating the air.

Reaching between us, he circles a fingertip over my clit, the movement not gentle, but firm, insistent. I shove one hand at his shoulder; I'm so sensitive from my orgasm, I couldn't possibly…

"Fuck," I gasp. Electricity snaps inside me, right behind the tiny bundle of nerves. My hips jerking, trying to evade his caress. Or maybe my body's begging for more. Right now, swept up in this carnal storm, I don't know. How can he... I can't...

"Give it to me, Eden. I need it again," he grates, the words muffled against my skin.

My body understands what my brain is unable to grasp; it obeys what my head is denying.

An orgasm slams into me, squeezing my throat so the cry there is trapped. My whole body seizes, pleasure turning me into a star that flames so bright and hot, it winks out. Above me, Knox growls. He levers off me but continues shuttling through my sex in short, fast strokes. His skin pulls taut over his sharp cheekbones, the emerald of his eyes nearly black. His mouth is pulled into a feral snarl, and with one, two, four more thrusts, his guttural groan echoes in the room as he comes.

Jesus, he's a thing of beauty. Naked but tortured passion. A perfect reflection of the cataclysmic event inside of me. His hips slow, finally stopping, and his head drops, his hair swinging forward and hiding his face from me.

Only our serrated breaths reverberate in the room, but the muted sounds from the party beyond the closed bedroom door penetrate, vividly and jarringly reminding me of where we are.

Who we are.

What we've done.

I shiver and, freeing my fingers from his hair, allow my arms to fall to the mattress.

I've just had sex with Knox.

Connor's brother. My brother-in-law.

There's no taking it back; there's no going back. We've crossed a line that definitely changes our relationship and could permanently damage it. If anyone outside these four walls ever suspected what's taken place inside them, we both could lose our friends, our family.

Without the scorching heat of lust to cloud my mind, the same question rises like a specter to haunt me.

What have we done?

Knox raises his head, and his eyes clash with mine. Every damn thing I'm thinking and feeling is probably reflected in my gaze; I'm shitty at hiding anything. Unlike Knox, whose face is the equivalent of an impenetrable steel vault. Usually. But as he straightens and shifts off the bed, his hooded stare gimmers like jade fire in the dim room. Swollen lips damp from our kiss, hair tangled from my fingers, skin taut and flushed from sex—he's the epitome of erotic satisfaction.

Without releasing me from his visual snare, he removes the condom and takes care of it. In seconds, he's crawled back between my thighs and is crouched over me on his palms and knees.

"I shouldn't have touched you."

His statement is bald, rough, and squeezes my heart in a vise grip. I close my eyes, needing to block out his harshly beautiful face, block out his terrible—but true—words. The pleasure that still hums through my body slowly dissipates, leaving a heavy weight on my chest. And that weight is composed of anger, pain…regret. Not mine, but his.

I turn my head, eyes still closed and shutting him out. "I'm—"

"I promised I wouldn't. And not just myself. Mom."

That admission, said in the same stark, abrupt tone, jerks my head and attention back to him. I stare at him, stunned. Speechless. But my mind more than makes up for my paralyzed vocal cords. *A promise? To Katherine? How was that possible? How did she know about…whatever was going on between Knox and me?*

Shock ebbs, and dread washes in. Oh, Jesus. Did she hate me now? Think I'd betrayed her and Connor?

"H-how...?" I stutter. Pause. Shake my head. And try again. "How does she...?" But I can't say it. The lump in my throat won't allow me to finish the question.

"She doesn't know about what's happened between us these past weeks."

Relief floods in, leaving me so weak, I'm thankful I'm already on my back. Immediately, remorse and guilt swell behind the relief. Because I'm relegating Knox to the status of a dirty secret, and he's worth more than that. Still...the fear of losing my family, their respect and love...

"I made this promise to her two years ago."

"What are you talking about?" I demand, frowning, confused. I don't need to ask about the "two years ago." There's only one event that changed all of our lives then. But why in the hell would the topic of Knox and I come up that night?

If possible, Knox's expression becomes harder. No, no, not harder. More closed off. Shuttered to any emotion. Even his eyes take on the flat, dull sheen of stone. Green stones that stare down at me.

That shut-down demeanor only solidifies the dread pooling in my chest to a brick of lead. Part of me doesn't want to know the answer to my question. Because I recognize that face. It's the same one he wore after Katherine lashed out at him at the dinner table those weeks ago.

"Knox," I whisper, lifting and touching trembling fingers to his cheek.

"She didn't only blame me for Connor's death. She accused me of wanting him to die. So I could have you."

Jesus Christ. My arm drops to the bed. Disgust rolls through me, over me, snatching me up in a blazing whirlwind, and I'm consumed by it. How can he state something so...so profane in that hollow, almost matter-of-fact voice? How is he not howling at the injustice of that accusation, the ugliness of it?

I part my lips to ask that very question when I glance up and look into his eyes. And I have my answer.

Oh, he's *affected*.

But it's not the fire of anger burning in his stare. It's not *burning* at all. Instead, shadows swirl in his eyes, darkening them. Still, I can decipher the emotions churning in them.

Grief. Pain.

Once more I lift my hand—both hands—to his face, cupping it, tipping his head down so he has no choice but to meet my gaze as I say, "That's. Utter. And. Complete. Bullshit."

"She was right," he rasps, that dead quality in his voice finally gone. But the replacement, the hoarseness and heaviness as if a thousand-pound weight bore the tone down, is just as terrible.

"No." I shake my head. "No," I repeat, vehemently. Louder.

"Not about wanting Connor's death. Never that. I could never—" He breaks off, and his head briefly drops before he raises it and meets my scrutiny again.

"Knox, you don't need to tell me that," I insist, stroking my thumb across his cheekbone. "You loved Connor—"

"I wanted you," he states. Flatly. His body is a statue of skin and blood above me. The rise and fall of his chest the only movement. "I wanted you even while you were married to my brother."

"What?" An electric shock ripples through me, and I blink at him, not fully comprehending what he said. Not certain I heard him. Not with this dull roar infiltrating my head.

"Yeah, Eden. I've wanted you even when you wore my brother's ring. And I don't know how, but Mom somehow guessed it." He shakes his head. "Here I'd thought I'd done a damn good job of hiding it."

"You did," I assure him, still unable to speak above a whisper. *Years.* Knox had desired me for *years.* "I never knew…" I trail off.

"You weren't supposed to. You were Connor's, and if he were here, alive, you still would be. And nothing, *nothing* would've made me interfere in that. But I guess I fucked up somewhere, because Mom knew. She never said anything, until the night he died. And when she calmed down after making those accusations, she made me promise to leave you alone because you belonged to Connor. So, I did. I promised I'd never touch you. Never claim you for myself." He pauses, and in his gaze, I read what's coming next. I tense my fingers, already sliding them down toward his mouth to cover it. To prevent him from uttering those words I don't want to hear. No matter how true I know they are. "I broke one part of that vow. I won't break the other."

He'd touched me. But he wouldn't claim me.

Of course, he can't. If his family—*our* family—discovered about what had been happening between us… If *Katherine* discovered it… Both of us would lose everything important to us. The people we loved most.

I knew all of this. Agreed with it.

And yet his words still strike me in the chest like a balled fist.

"I've already fucked up. But if all we have is tonight, I'm not wasting it. So don't say anything about leaving this room. Think about it, because I am, too. If I had any kind of dignity or conscience, I would let you go. But I don't. Not right now. No one's going to come looking for us. Hakim's let me use this room before when I've crashed here after being too drunk or tired to drive home. So for the next few hours, we lock ourselves in and fuck whatever this is out of our system," he murmurs. "Please."

Since speaking is beyond my capability at the moment, I nod. Because the perverted, twisted thing is that after two mind-blowing orgasms, my body is heating for him again. I'm already aching for his possession once more.

And as he lowers his head and takes my mouth, I let tomorrow—and all the problems and questions that remain unresolved—take care of itself.

Chapter Nine

Knox

Breathing deep, I grasp the two ends of the towel hanging from the pull-up bar and slowly heave myself up until my chin passes my hands. Just as deliberately, I lower my body, then repeat the exercise again and again. By the time my feet finally hit the floor, my arms, shoulders, and lungs are crying out for a break. But I move right into the next rotation of grip work. And from there, on to a session of Farmer's Walks, carrying a stupidly heavy set of weights back and forth across the gym.

If I focus on my body, then I can't dwell on the thoughts impatiently knocking on my brain, just waiting for the slightest crack to sneak in and bombard me. At least that's the theory. Nothing short of a lobotomy could erase the memories of the night before in the guest bedroom of Hakim's house from my mind. And I even have my doubts about that working.

Bedroom. That one little slip is all it takes for the rest of the flashbacks to bum-rush my head and fill it with pictures of

Eden and me with HD clarity.

I'd spent two weeks, most of them out of town at tattoo expos, feverishly working and fortifying my resolve not to surrender to the need and lust that had entrenched themselves under my skin, infiltrated my blood, metastasized in my organs. Yet, the reasons why I had to prevent any more nights like the one at her apartment from every happening again vanished like smoke when she walked into Hakim's house with another man.

Jealousy isn't a foreign emotion to me. For three years, I roasted in it as I silently watched Connor and Eden date and marry. And after he died, sick fuck that I am, I strangled on envy because of how she mourned him, couldn't see anyone else because of her love and grief for him, while I mourned him, too. I never claimed to be a good man. A good man doesn't crave what his brother has, doesn't love his brother's wife. The only honorable thing I could credit to myself was keeping my hands off her, maintaining a platonic relationship.

Then I fucked that up, too.

Jesus. I quit mid-Farmer's Walk and set the dumbbells down on the floor. Straightening, I tip my head back and stare blindly up at the ceiling. Will my johnson not to tent the front of my running shorts. It was ten on a Sunday morning in Jake's, not my usual 6 a.m., so other people are here working out. Damn if I'm going to grant them a show of How to Let Your Dick Call the Shots.

Snatching up my water bottle off the floor, I drink about half of it. Maybe trying to drown out the reel of images from last night and early this morning. I didn't unlock that door until almost three o'clock, after I'd given her two more orgasms, and I'd been balls-deep inside her another time. The party had still been going strong, and thankfully, no one had noticed our absence. But, yeah, I hadn't been thinking with my responsible head, and taking that chance had been foolish.

And my fear is I would do it again in a nanosecond.

Even after telling her about my promise to Mom.

Even acknowledging that I was only honoring the letter of that vow, not the spirit.

"So, the rumors are true," a smooth, deep voice drawls. "I'd heard Hard Knox Gordon is still in fighting shape. I'm glad I came down here to check it out for myself."

Lowering my bottle, I turn, but not to identify the speaker; I already know who's behind me. Israel Clarkson, three-time former BFC heavyweight champion. Well, four-time, counting another win in the years since I've retired. A thick, muddied mixture of joy, sadness, and anger roils in my chest as I meet the familiar brown gaze. Joy, because I missed the veteran fighter who'd also been a friend as well as my fiercest competitor. Sadness for the same reason. And anger, because it didn't require the deduction skills of Sherlock Holmes to figure out why he stood in a Chicago gym thousands of miles from his Florida home.

It's been more than two weeks since Jake first broached the subject about returning to the BFC to fight Israel. I should've guessed he'd been up to something, since he hadn't been nagging me about an answer.

Now I knew what that "something" was.

"You make it sound like you just happened to be in the neighborhood," I say, arching an eyebrow. "More like you were called and told to get up here so you could kick my ass into agreeing to this exhibition match."

"Okay, so Jake might've been the source of those rumors." Israel grinned, completely unashamed of playing errand boy for my ex-trainer. "When Jake Reece asks—" I snort at the "ask." Right. Most likely ordered. Israel smile widens, confirming my assumption. "Like I was saying, when Jake asks me to come and talk to an old friend, how can I deny him?" Israel crosses his arms over his massive chest. "Especially when said friend hasn't reached out to me in two years."

I smother the urge to fidget like a young boy found peeking into the girls' bathroom. When I left the BFC, I also stepped completely away from the world of MMA, including the camaraderie. When several fighters visited the shop a few weeks ago for tattoos, that was the closest I'd come to it. I don't even watch matches on TV. It hurts too much.

"Sorry." I don't offer excuses; I have none. None that are good enough.

Israel lifts his shoulder in a half shrug. "I get it." And from the understanding in his steady gaze, I believe he does. Good. Diving into my feelings in a gym reeking of sweat and disinfectant doesn't equate to my idea of a great morning. "Make up for it by hearing me out."

I glance over at the office tucked in the back corner of the gym, and through the large window with the warped blinds, Jake isn't even trying to pretend that he isn't staring at us.

"Why don't we go to Jake's office so he doesn't have to try and read lips?" I drawl, irritated and touched by both of the men's meddling and concern. It's hard to tell strong, tough men like Israel and Jake to mind their own damn business when it's obvious they care. But my mind is made up. I'm not returning to fighting. That's my past. And staying away is my penance.

We cross the gym, our progress slowed by several of the guys who're working out stopping us to fawn over Israel and shake his hand. When we finally enter Jake's office, I'm once more amazed at how scrupulously neat he keeps it. No papers scattered across the desk or trash overflowing from the can. It just reinforces that Mr. Clean image in my head.

"Israel." Jake stands and rounds his desk, clasping the fighter's hand and hauling him close for a half hug and slap on the back. "Sit down." He hikes his chin toward me. "You, too."

Chuckling, Israel sinks to one of the thrift-store chairs in front of the scarred desk, and I take the other.

"Well?" Jake presses, retaking his seat. "Did you talk some sense into him? Tell him this is an opportunity of a lifetime that the BFC rarely, if ever, extends to fighters? That he'd be a fucking idiot to pass it up?"

"Uh, no, we didn't get that far," Israel says, voice wry. "But—" He turns to me, waving a hand in Jake's direction. "What he said."

I snort. "You didn't have to fly all the way to Chicago for that." I meet Israel's unwavering gaze. "And I could've saved you the trip with a phone call, even though I'm glad to see you. My answer's no. I'm not coming back."

"No one's asking you to—" Jake growls, but Israel shakes his head, and my former trainer bites off the rest of his tirade.

"This isn't about you coming back to the BFC, to fighting. Look, most of us get why you retired. Losing Connor…" A shadow flickers across his face, but then it's gone in the next instant. "We can sympathize, but none of us could possibly understand all that you, Connor's wife, and your family suffered. But, I also know you, Knox. You're a fighter, through and through. A natural competitor. A lot of these guys, yeah, they train hard and get into this because of some supposed glory. But you're like me. It's your passion. Hell, man, I could tell that just by watching you condition out there. You might tell yourself you've stepped away, but you haven't. Not for real."

I don't say anything. Because as much as I resent it, he's striking at the heart of me. Addressing the part of me that whispers maybe returning wouldn't be a betrayal to my family, to my brother's memory. He's speaking to the selfish side of me that wants the exhilaration, the fierce, primal joy of stepping into a ring and facing another competitor. Of pitting my power and mind against his and coming out the best, the strongest.

"You can't be cool with the way you left things. Like I said, I understand why, but I know it can't sit well. Not with you." He turns fully toward me, propping his elbows on his thighs. "And to be honest, man, it doesn't with me, either. I hold this year's championship title, but I didn't beat the champion to get it. You won our last match, and I'm not satisfied until I can take the best, take you. I'm not going to lie. I want that chance." He pops up a finger. "One match. One time. That's all Reyes and the Powers That Be are asking. No one's pressuring you to return to the sport full-time. Just this one exhibition match. You'll not only earn some money to put toward your shop, another shop, or your family, but you can go out the way *you* want, and not how circumstances dictated."

I clench my jaw, throwing up mental blocks to prevent his words from stealing in and burrowing into my head, my heart. But those barriers might as well be made of smoke. He's hitting every weak spot in my armor. Everything he's saying, I've said to myself over the past two years. More often in the last few weeks since Jake brought the offer to me.

And Israel's right. How I walked away... It does leave a bad taste in my mouth. I've called it retirement, but in the secret recesses of my mind, I know what I did—I quit. And I'm no quitter.

But Connor... I thread my fingers together between my legs and stare down at them as if they contain the answers I'm seeking.

Accepting this match would be me putting myself first again. Being selfish again. Mom doesn't just blame me for Connor's death; she blames the sport, too. She would lose her shit if I returned to it. And Eden... She witnessed her husband die in the ring; she's never come out and said it, but

I know she's not a fan of it anymore. Understatement of the damn century.

"There's another thing to consider," Israel continues, voice quiet. "Reyes intends to donate a portion of the proceeds from the fight to a fund that will pay for the college education and training for a promising high school senior, securing him a spot in the BFC after he graduates. He's naming it the Connor Knox Scholarship Fund. Connor was the first fighter to die in a BFC ring. Reyes doesn't take that lightly." He sighs. "Announcing the scholarship along with the return of his brother and BFC champion to the ring would bring in money not just from tickets but sponsors and endorsements. I'm not trying to make this into emotional blackmail—"

"Isn't that what it is?" I grind out. Because, goddamn, it's working. A scholarship in Connor's name? He would get a kick out of that. Who am I kidding? He would fucking love it. And Israel's right. A sensationalized fight between the current and former heavyweight champions—the latter who also happens to be Connor's brother—would bring in mad money. Money that would, at least in part, go toward the fund. I can't ignore that.

Just like Reyes and Israel intended.

"Maybe," he concedes. "Yeah, it will bring the BFC a ton of publicity, promotion, and money. It won't hurt my career at all. And I'm not denying it's going to make us *at least* a half-million dollars richer. But it's also going to do some good, and if you want to honor Connor, this is a way to keep his name and legacy out there."

I close my eyes, my head bowing.

It's not the money; I couldn't give a damn about that.

But Connor having a legacy. Not dying in vain without the world knowing how smart and great a man he was...

"All right." I raise my head and meet first Jake's gaze, then Israel's. "I'll do it. I'll fight."

Chapter Ten

Knox

A couple of hours later, I hike my duffel bag over my head and shoulder and push through one of the double doors of the gym. My muscles pull tight, but it's good. The stretch gives me a bone-deep satisfaction. Israel and I spent an hour-and-a-half in the ring. And though I've sparred with other fighters in the gym over the last two years, none have been on Israel's level. That fierce surge of battle, of intense focus and, yeah, joy—there's no other word for it—had risen in me, and a part of me that I'd forced into a coma-like sleep didn't just wake, but came out swinging blows.

Yeah, I missed it.

And Jake, standing next to the ring, arms crossed and wearing a shit-eating smirk, knew it, too.

Fucker.

My own smirk tugs at the corner of my mouth as I step out into the late Sunday morning sunshine.

"Whoa. A smile. If I realized working out had this kind

of effect on you, I would've suggested you take off from the shop to get more hours in the gym a long time ago," the husky voice that cried out my name only hours ago drawls.

And like then, it's a hook-punch to the jaw, harder than any jab Israel could throw.

Eden pushes off the hood of my truck and strides toward me. Several questions bombard my brain at once: What is she doing here? How did she know where to find me? What's wrong? Is something wrong with my brothers, Mom?

But once I notice her expression is too relaxed for her to be delivering bad news, they all take a backseat to one thought.

God, she's so fucking beautiful.

Her thick, long hair is piled up in a bun on top of her head, revealing the slender, elegant column of her neck. Above the tight-fitting T-shirt that cups her perfect breasts, a purplish bruise mars her skin. A wild song of almost brutal possession sweeps through me, and I curl my fingers into the strap of my bag to keep from stalking the few feet that separate us, cupping the back of her neck, and pressing my mouth to that mark. Anyone catching sight of it would guess exactly what it is; does Eden realize it's visible? Or does she not care? My stupid, ass-blind heart latches on to the latter. I should warn her to cover the mark up before someone questions how she came by it—or, rather, who gave it to her. But the primitive, jealous side of me wants everyone to know it was my mouth that put it there. Mine. Just like the woman.

Fuck.

I drag a hand over my beard. Only anguish and disillusion lay down that crooked, rutted path. Last night had been an aberration, an anomaly. A mistake that I'm trying to regret. If I had any loyalty, any integrity, I'd regret it. But after being in that tight, snug body, I can't.

Eden stops in front of me, her long skirt swinging around

her feet. When she turns her face up to me, I inhale her scent, recalling how much richer and muskier it is between her thighs. My gut clenches, and blood pumps to my cock. If I hadn't changed my shorts for jeans after showering in the locker room, Eden would have a front row seat to where my thoughts have drifted.

"What are you doing here?" I ask, arousal roughening the question. Shit. When am I *not* hard around her?

Something flickers in her eyes, but it's gone before I can decipher the emotion behind it. At one time, I believed she was shitty at hiding her thoughts, but maybe I was wrong. Or she's just become better at hiding from me.

I hate that possibility.

"It's funny, really. I happened to be in the neighborhood, and just when I passed by, you walked out," she says, voice as dry as a Nevada summer day in the desert. Yeah, pretty damn dry. Yet, that emotion flashes in her gaze again, and this time, I decipher it before she manages to conceal it again. Discomfort. Uncertainty.

For the first time since we've known each other, Eden is nervous around me.

I hate that possibility, too.

"Let me try that again. Why are you here?"

A small half-smile quirks a corner of her mouth. "I want you to come with me."

"I did. Two times last night," I growl, the words escaping me before I can contain them.

I'm close enough to hear the catch in her breath and glimpse the heat flare in her eyes. Her gaze drops to my mouth, and I'm battling the urge to lower my head and taste that soft gasp for myself.

"I walked right into that one, didn't I?" she whispers. Shaking her head, she clears her throat, and continues, "Well, I came to find you—"

"How did you?" I interrupt, frowning.

"I called Jude, and he told me to look for you here." My frown deepens, but she waves a hand. "Don't worry, he's not suspicious about...about..."

"Us fucking?" I supply.

A tinge of red slashes across her cheekbones, almost concealing her freckles. But her chin notches up. "Yes," she says softly. "About us fucking."

Damn. Hearing *that* word on *her* lips. It's like she reached into my jeans, wrapped her fingers around my dick, and gave it a good, hard pump. And that the color in her face only deepens, makes it even sexier, hotter. *One night. One night.* The reminder tracks through my mind, but the leash on my control and will when it comes to her is ragged, tenuous.

"Anyway." She crosses her arms. Then drops them. Then looses a little, low chuckle. The laughter holds a bit of self-deprecation, and once more that nervousness emanates from her. "So, listen. I won tickets to a Cubs game a couple of weeks ago. They're playing the Nationals, and the seats are right behind the dugout. V and Shana could care less about baseball, and Jude and Simon had plans. That leaves you. Since I'm not going alone, you've been nominated to tag along with me."

Stunned, I stare at her. "We're going to a Cubs' game?" I repeat. A fist of emotion lodges in my throat, which, logically, I get is an overreaction to someone offering to take you to a ballgame, but...

Baseball, games... It had been our thing—my dad's and mine. Jude and Simon hadn't cared for the sport, so it'd become my special time with my father. Where the usually quiet, reserved man who worked nearly sixty hours a week would loosen up, relax, and become a boisterous, laughing, often obnoxious fan. And I'd felt special because he'd been that way with me.

I blink, bringing myself back to the present and away from one of the happiest times of my past.

"I need you to follow me back to my apartment," Eden continues, already heading back to her car that I now notice is parked behind mine.

"What?" I ask.

"Move your ass, Knox. Daylight's wasting." She glances over her shoulder at me, giving me a shy, slightly self-conscious smile that punches into my chest, grabs my heart, and squeezes it.

It's a thing of pure beauty. And, it's for me.

Does it make me an asshole that a fierce, greedy satisfaction howls within me? Maybe. Probably. But damn, it feels good. It makes me feel…like hers. Even if only for this brief moment.

And this brief moment has me walking after her.

A half hour later, a vise grip squeezes the fuck out of my chest at the sight of the people already congregated under the world-renowned, huge, red-and-white sign that reads WRIGLEY FIELD HOME OF CHICAGO CUBS.

"The game starts at one-thirty, and it's already one, so we're good on time," she says, staring out her window.

Good. I'm afraid of what's on my face. What it reveals.

"Since this is my first game, I intend to milk the whole experience—hot dogs, beer, foam finger. I might even pull a Miley Cyrus with that finger if I have enough beer." She snickers, but I remain focused on the road and maneuvering through the thick, Sunday game traffic and into the parking lot.

Once I find a space and park, she hops out, but I'm slower and quieter as we walk the couple of blocks to the stadium. The last time I stood outside this place was with my father years ago. Sixteen years, to be exact.

If I close my eyes, I can still feel the warm May breeze

on my face and arms. Can still smell the Irish Spring soap he used as long as I could remember. Can still hear his deep, gravel-rough voice griping about the Cubs' chances against the Cincinnati Reds.

I haven't been able to bring myself to attend another game. Not without him. And now, here I stand, with Eden.

"Hey." A soft, delicate hand curves around my bicep. "You okay?" Worry darkens her eyes, a frown drawing her eyebrows into a shallow V. "So, I have a confession to make. I didn't win the tickets; I bought them, and I didn't offer them to anyone else. You were my first and only choice. But is this"—she waved a hand toward the stadium—"all right? I've noticed that you always stop and look at that picture of you and your dad at the house. Jude mentioned you hadn't been to a game in a long time, so I thought, maybe..." Her voice trails off. "Did I fuck up?" When I don't immediately answer—*can't* immediately answer—she tips her head back, pinching the bridge of her nose. "I'm sorry, Knox. I overstepped. I just thought this might help us not be so strained around each other, and that it might be fun for you since it'd been so long—"

I ignore the part about things being weird between us to grab her and yank her against my chest, wrapping my arms around her—holding her so close and so hard, I'm probably causing her some discomfort, but I can't let go.

Not that she's trying to get away. Her arms close around me. Tight. Burying my face in her hair, I inhale her sweet, summer-and-peaches scent. Savor the feel of her breasts and thighs against mine, and the soft puff of her breath over my chest.

"No," I rasp. "It's fine. I'm—" I break off, clear my throat. After a moment, I continue. "Until now, I didn't realize how much I wanted to go to a game. Dad and I..."

I trail off, unable to voice what the games meant to me. I'd expected sadness after the shock of her surprise wore off. But instead, the sadness is tempered by the joy of those memories. Instead of the heartache I feared, and that kept from away from Wrigley for so long, there's a certain…comfort. And I owe that to Eden. Coming here with her—*her*—has softened the blow, made it pliable like melted wax, and has allowed my memories of Dad in, leaving the sorrow behind.

Lifting my head, I cup her jaw, tilt her chin up with the pad of my thumb.

"Thank you," I murmur, brushing my mouth over hers. Yeah, we're in a public place where anyone who knows us or our family might see us, but right now, I can't give a damn. Not when her lips part and her tongue is already sliding forward to tangle with mine. That ever-present hunger is there, simmering under my skin, but the kiss is gentle, tender.

"You're welcome," she whispers, her breath grazing my lips. She smiles, and I feel it curve over my mouth. Another, separate caress.

Reluctantly, I let her go and step back. It was foolish to risk the chance of someone catching us. But as she threads her fingers through mine and tugs me toward the stadium, I don't regret it.

Today, I'm going to be selfish because tomorrow, I'll be letting her go again.

There's no altering who we are.

But for a little while, we can be…not us.

• • •

"I had the best time," Eden announces as I twist the key in the ignition four hours later.

I snort. "You mean between heckling the ump, eating your weight in hot dogs, and hitting that old man in the back of the head with your foam finger, you actually watched the game?"

She laughs, and the warm, joy-filled sound echoes in the interior of the truck.

"I'm going to be honest. I don't watch a lot of baseball. And good God, it's loooong. But," she adds, "I had a great time. I'm glad we went."

"Yeah, me, too." I nod and snatch one last look at Wrigley Field. Funny, how I don't live far from it, but for years, I've actively gone out of my way to avoid it. Now, I'm staring at it like a long-lost friend.

Yeah, today was phenomenal. The best I've had in—fuck, too long to remember. To be relaxed, my only concerns drinking my beer before it got too warm and whether or not Chris Bryant would continue his on-base streak? It'd been... good for me. And God, fun.

Several times during the game, I almost told her about the upcoming exhibition event. But several times, I stopped myself. I didn't want to ruin the magic of the day, because instinct even now warns me she might not be supportive of me returning to MMA, even if only for one match. Not after having a ring-side seat to her husband's death in the ring. She's never been as vocal as Mom about my former career, but she's also never asked me about it. Matter of fact, she's never mentioned MMA, the BFC—except in terms of incorporating it with the shop's marketing—or if I even miss fighting.

So again, when I have the chance to bring it up, I don't.

Instead, I focus on the past few hours.

My world has been centered around the shop. In the last two years, it's felt like a sin to just be happy. Because Connor couldn't. But my little brother wouldn't want me to live this half-life in tribute to him. I can hear him now, roaring in my ear, "Fuck that, bro. Ride this thing until the brakes fall off."

"You know what? No fair bringing up my hitting the

older guy," Eden objects, laughing and dragging me out of my head. "I apologized, and he was sweet about it."

"Right. And when he squeezed your knee? Was that sweet, too? He was feeling you up." I shake my head, a grin tugging at the corner of my mouth. "You probably made his year."

"Nah, Jim was harmless."

"Jim?" I bark out a laugh. "You're on a first-name basis with him?"

"Yeah, we're friends now." My eyes are focused on getting us safely through the after-game traffic, but I hear the smile in her voice. "He usually brings his grandson to the games, but James started college this year and can't come with him like he used to. So, he was just a little lonely. He actually invited me and 'my young man' to come to Sunday brunch with him and his wife Holly next week." I glance at her, and she rolls her head on the rest to meet my gaze. "He said you don't talk a lot, but any man that passionate about the Cubs has to be a good one."

"Your young man?" I ask, trying to keep the dark, aroused growl out of my voice. But just hearing the possessive phrase turns me on. I tighten my fingers around the steering wheel so I don't jerk this vehicle to the side of the road and show her and every driver on the road what being hers would be like.

"Yeah." That softly spoken word strokes over me, through me. "He assumed we were together."

"Did you correct him?" I glance at her again, needing to see her expression when she answers. Thank God I've pulled to a stop at a red light, because I can't say with a certainty that I could tear my attention from her.

For a long moment, she doesn't reply, just returns my stare. The pulse at the base of her throat beats, and I want to feel that butterfly-wing flutter on the tip of my tongue.

"No," she admits, so hushed that if I wasn't straining to hear it, if I wasn't studying her mouth to see it, I would've missed her response.

"Why?" I press, my tone full of grit. "Did you want him to think you were mine?"

Her espresso eyes go impossibly darker, and they drop to my mouth, my chest, to my thighs where my cock is doing a damn good impression of a steel bar.

"Yes," she breathes as the light changes to green. "For today, yes."

Her answer is both pleasure and pain. Pleasure, because she's admitting to wanting me. And there's the pain because there's an expiration date stamped on us in bright red. And its "good until" date isn't days, but hours. But given that for years I'd thought even minutes were impossible, I'll take it. With gluttonous, dirty hands, too.

"Lift up your skirt," I order, driving into the intersection. Need sinks its claws into my gut. With traffic, we're only about fifteen minutes from her apartment, but this hunger for her can't wait. I want something to take the edge off. And though we're surrounded by cars in after-game traffic, my tinted windows provide some privacy.

Her swift catch of breath reaches my ears, and my grip on the steering wheel threatens to snap it into pieces while I wait to see whether she will obey me or not.

In the corner of my eye, her skirt inches up. The breath in my lungs deepens as the hem raises higher and higher and higher until it's bunched around her upper thighs. But it still isn't enough.

"Higher, baby," I rasp. "And take off your panties. I don't want anything between me and you."

Slow, a voice whispers caution inside my head. *Go slower with her.* Even though I was inside her last night, it was in the dark, in a locked room. Here, we're on the road, surrounded by other cars, and dusk is just beginning to fall. She's exposed, and I'm asking her to trust me. Go out on this limb with me.

Another hesitation, and I catch movement. A lift of her hips, and then her hands skimming down her golden, smooth legs. A moment later, more thighs until, fuck, her soft pussy with its trimly shaved, dark curls.

Air rushes in and out of my chest. Goddamn, she's beautiful. So innocent, yet so sensual.

Lowering a hand from the steering wheel, I lay it on the thigh closest to me. Stroke my palm over her silken skin. Ease my hand between her legs and slide two fingers into the most beautiful place in all of heaven and earth. Wet heat surrounds me, and I groan at the slick, tightness.

"Wider," I demand—beg. "Spread your legs wider for me, baby. Let me in."

This time she doesn't pause but parts for me, giving me more access to her. Shifting over a little, I push harder, deeper. Her cry breaks over my ears like the sweetest lullaby. The sting of fingernails bite into my arm, but she's not shoving me away. No, she's clinging to me. Lifting into my thrust.

"Knox, please." She whimpers. "Oh *God*…please."

The light in front of me switches to yellow, then red. Thank. *Christ*. Shifting all my attention down, I withdraw my fingers, and my jeans strangle my erection at the physical evidence of her desire glistening on my skin. Starving, I bring them to my mouth, lick and suck them clean. Her flavor… Musky, bold, sweet. That sample only makes me hungry for more. To lay her flat, hold her wide open, and dive into her, eat her until she's screaming and coming in me, on me.

She makes a sound—a cross between a groan and a sigh—and I look up to find her eyes on me. Watching me savor her. Lust gleams back at me. With a quick peek out my windshield to verify the light is still red, I graze her bottom lip with my damp fingers. Her breath puffs over my damp skin, and I press down on her tender flesh, then push forward until her tongue wraps around me…until she's tasting herself and me. It might as well be my cock she's licking, sucking. I shift my other hand from the wheel to cup and squeeze myself. The fierce ache wraps around my lower back, sizzles in my balls.

Sliding free of her mouth, I lower my hand back to her pussy and thrust. She keens, her hips bucking, raising into my stroke. One of her small hands clamps onto my thigh and the other, grabs the arm of the car. Head thrown back, delicate throat arched tight, she grinds against my hand. Fucking it.

The light turns again, and I ease off the brake. We're at a slow crawl in post-game traffic, and there's no telling how much longer until we reach her house. No telling how much longer before I can treat my cock to the delicious friction and vise-grip my fingers are enjoying. But she's still going to come for me.

I drive into her, burying as far as I can go, as hard as this almost awkward position will allow. But she's helping me, dancing for me, rolling those hips and meeting every thrust. Pressing the heel of my palm against her clit, I rub. Hard.

With a sharp cry, she explodes.

Her flesh ripples, seizing me, milking me. I continue to massage that pulsing bundle of nerves, so close to blowing, it would only take one bruising pump to my throbbing length. Her nails bite into my wrist as she holds me close, riding me, her serrated gasps a sexy soundtrack that I want to make her sing again.

Her touch falls away from me, and she relaxes. I slowly pull free of her hot, wet clasp. Grasping her skirt, I jerk it down harder than I intended.

Her harsh breathing gradually eases, but mine is loud and rough in the otherwise silent interior. Every bit of my focus is on making it to her place. And as the gridlock finally loosens, I probably break several traffic laws getting there.

Damn near forty torturous minutes later, her apartment building appears on the next block, and the road, so short before, seems to stretch farther and farther as the arousal in me rages so hot, so wild, I'm one living mass of lust and need.

I scan the street for a parking space. There. Not even three down from her building's front entrance. Within moments, I'm swinging my truck into the spot, shutting it off, and turning toward her. Tunneling my fingers into the bun on top of her head, I jerk her toward me, uncaring of the seat belt biting into my skin.

This kiss is the exact opposite of the one in the stadium parking lot. It's wild, ravenous, and sloppy. Slanting my head, I dive into her, tongues waging battle, twisting, tangling, sucking. She grips my hair, her nails scratching my scalp, the little prickles only shoving the fire burning me alive to nuclear.

"I'm coming upstairs," I growl against her mouth. "And I'm going to fuck you. If that's not what you want, then say something now, and I'll go. But if you get out of this car with me, I'm not leaving until I've had you in every way I've been fantasizing about for years."

My hand tightens in her hair. Damn it. I didn't mean to let that last part slip. Pray to God she didn't catch it. That's what a hard-on does. Makes you lose your damn mind and control over your mouth.

But as she grabs the car door handle, I breathe a side of relief. Nothing on her face or in her eyes reflects confusion or surprise. Then, she pushes open the door and steps out of the truck. A searing lust flashes brighter, harder, and it cremates any thought but getting inside her as quick as possible.

I follow her, a starving, malnourished dog after the sweetest treat.

Silence is thick and heavy between us, an invisible third as we enter her building and climb the stairs to her apartment.

By sheer will and discipline that I've only used when training and in the ring, I manage to not touch her. If I do before we step through her front door, I'll fuck her in the hallway, not caring who sees. I'll become the beast that lives inside me, single-focused on burying myself as deep inside her as I can, and screw everything else.

The click of the lock turning echoes in the hall like a bullet shot. Every sense is hyper-sensitized. Her citrus scent teases me. The heat from her petite body warms my chest and thighs. The shiver that ripples through her echoes in me. I'm one big exposed nerve where everything is hotter, brighter, louder. All because of her. Because of this need for her that I can't control now that I've touched her, tasted her. Had her.

Eden finally pushes open the front door and enters the apartment. I'm close behind her.

Easy. Give her space. Don't jump on her like some animal.
But I am *an animal.*

Shit, if I didn't already know that this woman drives me crazy, then the argument waging inside my head between my rational self and lust-crazed self does.

Inhaling a deep breath, I force myself to stop mid-stride. Try to scrabble together some of the much-lauded discipline I was known for while fighting. It costs me, though. When she turns around and studies me with that heavy-lidded gaze, the price is the air in my lungs. The restraint over the low, dark rumble in my chest.

"What's wrong?" she asks, the husky note like a waving red flag in front of a bull. "Are you..." Her feet shift into third position, and her shoulders draw back. "Have you changed your mind about...about," her voice drops to a whisper, "fucking me?"

Maybe it's the underlying hint of insecurity in the question.

Maybe it's the physical tells that betray her nerves.

Maybe it's hearing "fuck" on her lips.

Doesn't matter. Any of them—all of them—snap the threadbare ropes binding my control, and I'm across the room and on her in seconds.

Palming her face, I tilt her head back and crush my mouth to hers. It's a replica of the kiss in my truck. Hunger edged in desperation. As often as my tongue dives between her lips, and as eagerly as she meets me, giving me back every stroke, every lick, every moan, it's still not enough.

Goddamn. Will it ever be enough?

A foreboding wisp of unease curls in my chest, lingering before evaporating under the blaze of lust. No, I'm not thinking about tomorrow or even an hour from now. This moment is where I exist. All I have is this moment.

Impatient, I cup the back of her thighs and hoist her into the air. Her legs immediately lock around my waist, and I shift my hands to her ass, groaning as her flesh fills them. Unable to resist, I squeeze and mold, spreading her cheeks slightly apart through the thin material of her skirt.

She gasps, jerks her mouth from mine, and stares down at me, confusion and arousal meshing in her dark eyes. I can guess what she's feeling. A slight stinging stretch of that tight ring of muscle. I want that tiny hole. Want to watch it stretch around my finger, then my cock. Imagining the constriction of that smooth-as-glass passage as I work her, open her up for me has my chest rising and falling quicker. My dick hardening to the point of pain. Seeking to ease some of it, I grind her down on me, rolling her over my length.

Her whimper and my grunt mate in the air, melding into one needy sound. One more. Just one more of those teasing strokes. I drag her over me again, using my grip to circle her skirt-covered flesh over me, bumping the head of my erection, and hauling a hiss from my throat. Yeah, her clothes and mine separate us, but fuck if I can't feel the warmth of her sex, teasing me. Taunting me.

But now I can have her body. Have her.

Gritting my teeth, I stride down the short hall to the bedroom I left her alone in weeks ago. Not tonight, though. Tonight, I'm joining her on the bed I put together with my own hands.

Nudging open the door with my toe, I flick the switch on the wall then release my grip and ease her to the floor. For a moment, her arms tighten around my neck before sliding free, and she steps back, crossing them over her chest.

"Can you turn the lights—"

"No," I interrupt her. "I want to see you." Last night, all I'd had was the street lamp from outside Hakim's house. Not enough to discover if freckles scattered other parts of her body or if the shadows had hidden anything else from me.

She glances down, to the side, at some point over my shoulder. Anywhere but me.

"What's wrong, Eden?" An acidic burn sears the lining in my stomach as an insidious thought slides through my head, leaving a grimy trail that I can't scrub free. Did she prefer the dark because she could pretend I was someone else? Or anyone else, other than her dead husband's brother?

Or...Connor?

"I'm not Jenika. Or that girl in the bar. Or any of the women I've seen you with. The light kind of exposes that," she murmurs, then releases a strained chuckle. "This is ridiculous. I've never had any issues with my body. I don't know why..." She trails off, shaking her head.

I blink, understanding crashing into me. The hell. She couldn't possibly have doubts about whether I'll find her attractive. God, didn't she know that to me, she was perfect?

No, how could she? Since meeting her, I've had to bury every emotion toward her except a false brotherly affection, and I've become accustomed to hiding. But damn, I haven't been able to conceal my hunger or my dick around her lately. Still...

"You have that backward," I say into the silence. Her gaze jerks from the wall behind me to my face. "None of those women are you."

Her lips part, and she stares at me for several long seconds. A softness enters her eyes, and slowly, she lowers her arms. That signal of trust, of vulnerability, refuels the need inside me. The need to get my hands, mouth, dick on and in her.

"Take off your clothes," I order, not bothering to tone down the harshness in the command. By now, she has to get who she's invited into her bedroom, into her body. I'm not some gentleman or poet. I'm a rough, half-civilized fighter with zero pretty words.

Her response is to peel her shirt over her head, then pull down the zipper at her hip, and push her skirt down her legs, leaving her in only a pale-yellow bra. God*damn*. She never put her underwear back on. Are they still on the floor of my truck? Christ, I hope so. Then I'll have a keepsake of this night.

"Go on," I urge, and she obeys, popping the front clasp of her bra, and soon, that joins the rest of her clothing on the floor.

Fuck, she's gorgeous. A pagan goddess worthy of worship.

Her elegant neck slopes down to delicate shoulders and firm breasts with their dark brown nipples that fill my hands like they were created for them. With an adorable, slightly rounded belly and toned, lovely legs, she's any man's vision of a sensual, beautiful woman. And then there's the softest pussy between those thighs...

The impulse to rush her and fall on her like a predator with its prey rides me hard. I want to take her in big, ravenous bites until this hunger for her is satisfied.

But another, stronger longing reverberates in me, propelling me forward, shoving me to my knees in front of her. My arms wrap around her, and I press my forehead to the smooth skin between her breasts. The musk from her recent orgasm intertwines with her natural scent, and if any company could bottle the fragrance, they would make a killing at any perfume counter. It's sweet and alluring, a magical potion that in turns drives a man wild and makes him want to genuflect in awe and reverence.

And that's what I am to her, though she has no idea.

A devotee.

A worshipper.

Some people might think I'm a goddamn pervert or crazier than a shithouse rat for wanting my brother's wife. Some might even call it incestuous. But I don't see it that way. Because in my screwed-up head, Eden was mine first. I saw her first. I claimed her even though Connor charmed her and eventually won her. So though I can't ever have her for my own, I can at least take what is mine for a little while. Or maybe it's all bullshit, and I'm desperate to find any way to justify fucking my dead brother's wife.

For loving her.

Her hands tunnel through my hair and cradle my head. And that quick, lust amps up to compete with veneration. My hold on her tightens, and I turn my head, capture a nipple between my lips. A shudder shakes her, a moan drifting above my head. Her nails scratch my scalp, and I growl against her flesh, coiling my tongue around the stiff peak, and suck. She releases one of those sexy whimpers that have become my sexual currency, and I tug on the tip, grazing it lightly with my teeth before drawing on it again.

"Knox," she whines, bending over me, pressing her cheek to the top of my head. "Oh God, please. I need..."

I already know what she needs. And switching to the other breast and licking the pebbled point, I ease a finger between her legs. Her hips buck against my hand, a cry tearing from her as I trace a circle around her clit. The rich scent of her arousal is thicker, and my mouth waters for a taste. Giving her nipple one last suck, I trail my lips down her stomach, pausing to dip inside her navel, then continuing down, nuzzling the thatch of damp curls, replacing my finger with my tongue.

Her choked scream is a symphony to my ears. But then I don't hear anything but the dull roar in my ears as I tease and lap at that nerve-filled bundle of flesh. I groan into her sex, drowning in her flavor, the silken texture of her. I can't help myself; I feast on her. Suckling her, stroking through her folds, nipping the swollen lips sticky with the evidence of her arousal, lowering my head to plunge my tongue inside her. I'm a starving man pulled up to a table heavy with every temptation he's ever craved.

But I'm still hungry.

I slide a finger inside her, coating it in her wetness. I can't resist a couple of heavy thrusts, my knuckles bumping against her folds. With a low cry, she widens her legs, granting my hand more room. But as much as I love being inside her, I want something else.

Following the path that connects her sex to her ass, I dip between her crease and lightly trace the tiny entrance there. She stiffens, her hands freezing on my head. But I don't stop caressing her, letting her become accustomed to my touch on the place where I suspect no man has been.

"Knox?" she whispers, a quiver in her voice.

My answer is to rake my teeth over that pulsing nub and suck even as I drench my finger in her wet heat again and return to her ass. This time, I press, not entering but firmly resting my fingertip there.

Her hips roll against my mouth, a steady stream of mixed whimpers and muted screams escaping her. I don't let up, tormenting her clit with my tongue, so when I do slip my finger into the constricted ring of muscle she only tenses up a little, and her cry of pleasure only contains a hint of pain.

I hold still, don't slip any farther into the channel, but I don't let up on her pussy. I tongue it hard, granting her no mercy. And as she emits a long, rumbling moan that has me throbbing, I push deeper into her.

She explodes.

She quakes against my face, riding it, her legs trembling, her torso curling over my shoulder. Between the clench of her ass, the pulsing of her clit, and her gasping sobs, I could come right here, kneeling on her bedroom floor, my face buried in the closest to heaven I'll ever get near.

As her quaking ebbs into shivers, I finally lift my mouth from her, fighting the urge to dive back in, make her come again. And then again. Maybe she senses the struggle within me, because she weakly pushes at my head. I give in, but only because if I don't get inside her, my dick might kill me.

I straighten, with Eden over my shoulder in a fireman's carry. Crossing the short distance to the bed, I lay her on it. Her lashes flutter closed, her chest still rising and falling quickly, but her body is loose, relaxed.

Grabbing a fistful of my T-shirt, I jerk it over my head and drop it to the floor. My jeans and boxer briefs quickly join it, but not before I grab my wallet and remove several condoms and toss them on the bottom of the mattress. As I approach the bed, her eyes open and meet mine. A heat shimmers there, one that reflects the flames licking at me from the inside out. Wrapping my fingers around my length, I squeeze it, both easing and heightening the ache. My balls draw up, but I will the looming orgasm back from the crumbling edge.

I circle her slim ankle, then stroke my palm up the length of her leg until my fingertips graze the flesh I just devoured. Her breath catches, and her back arches, those beautiful breasts rising toward the ceiling. I tighten my grip on my flesh, the flash of pain clearing my head, shoving back the lust just enough that it keeps me from climbing on top of her, burying myself in her, and putting us both out of this beautiful misery.

Lifting a knee to the mattress, I lean over her, splaying my fingers over her stomach and gliding that hand up her abs, between her breasts, and around her throat, necklacing it. She stares at me, the fire in her chocolate gaze hotter, darker. And when I exert the slightest pressure, just the slightest, the flames are deeper. She likes it—the control, the hint of roughness, the dirtiness. Suddenly, my fist around my cock isn't enough to hold back the conflagration of lust threatening to consume me. I need inside her, that slick, tight, wet, almost bruising embrace locked around me. Straightening, I grab a condom and make fast work of opening the wrapper and rolling the protection down my length.

"Roll over, baby," I rasp, and with a grasp of her hip, I help her flip.

She goes to her hands and knees, that perfect ass in the air, the swollen, glistening folds visible and a lure to dive in and lose myself. The sudden longing to have all that beautiful, thick hair on my skin surges within me, and I loosen the strands from her top knot, growling as I twist my fist in them, savoring the silken caress

"Knox." Eden glances over her shoulder. "Please. Fuck me."

The request is gasoline poured over a ten-alarm fire. Scattering kisses down her spine, I circle the base of my cock, align it with the entrance to her pussy...and sink inside. Slowly. Steadily. Until I'm surrounded by her. Branded by her.

Owned by her.

For Eden, this is probably no more than a taboo scratching of an itch. For me, though. For me, it's a gift—an unforeseen gift that I've done nothing to deserve, but am too hungry, too desperate to turn away. I clench my jaw to trap any wayward words—or confessions—from escaping as I pull free of her body, dragging through her muscular walls that clutch at me, as if trying to prevent me from leaving her. When only the head remains just inside her, I push back in, groaning.

Pleasure strikes at the base of my skull, sizzles down my spine, and culminates like an electrical storm in my balls. One stroke. One goddamn stroke, and I'm so ready to blow, I'm shaking with the need. It's like bathing in fire while soaking in the coolest, most welcoming pool.

Her back arches, head thrown back, all that hair sticking to her damp skin. I should close my eyes, because looking at her will have me filling this condom with the next thrust. But I can't. Not when I'm hoarding every second of this for when she's again off-limits to me. When I'm alone, with only my hand and memories for company.

Abandoning her hair, I clasp her hips, and plunge deep. Over and over, I drive into her, savoring each plunge, each suck of her flesh releasing and welcoming me, each cry that breaks on her lips, each shudder that courses through her.

I shift my hands lower, cup her ass…spread the cheeks, exposing the tiny hole I teased earlier. Just like then, it lures me, and I want inside so fucking bad. Dipping a finger to where we're connected, I slide it through her soaked folds, and draw the drenched tip around the entrance.

Unlike last time, I don't wait, but slip inside. Again, she stills, tenses, pausing mid-stroke so only half of my stalk is buried inside her. Her harsh, loud pants echo in the room, and I continue to press forward, inching more and more of my finger in her ass.

"Relax, baby," I murmur, damn near choking on the groan as I slowly fill the narrow channel. It's so small, so tight, I would have to work to stretch it so she could take me. My hips jerk at the thought, shoving more of myself inside her. She keens, low and deep, and electrical charges trip through me, marching up and down my spine, lighting me up. "Relax and push back against my finger. You can take me, just like before."

Her head drops forward, her hair a dark curtain over her shoulders and hanging around her face. She does as I instruct, shifting backward, taking my cock and my finger. Watching it, I'm like a horse with blinders, unable to look away, completely focused on the sight of me sinking into both entrances. Jesus, how could I have gone twenty-nine years and not experience such mind-numbing pleasure? Before, sex has been about the finish, the orgasm, the oblivion. But now? Now, it's about the journey and the ending.

About Eden.

Flexing my hips, I thrust into her, and push the rest of my finger deep into her. Her scream rebounds off the walls, and the piercing sound shatters my control. I fill both parts of her again and again, riding both her pussy and ass hard. And she takes it, fucking craves it as she backs into me, harder, faster, her sobs damn near incoherent. Shifting my free hand from her hip, I sweep it down her lower belly and between her legs, seeking out and locating her clit. One stroke, two, over the bundle at the top of her sex, and her slick muscles clamp down on me.

"*Fuck*," I growl just as she comes, shaking, crying, her walls rippling around me, milking me. I drop down over her, pressing my chest to her spine, my palms bracketing her head. My hips snap back and forth, pounding into her, taking, claiming...

The orgasm barrels through me, snatching the air from my lungs, goddamn blinding me. It's pleasure, agony, ecstasy. An abyss that I catapult myself into like an Olympic diving champion...or a suicide jumper.

And as I sink to the mattress, my arms wrapped around this woman who I've craved and loved for five years, fuck if I can tell which one.

Chapter Eleven

Eden

I curl my legs under me on one of my dining room chairs, cradling a cup of coffee between my hands, warming them. At seven o'clock in the morning, the heat hasn't started to rise yet, the chill of the night still clinging to the hours after dawn. The low murmur of voices from the television I turned on after leaving the bedroom an hour ago keeps me company, providing much-needed background noise.

Much-needed because it keeps me from tumbling down the rabbit-hole that is the man fast asleep in my bed.

Unable to stop myself, I glance in the direction of the hall and room that I just spent the last few hours becoming a woman I didn't know existed. He drew something out of me—something a little scary, a little confusing, a whole hell of a lot exhilarating.

Maybe it's because we're fucking behind our family's backs, and it's wrong, forbidden, and taboo. Maybe it's the fact that he ripped away my inhibitions. Allowed me to do anything I wanted, no matter how dirty, how out-of-my-perceived-character, knowing no judgment would come from Knox. I can be free with him in a way I could never be with anyone else.

Including Connor.

I rub a palm over my heart, the ache there as real as if a sore, pink, newly healed scar marred my skin. Maybe because of my youth, because it'd been my first real relationship, because of my insecurities with my past, I'd become who Connor wanted me to be. No, that's not fair. I'd become who I believed he wanted me to be. His cheerleader, his support, the good, obedient wife whose only goal was to please him. Oh God, I loved him. I still do. And I would like to think as we grew older—as I matured from that nineteen-year-old girl who had seen too much in her life but was still so painfully naive and innocent—that we would've done so together, and he would've appreciated the woman I'm evolving into. We'll never know.

It doesn't change that in that bedroom, with Connor's brother, I discovered a side of my sensuality that emboldened me, empowered me.

I don't really know what to do with this woman.

I don't really know what to do with the man who showed me I like a little bit of dominance and a lot of dirty.

Guilt crawls under my skin, a place where the hottest of showers can't reach. How can I expect anyone else to accept what I did with Knox when *I'm* having the hardest time doing it? The sense of betrayal—that Knox unleashed a need in me that my own husband never had—snakes around my heart, slinks through my veins so even the coffee smells and tastes bitter in my nose, on my tongue.

Setting down the cup on the table, I rise from the chair and cross the floor to the window that looks out on the street. The cool air in the apartment slips under the T-shirt

I'd grabbed and pulled on. *His* T-shirt. Part of me itches to jerk it off; wearing his clothing imbued with his scent is too intimate. But the same impulse that had me tugging it on in the first place stills my hands, an impulse I don't understand and am too much of a coward to question.

"Why didn't you wake me?"

I jump at the gravel-rough rumble behind me. Jesus. I hadn't even heard him walk into the room. Turning, I meet an emerald gaze still a little hazy with sleep. Knox first thing in the morning, fresh from bed is…sexy as hell. Hair tangled from a pillow as well as my fingers; full, kiss-swollen lips; thick scruff; hard, inked, bare chest and arms; jeans unzipped and hanging low on his slim hips. Hell, even his bare feet conjure thoughts of him naked and sweating, hips working as he drives into me, gifting me with orgasm after orgasm.

"I know how hard sleep is to come by for you," I reply to his question, avoiding the power of his stare by ducking around his big frame and heading for the kitchen. "I wasn't going to disturb you. Besides, it's my morning to open the shop." Knox and I trade off mornings opening since we're often both there so late in the evening.

Plucking out the pod I used to brew my coffee, I replace it with a new one, and press the button to start a fresh cup.

"I needed to go to the gym," he mutters.

I look up from the utterly fascinating process of coffee spouting into a mug to catch him tunnel his fingers through his hair, drawing it back from his face. God, the man is just beautiful. Everything masculine, sensual, and raw. Those cheekbones could cut glass like the purest diamond, and his mouth… Whew. The phantom caress of it over my breasts and inner thighs has my belly twisting with renewed desire.

"Missing one morning won't turn you into the Pillsbury Doughboy," I grumble. The last of the brew hisses into the cup, and I open the refrigerator and pull out the creamer, adding just a splash to the coffee before handing it to him. No sugar, just like he takes it. In the shop, fixing him a cup doesn't seem intimate, but here, in my kitchen, him barechested and me in his T-shirt? A whole different ball game.

"Thanks." He accepts the mug, and his gaze drops over my body. It's a visual caress that lingers on my unbound breasts, my legs before returning to my face. "And thanks for letting me sleep," he murmurs.

"How long has it been since you slept this time?" I ask, but he's probably going to shrug it off, like he usually does.

"Last night would have been four nights," he says, shocking me with his candidness as well as his answer.

"Damn it, Knox." On instinct, I reach out to him, stroke the bruises under his eyes, which aren't as deep as they were the night of Hakim's party, but still there, not erased by the hours he caught in my bed. "That's not normal or healthy. And you were at the gym yesterday after not sleeping for three days? What the hell? That's dangerous. Going without sleep for so long is dangerous. When are you going to admit you have a problem and go get some help for it?"

Fear for him loosens my tongue, when all along I've held it, not wanting to push. But forget that now.

"I got it handled," he says, tone quiet and chock full of "leave it alone" as he sets his cup on the counter.

"Right," I snap, shifting my hand to his jaw, then dropping my arm to my side. "You think I can't pinpoint when your insomnia started?"

He stiffens, his face suddenly resembling one on Mount Rushmore. Y'know, if George Washington was a Spartan with a stare that could freeze a man on the spot and weaken his bladder.

Damn good thing I'm not a man.

"Let it go," he orders in that quiet way of his that brooks no argument and expects obedience.

"I might have been almost comatose for the first six months after Connor died, but I'm not stupid." I move closer, right into his personal space. "You won't talk about it, but do you think I can't guess what keeps you up? What you dream of when you finally do sleep?"

He remains silent, but that's answer enough.

And my heart cracks and splinters in my chest.

From what Connor had told me, Knox had been the strong one in their family, the caretaker since age fourteen when their father died. Everyone had leaned on him, looked to him, even their mother, who is still fragile two years after Connor's death. But who had taken care of him? Who did it now?

No one.

Not because his family didn't care. No, the Gordon family, even with their issues, loved one another, were loyal, and would do anything for each other. But their view of their older brother and son had been skewed for fifteen years. They only saw the strength and not the hurt.

The brokenness.

Maybe because I hadn't been born into their clan, I could perceive what they couldn't.

Or maybe because I spent so much time looking.

"Knox," I whisper, risking rejection and cupping his cheek again. "Sometimes I see it, too. The nightmares—they switch up. There's the one where I'm at ringside instead of my seat, watching that fist come toward him in slow motion. I'm yelling at him to duck, feint, move, *anything*. But I can't get the words out; they're trapped in my throat but echoing in my head. And I can't do anything but watch the blow connect and him hit the mat." Even now, that sense of helplessness strangles me, jams up my chest. "And then, there's the one where we're in the locker room, and he's stretched out on the examination table. But instead of lying there motionless, he's smiling, laughing, talking. He's okay." I bow my head, squeeze my eyes closed. "I honestly don't know which one is worse. That I replay his death or that I wake up, and for a few blissful, euphoric seconds, I believe he's alive."

A big hand cradles the back of my neck and tugs me forward. My forehead meets Knox's chest, and I inhale his earth and Christmas scent. It comforts me almost as much as those months of grief counseling did. Grief counseling that *Knox* had made me attend. I wrap my arms around him. Hold him tight, as if my embrace alone is keeping him here. Yes, the thought is melodramatic as hell, but I can't shake it.

"I'm so sorry," he croaks into my hair. "So fucking sorry, baby. It's my fault. I should've—"

"No." My head jerks up, and anger sparks, catching fire and spreading through me. "Don't you ever say that again. Katherine was wrong to blame you that night and any time since. Just like she was wrong to accuse you of wanting your brother's death. *Wrong*." Though I'd still been at the hospital when Knox and his brothers had broken the news to Katherine, Jude had later told me about the ugly accusations and blame that she'd fired at Knox. And even drowning in my grief, I'd been as horrified then as I am now. "Connor had a brain aneurysm. It could've ruptured with him doing something as simple as walking down the street. It was Connor's decision to go into MMA. His choice to step into that ring. Do you understand me? His. Choice. And what we now know of brain aneurysms and the percentage of people surviving ruptures, I can't even say for certain that if he'd known about it, he wouldn't have played the odds—still going into the fight, believing he would've been safe. That nothing could happen to him."

His jade gaze darkens, and his mouth hardens as if words are shoving against his lips and he's barricading them. It doesn't take a Magic 8-Ball to guess what those words would be. Another claim of fault, of misplaced responsibility.

Unraveling my arms from around him, I grab his wrists and draw his hands down between us. Clasping them in mine, I can't help but appreciate the differences between us. His hands are so huge, capable of delivering a beating but also of extreme gentleness. I rub my thumbs over the backs of his fingers and thumbs—over the words STILL I RISE inked onto them just under his knuckles.

"I've always wondered how an Irish fighter came to have Maya Angelou's words tattooed on him," I admit. "And why this poem."

"Grace, my trainer Jake's mother, became a second mother to me when I was younger. Jake offered me an outlet for my rage after my dad died by teaching me to channel it into boxing, martial arts, and wrestling. But Grace"—his fingers curl around mine—"she saved my mind. Sometimes I think my soul. I was so angry, and she mothered me when mine was...unable to. When Grace died four years ago, I had this done in memory of her. It was her favorite poem by her favorite poet."

Tears sting my eyes, and I rapidly blink to fight them back. It's the first time I've ever heard him speak anything even remotely critical of Katherine—including last night when he told me about her abominable accusation—and my heart aches at his reluctance to utter even that. His love for both the women in his life who raised him is apparent.

It also strikes me that I was wrong; someone had taken care of him, looked out for him. And her name was Grace. I've never met the woman—never heard of her before now—but I'm grateful to and for her.

"I first noticed the tattoo when I started working here, and do you know what I thought when I saw it? Well besides, damn, dude is gorgeous, has a beard, *and* great taste in literature? No wonder he pulls a lot of ass." His soft snort has the corner of my mouth quirking, but the amusement fades as I caress the words once more. "I thought, he's an eagle. Sue me, I'd just watched a show on Animal Planet about them. But they use the winds of a storm to gain altitude and rise above it. That's you, Knox. You're the eagle with the wind. The things that force other people to ground, to seek shelter and hide, things that would devastate them, you use them to soar."

I lift my gaze from his tattooed fingers to meet his gaze. And almost flinch from the emotion saturating his stare. Gone is the Sphinx, and in his place stands the battered and scarred warrior who's witnessed horrors but still survived and goes on. His jaw works, and his nostrils flare. But before I can decipher the origin and details of that tempest in his eyes, he hauls me against him, burrows his fingers in my hair, drags my head back, and covers my mouth with his.

The kiss is hungry, carnal, wild…and desperate. I taste it in the aggressive thrust of his tongue, the clench and release of his fists in my hair, the almost frantic angling of my head so he can dive deeper inside me, demand more from me. And I give it. Whatever this man who never asks for anything—doesn't expect anything from others—needs from me, I'll give it.

God, I'd been right to be wary of getting too deep with Knox, this man with the stony face, heartbreaking eyes, and magical mouth, hands, and dick. He could so easily have me losing myself again.

That sends a shard of unease slicing me, but not enough to pierce the dense fog of lust that encases us.

Dimly, I catch the ringtone of my cell phone on the dining room table, and ignore it, raising on my toes to open my mouth wider under his and meet him in this erotic battle we're labeling a kiss.

But after a moment of silence, the phone starts again.

Groaning, I drop to the soles of my feet and tilt my head back. It's Monday morning; that could be Jude or any of the other tattoo artists on the other end, even though it's still early.

It could be Kathrine or Dan.

As soon as the idea passes through my head, I can't eject it. Or all the other thoughts that follow. Last night. Knox in my kitchen, half-naked this morning. The consequences if anyone found out. Was sex between us a one-time thing—okay, two-time thing—or…just what the hell are we doing?

Sighing, I scrub my palms down my face and edge around him. Seconds later, I pick up the phone just as it stops ringing. A missed call from Simon. With a swipe of my thumb, his voicemail fills the room.

"Hey, Eden. I've been trying to reach Knox, but knowing him, he's probably left his phone somewhere. That's bullshit." His chuckle echoes from the cell. "He's probably just not answering. Anyway, when you see him today, could you let him know I have those two new pieces he wanted? I'll bring them by the shop this afternoon. Thanks, sis. Love you."

The voicemail clicks off, and "sis" and "love you" ping-pong off the walls of my skull, magnifying with each rebound.

Would he continue to call me his sister and show me that easy affection if he suspected that not four hours ago I—his brother's widow—had been pinned under his other brother's body, begging him to fuck me harder, faster? Would he, or Jude, or Katherine, be able to look at me, accept me, call me family…love me?

The possibility of losing them, the only people in this world who have ever really loved and accepted me, strikes me in the heart like a finely-honed dagger. Being abandoned again—it's the only nightmare that competes with those about Connor.

Family isn't everything only to those who've never been without one, who've always been blessed with the presence and security of one and take that precious gift for granted.

But... When I'm with Knox, it's like that breathless expectation of Christmas Eve mixed with the exhilarating, stomach-twisting combination of pleasure and excitement similar to catching a glimpse of your crush down the high school hallway. I feel vibrant, sharp, *alive* when I'm around him. And after two years of living in that awful in-between like a zombie—breathing but dead inside—it's addictive; *he's* addictive.

"I would never make you choose, Eden," Knox says, studying me from the distance that separates us.

God, does the man have mind-reading abilities?

I carefully replace my cell on the dining room table then meet his unwavering gaze. Unlike before the kiss, his normal, impenetrable expression has returned. And a part of me mourns that glimpse into the tortured man beneath. Even for a brief amount of time, he let me in.

"I don't want to choose." God, I can't believe I'm saying this...*doing* this. "I want both. At least for as long as I can. As long as we can."

An emotion spasms across his face before his harshly beautiful features resume their usual inscrutability. He shakes his head, and I can practically see the "no" on his lips before he utters it. "Eden..."

"I know this can't go anywhere, and I'm not asking you for a relationship or forever. But if we're careful, if we agree to keep this between us, why can't we have each other? For the first time since..." I trail off, unable to say Connor's name in a hot-sex-with-no-strings-attached conversation with his brother. "I don't have to be anyone but myself with you. Yes, I want to fuck you until I can't move," I say, the flash of heat in his gaze a match to the desire that's always at a low simmer inside me. "But it's more than that. I'm not a widow, a daughter, or a lifeline with you. I'm not...alone."

The truth of that staggers me. I have been alone. I've lived the past two years with this invisible shield of grief between me and the world.

Except with Knox.

Somehow, he slipped past it, touched my wounded heart, gave me a job, guided me back to the woman I was on my way to becoming. And then he showed me the sexual, uninhibited woman I didn't know existed.

Yes, asking him to enter into a secret, temporary friends-with-benefits pact with me is probably the epitome of selfishness. But I don't rescind my request. And I want him to give in. More than my next breath, I want it. Want him.

"You're my brother's wife," he states matter-of-factly. As if that should settle the discussion.

"Widow," I correct. "And you didn't seem to care about that last night...or this morning." Not when he'd guided me down his body and rolled his hips, pushing his dick in my mouth.

He doesn't address my point, but there's another flare of fire in his emerald gaze. "You believe you're ready for the consequences if someone found out about us, but you're not. I've already had a taste of disapproval. I don't think you could deal. It's heavy, baby. And you've already lost so much, I don't want to be responsible for you losing more."

Translation: He didn't think he was *worth* me losing more.

Knox was the fighter, but now, at this moment, I want to climb into a ring and go ten rounds with any and every person who'd ever uttered a word or committed an action that entrenched his blasphemous belief in his own unworthiness.

Aren't you doing the same thing? a sibilant whisper slithers through my mind.

No, I deny vehemently. He's not second best. If we were different people and under different circumstances, I would stare down any woman who dared glance in his direction, and proudly walk around with a sign declaring who he belonged to.

But we are who we are, and nothing can change that.

He deserves a woman who can claim him as hers. Who can be his. And I'm not that woman. I won't shatter his relationship with his mother, and I don't want to risk the rest of his family's love and respect for either of us.

But for a little while, I'd like to be her, even if under the somewhat deceitful blanket of secrecy.

"No one would find out if we're careful," I counter his argument. "And for the record, you wouldn't be responsible if someone did discover the truth. I would. I'm a full-grown woman and am capable of weighing the consequences of my decisions. And you using the excuse of 'protecting' me from my own choices is insulting."

He crosses his arms over his chest, arching a dark eyebrow. "So, I would be your dirty little secret?" His voice is rough, black gravel, but still, I sense that he's not angry or offended.

"And I'll be yours," I reply.

His eyes narrow. "There could never be anything dirty about you, Eden."

Damn. This man.

"Is that a yes?" I press.

There's a long moment of silence, and it vibrates with the tension between us.

"Yes."

The relief and joy that washes through me should be a warning that I'm in so much deeper than I want to admit. But right now, denial is my bestie, and we're rolling together.

And frankly, need trumps everything else. My palms tingle and itch with the desire to erase the distance between us and stroke the amazing chest that's calling to me like a pint of strawberry cheesecake ice cream.

But we have one last thing to settle.

"One last thing," I say, injecting as much *I'm not taking no shit* into my tone as possible. "I think you should stay home from the shop today. Or at least not come in until late afternoon."

"Why would I do that?" he asks, frowning.

"So you can get some more sleep. You seemed to be able to do it here in my bed. So maybe it's a change in environment that helped."

"It wasn't the environment, Eden," he growls. "It was the woman. Don't doubt that."

The bald, no-ruffles-or-adornment statement is somehow as hot as the filthiest thing he's ever uttered to me. Christ, I want to climb him like a jungle gym. With a will that must be divinely given, I focus.

"And I want you to promise me you'll go see someone about the insomnia and nightmares."

His frown clears, and the Sphinx returns. "That's not necessary—"

"Yes, it is, damn it," I snap, frustration over his stubbornness and fear for him sharpening my objection even further. "What if one day you crash behind the steering wheel? Or your health is jeopardized? There was a time I didn't want to go see a therapist, and you made me. Matter of fact, you drove me there and walked me up to the office." I curl my fingers into my palm, my nails biting into the skin. "Please, Knox. One session. That's all I'm asking."

I'm not above emotional blackmail, and I'm ready to haul out the big guns—the "Connor wouldn't have wanted you to be suffering like this" guns—when he finally nods. He doesn't look happy about it at all, but that's okay. Because as long as I've known him, Knox hasn't broken his word. If he says he'll go, he'll go.

I swallow a sigh of relief and zip my mouth. As my mom used to say, never miss a good opportunity to shut the hell up. But I surrender to the need to touch him, and cross the floor to the kitchen, pausing before him, close enough that my breasts graze the solid wall of his chest and my thighs press to his. Sliding my hands over his cut hips and up his back, I tilt my head up.

His scrutiny is hot, piercing, and on anyone else, unnerving. It's as if anatomy is just tissue paper, and he tears past it to the heart, the soul, to places you don't even like admitting are there.

"Are you sure this is what you want?" he rumbles, thrusting his big but elegant fingers into my hair.

"Yes, I'm sure *you're* who I want," I reply.

He doesn't speak, but that storm of arousal that darkens his gaze. Yeah, it's answer enough.

As is his hoisting me into the air, his strength slugging the breath from my lungs.

As is his mouth tenderly but hungrily taking mine as he sets me on the counter.

As is my hand dipping into his jeans and freeing him.

As is his slowly lowering me onto his cock, filling me, stretching me.

Yeah, I don't need words.

Chapter Twelve

Knox

"I've been waiting on this tat for months, man," the guy in my chair chatters.

I know Caleb from the gym. He's twenty-one, built like a bull, hungry to train, and reminds me of an excited puppy, complete with tail-wagging and face-licking. He gossips like teen girls at a sleepover and is never without a wide grin—unless he's in the ring. Then he transforms into this focused, fierce beast that can put the fear of God into almost anyone who comes at him. One day, after he gains maturity and much more experience, he's going to fucking grab the MMA world by the throat and shake it like a pit bull. Which will be a vast improvement over the ass-shaking, face-licking puppy.

He's bugged me for months about coming in for a tattoo. With the exception of my old friends and fighters from the BFC, I prefer to keep my private life and professional life separate. I don't mind any of the guys from the gym coming in, but I usually don't ink them. Caleb, though? His persistence made me cave. Have I mentioned it's impossible not to like the guy?

"Yeah, well, if you don't stop moving, you're going to wish you had kept on waiting." Because his mother will end up sporting a lopsided eye that makes her seem like she's eternally squinting in this portrait tattoo.

"Sorry." For five entire seconds he's quiet, then, "Who's that out front? Damn, yo, she's hot as fuck."

Irritation punches me in the chest, hard and fast. Dragging in a deep breath, I deliberately release it, concentrating on keeping my hand steady. Then I straighten, turning toward my station on the pretense of refilling my needle with ink. Either that or Mom end ups up looking like Forest Whitaker.

"Eden," I grit out. "She's my office manager."

"So, she single?" He cranes his neck as if he can see out the door, down the hall, and out front where Eden is manning the desk.

Fuck no. "She's my sister-in-law," I reply, which basically informs the kid that she's off-limits.

And he apparently takes it that way, because he nods. "Gotcha. That explains the 'touch her, and I'll feed you your balls for lunch' tone. 'Cause you're giving me a lot of tone," he drawls.

I snort, returning to his arm. My tone has shit to do with who Eden was married to, and everything with my leaving her bed and apartment this morning after spending the night.

It's been a month since our "dirty little secret" talk in her kitchen. A month since we've become lovers who have spent every spare minute outside of the shop together. And it's been the best four weeks of my life.

Mentally, I wince at the emo words. Eden is everything good. And she makes me feel that way. I'm whole when I'm with her, at peace, as happy as that day at Wrigley Stadium. I'm even sleeping more, although I've still held out against seeing a therapist. I'll go; I promised her. But every minute is a gift. Mainly because I can't hide from the fact that I'm running against a ticking clock, cramming years into however long this arrangement lasts. Because there's no doubt that it can't last. Not with my promise and our circumstances hanging over our heads.

I meant what I told Eden that morning; I refuse to make her choose between my family and me. The fact is, she needs them more than me. They give her security, fill that hole created by a shitty childhood, offer her sanctuary.

While me?

I can't even give her the truth.

Every morning, I leave her apartment and head out to the gym, where I train for the fight that is now just weeks away. I've had countless opportunities to tell her about it, but every time that opening comes, I retreat, shying away like a slinking coward.

Part of me wants to tell Eden about the exhibition match. Lies have never sat well with me, which is ironic considering I've spent the last five years of my life living the lie of a platonic brother-in-law. But the other half of me is terrified of losing this slice in time with Eden—with the woman I've been in love and lust with for so long—that I have somehow, through some twist of fate, been offered. I'm not fooling myself into believing it's more, but it's all I have—all I'll ever have. And I'm not ready to let it go. Not yet.

So I've remained quiet.

And that silence weighs on me.

"I've been meaning to ask you if you think you can give me some time next week? I know you've been putting in more hours, and I can come to the gym in the morning or the evening. Doesn't matter to me," Caleb asks. Even though I've warned him about moving, his shoulders hunch as if preparing for me to say no. I bet he's heard that often in his twenty-one years—that and worse. Much worse. Though we come from different backgrounds, we both sought out fighting for the same reasons—an escape.

He's right; with the match so close, I return to the gym after work for a couple more hours before heading to Eden's place. Jake has been working the hell out of me, and every minute is packed with some kind of conditioning, but I refuse to be one more person who disappoints Caleb.

"Yeah," I agree. "Come through tomorrow morning. I'll be there at five. We can work out for an hour before I start with Jake."

His grin lights up his whole face, and he appears younger than his age. "Thanks, Knox. I really appreciate it."

"No worries." I nod. "Now, for real, can you stop moving so I can finish this?"

"Oh, yeah, yeah, my bad." Another three minutes of silence. "Damn, I can't wait to see you fight again. This is going to be the rematch of the fucking century," he crows.

"You're returning to MMA?" a low voice asks carefully from the cracked doorway.

Ice slides through my veins, transforming my blood into frost, freezing the breath in my lungs. Forcing my arm down and away from Caleb, I slowly rotate on my stool and face the door.

Eden stares at me, for once, her normally easy-to-read expression shuttered.

If her question hadn't clued me in that she overheard Caleb, that inscrutable mask would have.

Denial and fear howl in my head as the ice in my chest starts to thaw, and the panic claws at me, sinking its talons deep, drawing blood that carries the metallic taste of dread.

I could lie.

I could evade the question and brush off Caleb's statement as misinformation.

But I don't. I can't.

"Yes."

For a second, that mask cracks, betraying the anger and gut-wrenching betrayal swirling beneath.

Completely oblivious, Caleb grins at her. "Yep, he's facing Israel Clarkson again. A rematch of one of the best BFC fights ever. I wish I could go to Reno to see it live." He sighs.

"In Reno?" she echoes, a thread of accusation running through her voice. Yes, Reno. The city where Connor died. But most of the big BFC matches happen there or Vegas, both cities being hugely popular locations. "When?"

The rawness in the hoarse question snaps my paralysis, and I stand, crossing the room to her. But she steps back, retreating from me, stabbing me in the chest. Her emotions radiate outward like a radar beacon, gaining heat and speed with each pulse.

"In about three weeks. November."

She nods. "November," she repeats in that flat tone that tells me nothing...and everything. "Do you mind if I leave for the rest of the day?"

We stare at each other for several long moments, and that silence is rife with condemnation and so much hurt that I curl my fingers around the doorjamb to keep from lurching forward.

"No," I rasp. "I don't mind."

Her lips part as if she's going to say something to me. And I wait, praying for anything but the cold that has turned her into this pillar of ice that's freezing me out.

But she turns and walks away.

Leaving me.

Jaw clenched against the pain throwing continuous haymakers against every organ in my body, I return to Caleb and his tattoo.

For once, he's quiet and remains that way.

Good, because whatever comes out of my mouth right now wouldn't sound human.

I finish his tattoo and make it through the rest of the afternoon and evening on autopilot. Reason cautions me to give Eden room, time. But every hour—every minute—that passes presses down on my rib cage, even as a sense of panic cranks up each time I glance at my watch or cell. By the time the last walk-in client leaves, I can't wait another moment.

Hiking my chin at Jude, I palm my keys and tug on my beanie. "Hey, do me a favor and lock up? I have to go."

My brother pauses in the middle of wiping down his tattoo chair and studies me for a beat before nodding. "Yeah, I got you."

I head out, and the entire twenty minutes to Eden's apartment, I battle the noose of dread and anxiety steadily tightening around my neck. Choking on the sense of foreboding…and resignation.

Minutes later, I stand in front of her door and knock. Not soon after we started having sex, she gave me a key to her place, since I often came in late. But using it now… Yeah, it doesn't seem right. Not when, after tonight, she'll most likely never want me inside again.

My chest seizes, and I focus on pushing air in and out of my lungs, like I would during a fight. Then I knock again.

The click of a lock disengaging reaches me first, and then the door swings open as if in slow motion. As if my mind is winding reality down so it captures each moment, to save it for later when mental snapshots are all I have left.

She stands in the doorway, and I take her in like a starving stray.

She's my everything.

It's not hard for me to admit that; I've wanted her from the moment I looked up and noticed her in that club's crowded

VIP lounge. Not long after, she met and fell in love with my brother and became a fixture in my family.

And since then, I've loved her.

As she stares at me with betrayal glinting in her dark gaze, I love her.

And when I walk out of here tonight with our relationship littering the floor like smashed glass, I'll still love her.

"Can I come in?" I ask.

She shifts backward, and I take that as her answer. Stepping past her, I enter the apartment that has become as familiar to me as my own place and close the door behind me.

She crosses her arms over her chest, and the gesture is so vulnerable, as if she has to protect herself from this conversation—from me—I jerk to a stop, granting her distance. Or maybe it's more for me, so I don't surrender to the temptation to reach for her, touch her.

Scrubbing a hand down my face, I scavenge my brain for a place to start, an excuse that would make any of this okay. But I'm coming up empty-handed on both. Nothing I could say is going to erase that disillusionment and betrayal, so all I can give her—what she deserves—is the truth.

"I'm sorry, Eden," I begin. "I should've told you about the fight."

"Why?" she asks, and I almost flinch from the thick hoarseness. Earlier at the shop, her face had been unreadable, shut down. But now, her hurt pours out of her.

"Why I agreed to the match, or why did I keep it from you?" I ask, my fingers aching with the need to brush her pale skin, smooth my thumbs down the elegant column of her throat, which has to be scratched and sore if her voice is any indication. Scratched and sore from crying.

Over me. My decision. My deception.

When I'd held her in my arms eighteen months ago while she broke down after her fist day in the shop, I'd vowed that she would never have another reason to cry and hurt.

And now, I'm the reason for both.

"Either." She shrugs a shoulder. "Both."

"The BFC approached me about a rematch against Israel Clarkson because of what happened with the first event."

"You mean Connor dying," she interrupts with a snap of temper.

"Yes," I agree. "When people think of that match, they don't remember the title fight. They recall it being the night Connor died. There's a shadow cast over it. So the BFC wants to redo the match. Also, that was the last fight of my career. Listen—" I shove a hand over my hair, fisting the strands. Exhaling, I try again. "I know I'm not explaining this well. At first I didn't accept the offer—"

"Does that matter?" she challenges, her chin tilting up. "You ended up agreeing."

"Yeah." I nod. "Because part of the proceeds from the event will fund a college scholarship in Connor's name and honor."

"Is that supposed to change my mind just because you throw out the 'It's for the kids' card?" she asks, her arms slowly loosening and dropping to her sides. Her voice lowers, trembles. "You think I give a damn about a scholarship when all I can see over and over again is my husband dying for this fucking sport? When all I can imagine is losing someone else I care about to it? I'm supposed to be happy about it because someone is going to write a check?" she demands. "Sorry if it makes me a selfish bitch, but I can't. I won't."

Losing someone else I care about...

The admission twists something inside me so hard, I struggle not to flinch. Pain and joy flare in me for what's said and what isn't. She cares for me.

But she doesn't love me.

The omission of that word is as huge and bright as a

blinking, neon Vegas sign.

Breathing past the vise grip squeezing the fuck out of me, I refocus on her and the fear that's practically pouring out of her. "Eden, I'm not returning to the BFC. It's one exhibition match. That's it."

Her harsh, sharp-as-glass laugh echoes in the room. "Right, Knox. One time." Another of those serrated, cutting chuckles. "I've spent five years of my life around the Gordon men. Do you really believe I don't know you? You're all competitors, fighters in one way or another. You more than the others. I remember seeing you in the ring. You loved it, were born for it. You were so *alive* there. More than I've ever seen you anywhere else or since. Once won't be enough for you."

"I'm not Connor," I say quietly. In so many ways, I'm not my brother.

For a moment, her eyes soften, her lips tremble, and she shakes her head. "No, you're not. You're not impulsive or rash. You're steadier, more responsible. You're also a better, more seasoned fighter. For you, this isn't a lark, an adventure; this is your passion. And that's why I'm more scared for you than I ever was for him."

"You're partly right," I concede. "I do feel alive when I'm in the ring. Fighting has been in my life for so long, it's a part of me. It saved me when I could've easily gone in a very bad direction. But it's not my passion. Not even art, tattooing, or the shop are. Yeah, they focus me, offer me an outlet, a purpose, a drive. But my passion? No. Only one thing—one person—can claim that position. You."

The truth rolls out of me like rapids swollen by a violent, sudden rainfall. I have shit to lose. Hell, I'm losing it at this moment, watching it move farther and farther away, and all I can do is stand still like a goddamn spectator. But this game was fixed before it even started. The score decided, the victor chosen. Yet, I still played, and it's only now when the inevitable is crashing into me, rupturing inside me like a grenade, that I can admit to that tiny, infinitesimal sliver of hope that had lodged in my heart like a grain of sand. Hope that this could possibly have a different ending.

Yeah, that hope has been crushed under the heel of reality, and all I have left is the truth. Pride is for shit when you have nothing else left.

"I would never make you choose between fighting and me," Eden whispers, eyes searching my face. Confusion and a deepening, dawning understanding darkening her eyes.

"You don't get it, Eden," I growl, my fingers curling into fists as I battle the need to cross the room, chew up the distance between us, and tangle myself in her hair. Make her look at me and see. Fucking *see*. "There *is no* choice. I made it two years ago. Hell, five years ago. You. I chose to step back and not pursue you when I saw how happy Connor made you. I chose to shut down my heart and settle for meaningless fucks because no woman would ever or could ever be you. I chose to hire you even though being around you day in and day out was torture. I chose to be your fuck buddy because it's all I could have of you, and I'm enough of a selfish bastard to grab it with both hands. It's *always* been you, Eden. Even knowing you're not mine, would never be mine, it's always been you."

"Knox," she breathes, stumbling back a step, her fingers splayed over her chest.

I ignore the pain that cremates me from the inside out. Ignore. Yeah, not possible. I push past it.

"I told you I've wanted you for years. And that's true. But what I didn't say was that I've loved you for almost the same amount of time. Even while you were with my brother," I state just in case she doesn't fully grasp the complete fuckery of this emotional ménage she hadn't even know she was a part of. "Your marriage to Connor didn't kill it; neither did his death. And walking out of here knowing you hate me won't, either."

She shakes her head, still pale, hand still pressed over her heart. "I don't hate you, Knox—"

"Not yet," I cut her off. Partly because I need to get this out while I can. And the other part because if she utters how she loves me but not in the same way, I might punch a hole through her wall, screwing up any chance of her getting back a security deposit. "Connor's death. That's on my head. My hands." I spread my hands open in front of me and stare down at them as if I can see blood painting my skin.

"I told you—don't ever say that again," Eden snaps, some of the fire my announcement leeched out of her returning. "It's not your fault—"

Once more I interrupt her. "I could've stopped the fight," I state, laying out the bald, ugly truth I've been hiding between us. And as her arm drops to her side, I can't do anything but stand witness as what I was terrified of most comes to pass.

Her eyes darken, and she moves those elegant fingers up her chest and circles her neck. Her knees buckle, and she slides toward the floor, the couch breaking her fall. Heart barreling toward my throat, I lurch toward her, but she slams a hand up, palm out in the age-old sign of *Stop right the fuck where you are*. Her lips form around a word, but no sound comes out. But I can read it. *What?*

Answer. She wants an explanation, not my touch.

"The BFC office wanted an event where they could promote both the Gordon brothers," I continue. "They knew it would bring in mad money, sell the most tickets. A championship match as well as the heavyweight champion's younger brother—it was marketing gold. And I went along with it because not only did I get a kick out of being on the same ticket as my brother, but I wanted that title match against Israel. In my heart, I knew Connor wasn't ready for the match. I tried to talk to him about it, but he was stubborn. Got pissed when I suggested he wait, that he didn't need to step into that ring because of the head office. He felt he had so much to prove. 'Cause of me, maybe. I know he got tired of being compared to me whether he won or lost. And there's nothing wrong with desiring to be your own man, but I think it pushed him into accepting that match."

Connor had always been the best at what he set his mind to; damn, the man had graduated high school and college early. Had been courted by top accounting firms, promising him any and everything if he'd join them. But he'd chosen to enter MMA. And as talented, as hard-working as he was, he still wasn't the best there. Given time, he possibly could've been, but Eden had been right about the Gordon men: we're competitive as fuck. And someday hadn't been coming fast enough for Connor. Yet, that determination and drive were two traits I loved most about him.

"I tried to tell him that," she whispered, her wide eyes so dark they almost appeared black. Shock. Her arms were back around herself, as if holding herself together so she didn't shatter into pieces.

"I could've had the fight pulled," I repeat, refusing to look away from her. Like a masochist, needing to glimpse the moment when disgust and rage entered her gaze. "Yeah, I believed the worst that would happen was Connor would take an ass-kicking, not die. But my beliefs and assumptions don't amount to shit. If I'd told them I wouldn't fight unless they pulled Connor's match, his death wouldn't have happened. He would've been mad as hell, but he would also be here. But I didn't. And that's on me."

Saying the secret that has weighed me down for two long years out loud is...freeing. Cathartic, in a way. I'm no longer hiding. The burden of my brother's death—I don't know if I'll ever be free of it. Maybe. In time.

But this truth is a double-edged sword. It slices away the chains of the secret that has held me bound. But it also severs the bonds of relationship between us.

She doesn't utter a word, just stares at me. And her silence is as much of an indictment as if she started screaming and hurling accusations at me.

I knew it—I knew she would realize I'm to blame. And I'd prepared for it. Or I thought I had. Nothing could've readied me for the searing agony razing me to the ground. But I throw up fire-retardant walls, blocking the memories that are already trying to crowd in and overwhelm me, mocking what I had for a brief time and lost.

"I don't expect you to forgive me," I continue, voice flat, revealing none of the chaos whipping and swirling inside me. "But when I walk out of here, I'm going to try and forgive myself. I can't..." I cut off, clenching my jaw and glancing away before returning my gaze back to her, unable, even in these last few moments, to *not* look at her. "I can't live this half-life anymore. I've spent the years since my father died enslaved to something—my anger, my career, my guilt...my love for you. I want to be free. Not of loving you; it would be easier to stop breathing. But of holding myself hostage to a woman who can't return what I want...what I need. I convinced myself that even a little of you for whatever time I could grab would be enough. But it's not. Maybe for the first time, I'm beginning to believe I deserve more. I don't know, but one thing I *do* know is this"—I wave a hand between us—"isn't healthy. Not for you. And not for me. Eden." I pause but then push out the rest. "Never doubt for one second that I fucking want you more than life. But I won't hold *you* hostage to that, either."

Only then do my feet unglue from the floor, and I move toward her. I stroke a hand down the length of her hair. My muscles tense, and my heart thuds heavily against my rib cage, bracing for a possible rejection of my touch. Could be shock, but she doesn't flinch or avoid my touch. Bending over her, I press my lips to the top of her head, inhaling her warm, sweet scent, searing the sensation of the dark strands under my palm into my sensory memory.

After a moment, I straighten, and without glancing around, I retrace my steps and exit the apartment.

I don't look back.

Not when I descend the steps.

Not when I push out the building.

Not when I climb into my truck and pull off.

A clean break is supposed to be the easiest to heal.

I'm going to find out.

Chapter Thirteen

Eden

I pull up into Katherine and Dan's driveway and cut off my engine. Closing my eyes, I drag in a breath and sit there behind the wheel, needing to gather myself before I go into the house I used to call home.

Sunday dinner.

Sighing, I lift my lashes and stare out my driver's side window at the front of the house. The last one I'd attended had been two weeks ago, without Knox. Before the world as I'd known it for the past eighteen months had imploded and left me reeling, a leaf swirling and tumbling on a strong, uncontrollable wind. That's how I feel right now. Out of control. Adrift. Lost.

The person who'd been the mainstay, the grounding force in my life for a year-and-a-half is gone. Physically to Reno, having decided pretty much right after we last saw each other to spend the next few weeks there, training and preparing for his fight. Emotionally? He was so much farther than seventeen-hundred miles across the country.

It'd been a little over two weeks since I discovered his intention to return to MMA.

I chuckle, and the brittle, raw sound echoes in the confines of the car.

As if his plan to fight was the only thing he'd disclosed.

The most Knox had ever spoken at one time, and it's to tell me he loves me—has been in love with me almost from the moment he saw me five years ago—and that he's responsible for Connor's death.

Seventeen days later, and I'm still reeling over both revelations. I swallow, the fist of hurt and disbelief hindering the action.

His words had crashed into me like a brick through a window, shattering every belief and idea I had about him—about us. For so long I'd seen Knox as this stalwart, quiet sentinel incapable of weakness and human emotions like fear. Not him, who stepped into an octagon and faced down men intent on beating him to a bloody mess. He'd been that pillar of strength we all looked to, especially me, for security, for sanctuary. Even after sex changed us, he'd still been my... rock.

But the Thursday before last, in my living room, he'd changed that with nine, phonetically simple but Big Bang-universe-altering words...

I told you I've wanted you for years.... But what I didn't say was that I've loved you for almost the same amount of time.

He's still strong and powerful. But incapable of weakness, of human emotions? That image is shot to hell and back. Knox Gordon is not only capable of emotion, he is a seething cauldron of it, just with a tightly screwed top.

And I'm his Achilles heel.

I'm still not sure how I feel about that.

Not sure how I feel about anything, since my MO lately has been to shut down everything but what is strictly required to get through the day. Because something else became abundantly clear when Knox left. My world turned from vivid technicolor to muted blacks and grays.

I'm empty. Lonely.

A rap on the window startles me, jerking me out of my morose thoughts.

Jude peers through the window, frowning.

Forcing a smile to my lips, I pull on the handle and open the car door. Stepping out and closing it behind me, I shrug at my brother-in-law. "Hi, Jude."

His frown doesn't clear. God, with a black beanie pulled over his short hair and a couple of day's growth of dark blonde and brown hair darkening his jaw and bracketing his mouth, he resembles Knox. It twists a knife in my chest, and my smile wobbles before I can catch it.

And like his brother, he misses nothing. "What's going on?"

Since, *I think your brother broke m*e, most likely won't go over well, I stick with, "Nothing. Just got some things on my mind."

"Is this about—*damn it*," he growls, snatching his phone from his back pocket and quickly swiping a thumb across the screen. "Are you sure this isn't about—*shit*." His phone vibrates in his hand again, and once more, he touches the screen, ending the cell's shaking.

"Ana?" I ask, though I really don't need to. Only one person irritates Jude to this extent, and that's his ex-girlfriend. Correction. Crazy ass ex-girlfriend who's apparently never seen *Frozen* because the girl refuses to *let it go*.

"Yeah," he grunts. "I'm not going to deal with this all night." He powers down the cell then stuffs it into the back pocket of his jeans. "You sure you okay?" he asks, those narrowed, green eyes fixed on me. Right now, it hurts to look into them since they remind me of his absentee brother.

"Yes." I walk ahead. "And I'm hungry, so let's head inside." Lie.

As soon as we walk into his mother's house moments later, the aroma of roast hits me. Normally, I would be drooling over one of my favorite dishes, but today, my stomach tightens, lurching a bit in protest. My appetite has been zero lately, and the last thing I'm looking forward to is Katherine commenting on me picking over my plate and asking why I'm not eating.

Yeah, answering that truthfully is off the table.

"I was wondering where the two of you were," Kathrine called as Jude closed the door behind us. She smiled, holding a platter in her hands. "Well, don't just stand there, everyone else is here. You're the last to arrive. Let's eat."

Following her into the dining room, I greet Simon and Dan with a wave and hug. Unbidden, my gaze slides to the sixth and empty chair on the other side of the table across from me. No, everyone isn't here; Knox is absent. And irritation snaps inside me that Katherine doesn't seem bothered over one of her sons not being there.

As soon as the thought pops into my head, it feels disloyal, and I shove it down. But stubbornly, it refuses to be cowed.

Maybe it shouldn't be.

Dinner crawls by, and even though the food looks delicious and perfect as always, it might as well as be cigarette ashes on my tongue. And that I can't stop from glancing at the empty chair doesn't help matters, either.

"Would anyone like coffee?" Katherine asks, rising from the table and gathering her husband's plate and mine. All of us, except for Jude, answer in the affirmative, and she smiles again. She's in a lighter mood today, meaning it's one of her better days.

Simon stands as well and helps his mother clear the rest of the dishes. He follows her into the kitchen, returning minutes later with a tray full of cups and saucers.

"How's Knox doing?" Dan asks, taking a coffee cup off the tray. "He had to work?"

"He's fine," Simon replies, removing the cups from the tray and placing them in front of him. "And no, he's in Reno, not the shop."

"Reno?" Katherine echoes, entering the room with a coffee urn. "What's he doing there?"

My stomach clenches, dread curling in it, and my gaze meets Jude's. His eyebrow arches, and I give my head a small shake, understanding his unspoken question. No, I hadn't said anything to their parents.

"Jude?" Katherine presses, standing behind Dan's chair.

"He's there preparing for a fight," Jude answers.

Silence permeates the room, heavy, thick, and vibrating with tension.

"Since when did he start fighting again?" Dan frowns.

Katherine set the coffee pot down on the table with an ominous thud.

"It's an exhibition match," Simon explains, his solemn gaze on his mother.

"A portion of the proceeds will be donated to a scholarship in Connor's name. It's specifically for kids from low-income backgrounds who couldn't afford college otherwise, and whose dream is to enter MMA," I add. Katherine's attention swings to me, and I meet it without wavering. Yeah, I hadn't wanted to hear anything about this fund when Knox had first told me. But I'd ended up searching the BFC's website for more information on the proposed scholarship and reading more about it. The tribute they'd posted to Connor at the bottom had been beautiful and had drawn tears to my eyes. "He would've loved knowing this is his legacy."

But it's as if I were speaking in another language. Her blue eyes narrow, and her mouth firms into a hard, grim line.

"Are you telling me he rejoined that sport after it took his brother's life?" she demands, voice low, dark, and nearly trembling with anger.

"Katherine..." I murmur.

"No," she cuts me off, voice sharp. "Don't you dare defend him. How could he do this?"

Her question reverberates in the room, and my jaw clenches, swallowing down a barrage of words that shove and push at my throat.

How would Katherine react if I relayed Knox's second admission to her? Would she heap more vitriol on him, seeing as she already blamed Knox for introducing Connor to the sport that had killed him?

I can't lie; his confession stunned me. Not because Knox didn't stop Connor's match when he had the opportunity. No, contrary to what Knox believed, there's no way in hell Connor wouldn't have marched into that Octagon anyway. We'd talked about it many times leading up to it. He'd been determined, even if Knox didn't approve. Yeah, I've known all this time that Knox hadn't agreed with Connor fighting this particular match. Connor had been upset that his older brother hadn't had confidence in him. I'd tried to explain that hadn't been the case, but Connor had a lot to prove to the BFC, the reporters, the fans, and more importantly, his brother.

So, yes, that's why I'd been struck speechless when Knox had dropped his bombshell—that he'd been walking around for two years with that enormous burden of guilt and blame on his massive shoulders for nothing. And *God*, those shoulders were indeed massive, so I can just imagine the amount of pain he's been carrying. I wanted to cry for him, but I'd been stunned, frozen. And by the time I could force my vocal cords to speak, he'd already left.

And didn't return. Not to my apartment or the shop.

He left without me telling him I didn't blame him, too quickly for me to catch up to him to deliver that message. And he hasn't answered or returned any of my phone calls since. I wanted to assure him that in no way did I hold him at fault. That my lack of reaction hadn't been due to resentment but shock. He'd just confessed the burden he'd been carrying around for two years, admitted he'd loved me, then followed it up with talk of my being unhealthy for him. With all that hitting me at once, I'd been confused, paralyzed. And by the time I'd fought through the surprise, he'd left.

Now, sitting at his mother's table with her bitterness damn near humming in the air, I understand why he didn't wait. Because of the venom that emanated from his mother. Since Connor's death, Knox had been the sacrificial lamb in this family. He'd been made to feel an outsider, an interloper by his own mother. So, if Katherine felt that way, how could he possibly believe I wouldn't?

Dismay slides into my chest, and I could kick myself for my slow reaction.

I would never make you choose, Eden.

The words from that morning in my kitchen bounce off the walls of my skull, gaining volume and speed. Why hadn't I seen it then? *How* hadn't I seen it?

He wouldn't make me choose because he didn't believe I would pick him. He was convinced he would always come in second place with me—to his family, to Connor.

And why wouldn't he assume that? Out of my fear of losing, I hadn't realized all that I could gain. *Who* I could gain.

Oh Christ.

"Mom, calm down," Jude tries to soothe his mother. "It's just one match. He's not going back to fighting full-time."

"Honey," Dan murmurs, setting a comforting hand on her arm. "If it's for a scholarship honoring Connor…"

"What good is that?" she demands, and I'm reminded of my own caustic response with Knox. And am ashamed. "My boy isn't here. Is it going to bring him back? I don't care about anyone else's son when mine is in the ground." Her voice cracks, and the grief echoes in my chest. Dan stands and reaches for her, but she vehemently shakes her head, pressing her open palm to his chest. Resignation crosses his face before he sinks back down into his chair. Her gaze, damp yet hot with anger, scans the table, lighting on Jude, Simon, and me. "Don't any of you dare defend this to me. It's unforgivable. Connor isn't here because of that damn sport. A sport Knox introduced him to. It's his fault—"

"Stop it," I whisper.

"Selfish. He's only thinking of himself," she continues in her tirade. "No son of mine—"

"*Stop it.*"

She breaks off, blinks, stares at me. Her fingers flutter to her throat, and a moment later, she frowns.

"Eden, what's…" She shakes her head. "I'm sorry. This has to be upsetting for you, honey. I'm sorry…"

"Yes, it's upsetting," I say, anger and, yes, fear swirling in my chest in a thick, cloying soup. "Hearing you talk about your son like that is very upsetting. And hurtful. And wrong," I rasp.

Her brows furrow as if she's confused that I'm defending Knox. "Eden," she whispers.

"No," I state, sitting back in my chair, straightening my shoulders. I drag in a breath, and it shudders out of my lungs, but I push past the terrible fear of causing her pain, of losing her love. "You're wrong. Wrong to blame Knox for Connor's death. For Connor's decisions."

"Eden." Dan clears his throat. "I don't think this is the

proper time to discuss this. Not now."

"Then when?" Jude interjects, his tone frigid. "When is a good time to finally talk about how our mother has punished her oldest son for living because one of us died?"

I flinch. Because underneath the freezing note is hurt, so much hurt. For Knox? For himself? Maybe both of them. Katherine pales, a whimper escaping her as pain flashes in her blue eyes. Dan shoots from his chair and, catching her shoulders, helps lower her to his seat.

"That's enough," he barks, displaying a rare temper. "She's your mother, and you will show her respect."

"It's not enough, Dan," I reply before Jude, who is glaring at his stepfather, can. "This needs to be said. Katherine," I shift my regard to her, and despair spears me through the chest as she stares at her other son, her anguish a tangible thing. But at her name, she switches her attention to me. "Connor died because of a brain aneurysm. Yes, the punch he received in the fight ruptured it, but so would've falling out of the bed and hitting his head. Or if he'd taken a job at a bank, so would've tripping and knocking his head against his desk. He loved playing basketball. A misplaced elbow or hard foul would've accomplished the same thing. It's not fair; God, I know, it's not fair, but it's what happened. Blaming Knox isn't going to bring him back. Making Knox suffer for choices that weren't his *but Connor's alone*, won't make his death make any more sense or bring you any peace."

"That's not true," she whispers, tears filling her eyes. "I'm not trying to make him suffer..."

"Yes, you are," I object softly, even though her refusal and denial to admit her resentment toward her son frustrates me. Angers me. "And you're killing him inside. Do you know that he blames himself? That he hasn't really slept in two years because nightmares and the guilt of losing his younger brother tortures him? And then when he comes to this house, he faces more accusations. You're. Tearing. Him. Apart," I grind out. "He's honorable, faithful, hard-working, loyal, *good*. He's everything good, and you are slowly destroying him."

Again, a deep silence hangs over the room, this one weighty with shock.

And I'm not immune. My breath whistles from between my lips, my heart working overtime. Images from the past and the present bombard me.

Knox, barging into my room upstairs and forcing me out of the bed.

Knox, holding me as I wept my grief.

Knox, sitting in a seat at Wrigley Stadium, relaxed, watching the baseball game, wearing a faint, but real, smile.

Knox, asleep in my bed, hair tangled around his face, vulnerable.

Knox, declaring his love for me.

Christ, I'm so *stupid*.

He sees me in a way no one else ever has—including Connor. That doesn't diminish my love for Connor. My love for him was with all the rosy, unicorn-and-rainbows, hero worship of a girl who found her knight in shining armor. He was there for me when I so desperately needed to see that not all men hurt, reject, and abandon.

And Knox. *Oh God*, Knox.

My love for him is that of a woman who has experienced the suffering of life and has come out stronger, forged into unbreakable steel. A woman who understands that she doesn't need a man by her side to complete the picture of who she is but *chooses* to want him there. My love for him is with the knowledge that heroes aren't shiny, golden-haired, perfect gods. They're men. Scarred, battered, wounded men with feet of clay...and hearts of the purest, most precious gold.

I wouldn't lose my independence or myself with him. No, Knox had spent the last eighteen months helping me find out who Eden Gordon was and celebrating her. Supporting her. Encouraging her. He didn't want to strip me of my identity but help me find it.

I. Love. Him.

"What?" Katherine breathes.

I blink. Well, damn. I guess I must've said that aloud. But I'm not ashamed of it. The exact opposite. Pride, and a lightness I haven't experienced in…years. Disbelief and joy ring through me. But so do the remnants of apprehension. Even as I acknowledge my love for Knox, I'm sitting at the family table facing my biggest fears. Rejection. Abandonment.

But when I think of the alternative—of not being able to freely love Knox, of not waking up to him, curling up next to his big, powerful body—there isn't a decision.

Well, yes there is.

It's Knox. It'll always be Knox.

"I love him," I repeat, and am surprised and pleased that it doesn't shake but sounds firm…proud.

I glance around the dinner table, and Jude, not appearing the least bit shocked, arches an eyebrow at me and nods. Simon is wearing a half-grin and winks. Katherine and Dan, though… I swallow a sigh. The astonishment is thawing from Katherine's expression, and a storm cloud is gathering. An ugly one.

"Katherine, I love you. You're more of a mother to me than my own," I say, gently, because no matter all that has gone down at this table, and what our relationship might resemble in the future, she's been there for me. Loved me when my own parents hadn't. "I loved Connor. And when he died, I wanted to crawl into that grave with him. But I didn't. And by some miracle, I've fallen in love again—with Knox. And he is a miracle. One I didn't see coming, wasn't expecting. I know this is going to be hard for you to accept—I don't even know if you can. And…and I'm okay with that if you can't. I have to be. Because while I love you, I can't live my life in memoriam of Connor."

I push my chair back and stand, clutching the edge of the table. And my heart cracks at the disgust twisting Katherine's mouth. Still, I breathe through the stinging.

"I love you," I repeat. "So much. But I'm going after him, and if he'll have me—if he'll believe that I want him—I'm going to claim him right back. One day, I hope you can…"

The emotion clogging my throat won't let me continue. I survey the room one more time. The oak dining room table. The elegant gold-and-blue striped wallpaper. The tasteful but beautiful chandelier. The people. I imprint it all on my brain because there's a chance I won't see it again for a while.

Jude and Simon stand, their eyes on their mom.

"Love you, sis," Simon murmurs, his long legs eating up the short distance between us. He wraps me in his arms, hugs me tight and hard. "It'll be okay," he whispers in my ear. "Now go get my stubborn-ass brother."

Tears burn my eyes, further trap my voice. I nod.

"Let me walk you out, Eden," Jude says, grasping my elbow once Simon lets go. "We have plans to make for how soon we can get you to Reno."

I glance at Katherine once last time, but her head is bent, and a part of me wants to go to her, embrace her, inhale her familiar perfume. But I, more than anyone, understand about time and space.

Returning my gaze to Jude, who brushes his knuckles over my cheek, I nod again and turn, leaving my family behind.

But I'm walking toward my new family. Knox.

If he'll have me.

Chapter Fourteen

Knox

Jake finishes wrapping my right hand, and I flex the fingers and wrist while he works on the left. My gloves with the BFC logo sit on the table beside me, ready for me to pull on. I stare ahead, not really seeing the other long, rectangular table along the opposite wall. Since I never fight on a full stomach, it only holds bottles of water and sports drinks, protein bars, fruit, and other small snacks, nothing too heavy. Besides the table I'm sitting on, a couple of chairs bracket a long couch and low table.

Only Jake and I are in the private dressing room, just as I prefer. This week was packed with pre-event activities that required my presence—open workouts at one of the most popular casinos, media scrum, ceremonial weigh-ins, the dedication of the scholarship fund. Promotional shit has never been my favorite, and the ceremony that featured footage of Connor from his past fights and interviews had been bittersweet. Joyful and painful. Thank God I didn't have to speak too long or there might've been an ass-load of memes and GIFs of me breaking down crying.

One thing hits me like a bat over the top of my head as I attended all these events.

I don't miss it.

At all.

Even though it was my decision to leave Chicago much earlier than planned, I've been counting down the weeks, the days until I can return home. To my family. My shop. Tattooing.

Eden.

At first, I tried pushing her out of my mind. But about five minutes after I landed at Reno-Tahoe International Airport, it struck me how futile that was. Like trying not to eat. Or breathe. Or stop your heart from beating.

Jake tapped the back of my left hand and stood. "You good?" he asked, studying me with that scalpel-sharp stare. "Ready?"

"Yeah." I nod, reaching for my gloves.

"Good." He claps me on the shoulder. "You got about ten minutes. I'll come back for you."

I nod again as he turns and heads for the door. A peaceful quiet inhabits the room, and I'm thankful for it. Jumping off the table, I pace the floor, concentrating on the fight ahead. Most fighters would tell you preparation starts in the mind, and I agree. I envision moves, possible scenarios that could happen, how I'll handle them. A calm pours through me. Yeah, I'm ready.

I'm stronger than I've ever been. Focused. Rested. I haven't always been able to say that. But I did keep my promise to Eden. After the first two nights here without sleep, I hit the internet and found a therapist. I didn't say much, but even the little bit I did loosened the release valve. Enough for me to sleep without jerking awake with nightmares. So three days later, I returned. Talked some more. Slept some more. When I return to Chicago, I plan to continue seeing a counselor, because Eden can't be my security blanket. She was right; I need to go after my own healing.

A loud knock on the door echoes in the room, and I'm already grinning before it cracks open. Jude and Simon have never missed a fight, and they were supposed to land two hours ago. Damn, I missed them.

"It's about time you got—"

Fuck. The air snags in my lungs. No, my lungs stop working altogether. My body freezes, the same temperature as the cold air cycling through the arena's conditioning system. Everything in me goes still. Except my heart. That beats so hard, so fast my chest should've been rising and falling with it.

Eden.

Not Jude or Simon.

Eden stands in the doorway.

"Hey," she greets me softly. "Can I come in? I know it's right before you're about to go out there…" Her fingers tangle in front of her, and her feet are in third position.

"Yeah," I say, my voice working again. "Yeah," I repeat. "Come in."

A small, self-conscious smile flirts with her pretty mouth, and she moves forward into the room, closing the door behind her. I snatch those seconds to devour her, feast on her in greedy, visual gulps. It's been three weeks since I've seen her, and I'm starving.

Her long, beautiful hair hangs down over her delicate shoulders and slim back, framing the face that has haunted my dreams. That face bright with laughter. Twisted in passion as she comes. Soft and intense as she tells me how I soar.

Cool, blank in shock as I confess my love for her.

Yeah, her lovely features are branded in my brain, and yet

memories have nothing on reality. Her dark eyes are deeper, her high cheekbones more defined, full mouth lusher, more sensual. And the scatter of freckles...sweeter.

Lowering my gaze, I swallow a groan and am thankful as hell for the cup protecting my dick inside my shorts. Her perfect breasts rise above the curved neckline of a gold dress that slides over her petite frame and sexy curves, hitting her mid-thigh. Sexy as fuck stilettoes of the same color jack her up several inches. She probably wouldn't have to rise up on her toes to kiss me now.

Curling my fingers into my palms, I squeeze them tight. The ache reminds me she's not mine to touch.

At some point over the three weeks here, I'd come to terms with that. When I'd told her I would no longer be hostage to my love for her, I'd meant it. Just as I refused to hold her chained to me. It's not Eden's fault she met and fell in love with my brother. And it's not her fault she can't love me the way I need. Does it hurt like fuck? Hell, yeah. But I won't punish her by cutting her out of my life, by making the shop an uncomfortable place so she leaves.

We'll find some way to make it work.

But I have to move on. For five years, I've shelved a part of myself, and I can't live that way anymore. Can I find someone else who will own my heart like her? I don't know. Still, I have to try because another thing I've discovered in these three weeks is I don't want to be alone. Connor has taught me life is too fucking short to not love, to not share your life with someone. And I want that.

None of those resolutions and decisions mean having her in the same room as me right now isn't carving a hole out of my chest. Or that I'm not aching with the need to touch her, inhale her scent, have her body pressed against mine.

"What are you doing here?" I ask. Hell, that seems to be my go-to question with her.

If her half-smile is any indicator, she's thinking the same thing.

"How did I know that was going to be the first thing you said to me?" she murmurs, confirming my suspicion. Her smile fades, and a sadness that clenches my gut enters her eyes. "Hi," she simply says. Then, "I've missed you."

I don't reply. I can't.

That sadness deepens, and she shakes her head. "I know you might not want to hear that from me." She laughs, the sound light, nervous. "You might not want me to be here. And I get that, but I still had to take a chance because," she pauses, drags in an audible breath, "because you're worth that chance. You're so worth it."

Shock punches me in the rib cage. Yeah, lungs and voice back to not being operational.

She hesitates, sighs. "First, I need you to know that what you told me about being responsible for Connor's death is bullshit. Like I told your mother, going into that ring was his decision—"

Holy *fuck*. *My mother*? Those words are defibrillator pads to my body.

"My mother? Eden, what're you talking about?" I rasp.

"Getting there. But I need you to understand that you are shouldering this burden that's not yours. No one could've convinced Connor not to fight. *No one*. And why should you have canceled your match? That would've been harming your career for Connor's, and he wouldn't have been grateful. He would've resented you like hell for it. No, I don't blame you for that. And neither should you. Knox—" She shakes her head. "You were his older brother, not his father, even though you had to kind of step into that role. And you're definitely not God. Let that guilt go. Please. You're too good to carry that around."

My heart strikes my chest wall, the thunderous drumming

deafening in my head. But it can't compare with the relief, the *release* that I can actually feel rise off my shoulders like a hot-air balloon slowly lifting off the ground. For the first time in two years, I can breathe easier. Not that her words magically erase the stain of the load that has weighed me down. No, the blemish has been there too long, settled too deep for that to happen in seconds. But... I drag in air through my nose. It helps. God, it helps. Because it's her.

"Second, I couldn't let you step into that octagon without knowing something." She rubs her palms down her dress-covered thighs, her head dipping. Seconds later, those shoulders draw back, and her chin hikes up. She meets my gaze, both defiant and vulnerable. "I love you. So much that I ache with it. I wish I could tell you I loved you from the moment I saw you, but I can't. And while I don't regret Connor, I am sorry that it took me so long to see you, really *see* you. Because you so deserve to be seen."

She steps forward, pauses, and an emotion flickers across her face. But then her full mouth firms, and she travels the distance separating us, not stopping until she's in my space, cupping my jaw.

"Knox, you're not second best to me. You just *are*. You're my comfort. My security. My joy. My heart." She leans forward, and her forehead rests against the hollow of my throat. "My everything," she whispers.

Something inside me snaps so hard, it's almost physical. A sound I've never made before—a cross between a groan and a shout—erupts from my throat. My arms are around her, crushing her to me, holding her so tight, I wouldn't be surprised if my embrace is bruising. But I can't let go. Not with her words ringing against my skull, reverberating in my chest, swirling in my gut.

Fisting her hair, I yank her head back and cover her lips with mine, thrusting my tongue between her lips, claiming her for my own. Finally.

Finally.

She moans into my mouth, meeting each stroke, each lick, each nip. I can't get enough of her taste, of her soft curves grafted to mine.

A throat cleared behind us, then Jake's rough, gravel-pitted voice said, "I hate to break this up, but there's a little matter of a match that starts in two minutes."

In that second, I couldn't give a damn about a fight. Not with the woman I've loved for so many years in my arms and her words ricocheting in my head.

My everything...my everything...my everything...

I'll never unhear it.

I'm not fooling myself. There will be people who will resent her love for me and mine for her. Mom definitely will. Especially since I broke my promise to her. Regret and sadness twinges inside my chest for that. And a part of me wants to ask her if she's certain that this—that *I'm*—what she wants. Because it will estrange her from the family she loves, the family we both love.

But then Eden tilts her head back, a wide grin illuminating her face, brighter than the arena lights, and I shove those doubts aside. She loves me. And right now, that's all that matters.

"He'll be right there," she says, not turning to Jake but stroking my cheekbone, the bridge of my nose, my mouth. "He has ass to kick."

The corner of my mouth quirks. "You going in there?"

She shakes her head, sadness flickering across her expression. "No, I can't. I'm sorry."

I press my mouth to hers in a brief, hard kiss. As if she needs to apologize. I understand why she can't watch another fight. "You'll be here when I get back?"

The sorrow evaporates under the heat of her smile.

"There's no other place I'd rather be. Go get him. For you. And for Connor."

I draw her close for another embrace, closing my eyes and savoring her. Then I pull away and charge out of the room. The sooner I win this match, the sooner I can get back to my woman.

Mine.

Goddamn, that feels good to finally be able to say.

• • •

I cradle Eden's hips. Lift her off me until only the tip of my cock remains between those beautiful, puffy, wet lips. I grit my teeth as I slowly lower her, watching as my flesh, glistening with the evidence of her need, disappears inside her.

"Fuck," I grunt, her flesh taking me deep, spasming around me. Christ, she feels so perfect. Squeezing me like a fist, sucking me like a mouth. My thighs tense, ass clenches. Electrical pulses sizzle in the soles of my feet, racing up my body, my spine, only to dart back down and tingle in my balls. They draw up tight, and it won't be long before I give in to that welcoming oblivion.

I spent three weeks without her. Yeah, I can't hold out.

Her fingernails bite into my shoulders, and, head thrown back onto her shoulders, she cries out. "Knox, please," she begs, hips twisting, writhing. "I need to come. So bad. Give it to me."

No way I can deny her. Not when she pleads so pretty like that.

Reaching between us, I circle her clit, even as I pound up inside her. Her sex ripples around me, sucking me deeper. I don't let up on that swollen nub, rubbing, massaging. With a hoarse scream, she convulses on top of me, her walls clamping down hard, milking me. Taking me over that edge with her.

Grabbing her ass, I hold her up and drive into her, fucking her, branding her as mine.

"*Mine*," I growl as I come, pouring so hard and long into her, a part of me is afraid it won't end. And the other part is worried it will.

As the sharp-edged pleasure eases, I leave the bed and quickly dispose of the condom in the bathroom, hating to be separated from Eden for even that long. Sliding in beside her, I tug her into my arms, and she eagerly curls around me, settling her head on my chest, bending her thigh over mine. She brushes her hand over my chest, resting it over my heart.

"Tell me again," I murmur into the darkness.

Soft lips graze my nipple, and my emptied cock twinges. "I'm yours," she whispers. "And I love you."

Rolling, I pin her under me, threading our fingers together and guiding her arms above her head. Lowering my head, I take her mouth, sliding my tongue between her lips, and she opens for me, welcoming me. Her taste, that silky moan she makes, her touch on my face, in my hair—none of it will ever get old. Ever.

"If I haven't said it before, let me say it now," she breathes. "I'm proud of you."

A warm glow throbs right over my heart. No, she hadn't been able to watch the fight, but after winning the match in the fifth round by unanimous decision, I returned to the dressing room. And no one celebrated harder than she did.

"Are you sure you're okay with retiring again?" she asks, gaze steady on me.

"I told you, I want my life in Chicago. With you."

She nods, smiles. "I just don't want you to have regrets."

"Never." I touch my lips to hers. "Now, you never did tell me about your conversation with my mother," I remind her, shifting between her legs. My cock rests against her pussy, and though I just came, I push against her, loving the soft, slick give of her folds.

She groans, but a smile tugs at her lips. "Seriously? You want to talk about your mother now?" She punctuates "now" with a roll of her hips.

"Not really, but yeah," I say.

She chuckles. "Fine." Taking a deep breath, she starts relaying the events of last Sunday's dinner. By the time she finishes, I'm stunned...and humbled.

I remember telling her I would never force her to choose between the family and me. Turns out I didn't have to.

"Eden." I shake my head. "I'm so—"

"No." She lays three fingers over my mouth, silencing me. "I'm not. Would I love if she could accept us? Yes. In a perfect world, that would be ideal. But she doesn't, and I don't know if she ever will. Your brothers seem okay with us together, but who knows how other people will react?"

"I'm not going to lie. Hurting Mom hurts me, too. Do I hate that I betrayed her trust by not keeping my promise to stay away from you? Yeah. Do I hate that your relationship with her might be damaged? Yeah, because I know how much you love her. I do, too. But am I willing to let you go again?" I clasp her fingers tighter. "No."

"I won't let you go either," she agrees. Untangling a hand from mine, she strokes her fingertips over my face. "Because as long as I have you, I have everything."

"Baby, you'll never have to worry about not having me. I don't even remember what it's like not to love you. And nothing will change that." I sweep a kiss over her lips. "I'm yours."

"I just have one favor to ask," she teases with a grin.

But my, "Anything," is resolute, final. And her grin softens to a smile so full of love that for a brief moment, I have to shut my eyes, or she'll see a grown man's eyes tear up. Maybe later, when I'm standing on the condo's balcony with no witnesses. But right now, in bed with my body already hardening? No, not going to happen.

"When we get back home, can you finally give me that tattoo?"

I laugh, and the joy-filled sound bounces off the walls of the shadowed bedroom.

"Done."

Acknowledgments

To God, my Father. You never cease to amaze me with how You continuously bless me with ideas, the words, and the heart of every story. Thank you for never leaving or forsaking me.

To Gary, the best husband in the world. Your faith lifts me up and keeps me going when mine fails. Your never-failing love and support are gifts that I cherish. Just like I cherish you.

To the beautiful and patient Kate Meader and Shelley Newham. Thank you for answering all my endless questions about Chicago. You helped me bring your beautiful city to life in the book, and I truly appreciate your kindness!

To the real Hakim Alston, or as I have called you from the time we were in diapers, Michael. When I decided to write a tattoo artist, there wasn't any other person who came to mind but you, one of the best artists out there. Thank you for answering all my questions and only sighing every other time when I called to pester you. FYI. I would've named the character Hakim after you anyway. You didn't need to extort it out of me. LOL!

To Breeze Yancie, my gorgeous niece. Thank you for hooking me up with the Drake lyrics. And for not calling me old—at least not to my face—when I asked you pop culture questions.

To Kevin Bryant, my wonderful son. Thank you for the *Naruto* rundown. And I promise you, I'm going to watch *Hunter X Hunter*. When you come back from college, I'll be caught up. Pinky swear!

To my mind-hive bestie, Juliette Cross. You know I love you, and providing me with the *Game of Thrones* research is just one reason why. And I'm even going to pretend there was no eye-rolling and ridicule involved on your end…

To Rachel Brooks, agent extraordinaire. Thank you for your patience, guidance, support and no-nonsense wisdom when I need it. I'm still getting my T-shirt made. I'll even give you credit. LOL!

To Tracy Montoya, my beard-and-man-bun-hating but ah-mazing editor. I promise, when I mention your name, no one in my family asks, "Who now?" 'Cause they all know who you are! I talk about you so much, they're like, "Oh, how's she doing?" LOL! Thank you for being just the best. I'm a better writer and author because of you. And because of you, I have the confidence and pride that every book that goes out into the wild is the best one I could write. And that's due to you. Thank you! Heart eyes to you!

About the Author

USA Today bestselling author Naima Simone's love of romance was first stirred by Johanna Lindsey, Sandra Brown, and Linda Howard many years ago. Well, not that many. She is only eighteen…ish. Though her first attempt at a romance novel starring Ralph Tresvant from New Edition never saw the light of day, her love of romance, reading, and writing has endured. Published since 2009, she spends her days—and nights—writing sizzling romances with a touch of humor and snark.

She is wife to Superman, or his non-Kryptonian, less bulletproof equivalent, and mother to the most awesome kids ever. They all live in perfect, sometimes domestically challenged bliss in the southern United States.

Come visit Naima at www.naimasimone.com.

Also by Naima Simone

ONLY FOR A NIGHT

ONLY FOR YOUR TOUCH

ONLY FOR YOU

SCORING WITH THE WRONG TWIN

SCORING OFF THE FIELD

SCORING THE PLAYER'S BABY

BEAUTY AND THE BACHELOR

THE MILLIONAIRE MAKEOVER

THE BACHELOR'S PROMISE

A MILLIONAIRE AT MIDNIGHT

WITNESS TO PASSION

KILLER CURVES

SECRETS AND SINS: GABRIEL

SECRETS AND SINS: MALACHIM

SECRETS AND SINS: RAPHAEL

SECRETS AND SINS: CHAYOT

If you love erotica, one-click these hot Scorched releases...

GOOD GIRL'S BAD LESSONS
a *Dirty Debts* novel by Carmen Falcone

Translator Emma Cavanaugh will do anything to win her ex-boyfriend back—including summoning her brother's best friend, Italian billionaire and playboy Nico Giordano, to give her much-needed lessons in the art of seducing and pleasing a man. Sex was never her thing, so if anyone is going to know how to teach her how to be bad it'll be Mr. Sex-on-A-Stick himself.

SNATCHED
an *Outlaw Warriors* novel by Cathleen Ross

Hellbent on revenge, Club Enforcer Troy DeLance kidnaps his prospect's sister as payback for a betrayal. If he has to tie Stacey Martin to his bed to make her stay, so be it. All the better if she likes it. Stacey will do anything to save her brother. Even surrendering in ways she never imagined to her beastly kidnapper. But as their relationship heats up, neither realizes someone else is plotting a more deadly payback...

Burned
a *Viking Bastards* novel by Christina Phillips

I offered her everything, and she threw it back in my face. Now she's back, for one week only, gorgeous, successful, and I can't keep away. She offers a way to heal our fractured past. She burned me so bad––there's no way I should even want to be near her. But the more she gives, the more I need. Until I discover the real reason she left, and my whole damn world implodes…

Fight Twice for Me:
Two Stepbrothers are Better than One
a *Fight for Me* novel by C.C. Wylde

The last place I wanted to be is at my ex's MMA club, especially since I've sworn off fighters. I never anticipated meeting the De La Cruz twins there. Could *anyone* resist a chance at a night of mind-blowing sex with them? It felt good to forget the rules… until I woke up to find out they were my new stepbrothers. It's about to get complicated.